Marshaling Her Heart

Books by Mary Connealy

From Bethany House Publishers

THE KINCAID BRIDES

Out of Control

In Too Deep

Over the Edge

TROUBLE IN TEXAS

Swept Away

Fired Up

Stuck Together

WILD AT HEART

Tried and True

Now and Forever

Fire and Ice

THE CIMARRON LEGACY

No Way Up

Long Time Gone

Too Far Down

HIGH SIERRA SWEETHEARTS

The Accidental Guardian

The Reluctant Warrior

The Unexpected Champion

BRIDES OF HOPE MOUNTAIN

Aiming for Love

Woman of Sunlight

Her Secret Song

BROTHERS IN ARMS

Braced for Love

A Man with a Past

Love on the Range

THE LUMBER BARON'S DAUGHTERS

The Element of Love

Inventions of the Heart

A Model of Devotion

WYOMING SUNRISE

Forged in Love

The Laws of Attraction

Marshaling Her Heart

The Boden Birthright: A CIMARRON LEGACY Novella (All for Love Collection)

Meeting Her Match: A MATCH MADE IN TEXAS Novella

Runaway Bride: A KINCAID BRIDES and TROUBLE IN TEXAS Novella (With This Ring? Collection)

The Tangled Ties That Bind: A KINCAID BRIDES Novella (Hearts Entwined Collection)

WYOMING SUNRISE
BOOK 3

Marshaling Her Heart

MARY CONNEALY

BETHANYHOUSE
a division of Baker Publishing Group
Minneapolis, Minnesota

Published by Bethany House Publishers
Minneapolis, Minnesota
www.bethanyhouse.com

Bethany House Publishers is a division of
Baker Publishing Group, Grand Rapids, Michigan

Printed in the United States of America

Library of Congress Cataloging-in-Publication Data
Names: Connealy, Mary, author.
Title: Marshaling her heart / Mary Connealy.
Description: Minneapolis, Minnesota : Bethany House, a division of Baker Publishing Group, [2023] | Series: Wyoming Sunrise ; 3
Identifiers: LCCN 2023012910 | ISBN 9780764241154 (paperback) | ISBN 9780764242205 (casebound) | ISBN 9781493443727 (ebook)
Subjects: LCGFT: Christian fiction. | Romance fiction. | Western fiction. Novels.
Classification: LCC PS3603.O544 M37 2023 | DDC 813/.6—dc23/eng/20230324
LC record available at https://lccn.loc.gov/2023012910

Scripture quotations are from the King James Version of the Bible.

This is a work of fiction. Names, characters, incidents, and dialogues are products of the author's imagination and are not to be construed as real. Any resemblance to actual events or persons, living or dead, is entirely coincidental.

Cover design by James Hall
Cover image by Magdalena Russocka / Trevillion Images

Author is represented by the Natasha Kern Literary Agency.

Baker Publishing Group publications use paper produced from sustainable forestry practices and post-consumer waste whenever possible.

23 24 25 26 27 28 29   7 6 5 4 3 2 1

To my mom, Dorothy Dunn Frew Moore

She lived for 94 years,
and to me each one of them was,
once I got to join her life,
an honor.

1

A soft tap on the window snapped Becky Pruitt awake. She was on her feet, gun in hand, her back pressed to the wall beside the window before even being fully awake just by pure reflex.

"Who's there?"

"Becky, it's me. Nate." Nate Paxton, her foreman. New at the job, he'd been with her just two years, but he was a man she'd come to trust.

It was strange, however, for him to come here in the night, so she remained cautious.

"What do you want at this hour?" She glanced at the lovely old clock she'd inherited from her grandmother and saw it was past midnight.

"I have something to tell you and I never got a chance today. No one else can know about this, only you. And it can't wait."

It was true they'd had a hectic day. Cattle to round up and get fattened up on grass she'd saved back before they took the long drive to Denver. She'd gone there the last two years and had gotten top dollar. She planned on it again. She'd talked to Nate plenty and they'd worked side by side, but all the other hands had been close by most of the day.

Becky swung the shutter open that covered her glass windows. She was mighty proud of that glass.

She shoved the window up.

"Come close. I can't yell this or the Grables will hear me, and not even they can know what's going on."

"Let me turn up the lantern," she said.

Nate reached through the window and caught her arm. "No light. It might draw attention."

She could just barely hear him, so she dropped to her knees and folded her arms on the windowsill. Her dark braid hung down long enough, it was pinned behind her arms. Nate had no business even coming to her window while she was in her nightgown. It was outrageous behavior. But she saw the intensity in his expression. He wasn't here for any improper reason. He had something to tell her in secret.

"What is it?"

Nate moved closer. Before he spoke, a black blur came diving through the window.

Brutus was here to save the day. He came to her side and nuzzled her hand, which she smoothed over his head.

Then there were paws at the window, and Lobo's muzzle appeared at Nate's side. She was Becky's other dog. Along with Brutus, the pair were parents for most of the

8

puppies in the county. Including the puppy Becky had given the Nolte family a couple of weeks ago. A puppy that had saved the Nolte family's life by warning them of approaching danger.

Lobo stood on her hind legs, put both paws on the windowsill, and poked her nose inside. She didn't dive in like Brutus. Lobo had a firm position on staying outside unless it was really important.

Since Lobo knew Nate well, she seemed content to rest her head on his arm. Nate ran a hand over her wolfish gray head. In appearance Lobo was more wolf than dog, but when she wasn't snarling at strangers, she had a gentle temperament that made Becky sure there was some dog in there somewhere.

Lobo licked Nate's hand. "Becky, I know I've got no business coming to your window, so I'll make this fast. I'm a former U.S. Marshal. I've been asked to go back to work."

Becky's arms dropped, and she sank back on her heels and forgot to whisper. "You snuck over here at night to quit?"

"Shhh! We can't wake the Grables." Jan and Roscoe Grable lived in the house. Jan cooked for Becky and Roscoe, Becky's ranch foreman before he'd busted up his knee, who cooked for the hands. They were on the far end of the house from Becky, but they weren't deaf.

Becky narrowed her eyes at her foreman. She quit reacting to every word he said. It was time to let him talk without interruptions.

"Go on."

"There's been another stagecoach robbery."

Becky gasped, then clamped her mouth shut. Waiting.

"The U.S. Marshals have decided the outriders aren't enough. Somehow this band of outlaws is getting inside information about stages that are carrying shipments of payrolls. Some to the area forts. Some to the mines around South Pass City and other places."

He paused. She didn't respond. He blinked a couple of times before continuing on.

"This last holdup was planned carefully. The gang knew just where to waylay the stage. They picked a narrow trail with good hideouts and rained bullets down on those with the stage. They killed four outriders, the driver, and the man riding shotgun, plus there were two passengers." Nate's mouth went tight with anger. He shoved both hands deep into his dark brown hair, and his brown eyes flashed. Then he drew a deep breath and exhaled slowly, looking as grim as the news he was imparting.

"I met my brother in Pine Valley yesterday."

"You said he was coming to visit, but you didn't bring him out." Becky felt like a few words wouldn't derail the story.

"He's a U.S. Marshal from Colorado, and he wasn't here for a family get-together. He came here to stop the Deadeye Gang. He'll bring in ten men—including himself. He asked if I'd work as a Marshal until we capture this gang, and I've agreed. They aren't going to tell anyone they're here. We've got a plan, and secrecy is imperative."

"What plan?"

Nate stared hard into Becky's eyes as if he were trying to read her mind. "I can't tell you all of it, but your co-operation is needed. If you're not interested, say so now and we'll try to set this up somewhere else."

"You can't tell me?"

Nate waited. Clearly expecting her to either agree or disagree and go on about her life while their secret plan unfolded around her and she remained ignorant.

When she said nothing, Nate said, "All you need to do is let me hire three men who come riding in, sometime in the next week or two. Sal will be one of them. They'll ask for work. It's time for the fall roundup, then the drive. You ride off with every single cowhand on the place to drive the herd to Denver, just like always. Leave me behind and these three new hands."

"I hire them and then ride off and let them go about their plan and not ask intrusive questions?"

"Yes. I'm sorry. You run this ranch like a savvy, experienced cattleman. I know you keep your eyes wide open and understand everything going on around you. This goes against all your hard-learned lessons."

"Three men, not ten?"

"Yes, three men just because you always leave a few behind. Those three and I will be the ones staying while you ride off."

"I don't go on the drive. You do. You know I don't like leaving the ranch for so long. I need to be here to run things."

"This year it'll be me. After you go, the other seven men will come in and we'll run this investigation out of the Idee."

Becky's Ranch had ID as its brand. It stood for Independence Day, marking the day she started her own spread and got out from under her father's thumb. It was known far and wide as the Idee.

"We need a place to lay low. The Deadeye Gang striking again so soon, and hitting so hard, has finally shocked the Marshals into taking action. And it's high time. We'd hoped the gang would calm down after the Wainwrights died. My brother Sal said they now figure the Wainwrights were the ones urging caution, slowing things down to keep the pressure off."

Becky covered her mouth with her fist, holding in the words. Peter and Henry Wainwright had owned the general store in Pine Valley. They'd lived respectable lives, but secretly they'd been involved in the area's murderous stagecoach robberies. They'd finally overplayed their hand when a young woman had seen Henry Wainwright where he wasn't supposed to be. Her testimony would have implicated Henry in a murder. They'd set out to kill Samantha Nolte, the stepdaughter of Becky's good friend Nell Nolte—a woman who was now the justice of the peace in Pine Valley.

When they'd attacked Samantha, they needed to go through Nell, her husband, Brand, and Brand's three daughters. The Wainwrights had lost. Becky and Nate had come on the scene with Brutus about the time it was all over. They and the sheriff had finished the Wainwrights and, they'd hoped, the Deadeye Gang.

It was not to be.

Nate went on giving Becky orders on how to run her ranch. He was doomed to disappointment, but she let him talk.

"With everyone gone from here, the Marshals and I will be free to slip around. No one lives nearby; we can come and go unnoticed. If anyone asks about strange men

12

in the area, I'll tell them they're new to the ranch. It's a decent plan, and we've got to take action and not delay. I know it goes against your nature to let your ranch be used like this. Let us do it anyway. Think of it as making a compromise to protect your own interests, just like any other hard-eyed businessman."

Becky was sorely afraid she was very hard-eyed right this minute. "You've brought your message. I need time to consider it."

"Three men will ride in together, including my brother. I intend to tell the other hands who he is, and the other two will be his saddle partners. I need to know right now if you're agreeable to hiring them."

Becky studied Nate. She trusted him. But turning her ranch over to his crew of Marshals, without even knowing what exactly was going on, didn't set right.

"I have time to think before your cohorts get here. When they do come, I'll hire them. But I'm not promising you anything now. I need more time. Your brother and his buddies can work here while I think about it."

Nate narrowed his eyes. Annoyance flashed across his features. He wasn't satisfied with her request for time. He glared at her for a few long seconds, as if he thought maybe she'd crumble in the face of his majestically strong will.

Too bad.

Then his gaze dropped to her body as though just now noticing she knelt before him in her nightgown. A mild blush rose on his cheeks, and his eyes quickly shifted to the windowsill. He tugged on the brim of his hat, turned, and scratched Lobo. Brutus licked Becky's fingers and jumped out the window to follow Nate and Lobo.

Becky stood to close the shutters as Nate popped back into view. Grinning just a bit, he said, "That's a mighty pretty nightgown, Miss Pruitt."

His head vanished then, and she heard him walk away. It took a bit to realize she was standing there with her jaw slightly dropped. Like a brainless sheep. Like a woman who'd never heard a word of flattery before. Which she had. From her pa's dreadful cowhands back when she was growing up without a ma at her pa's nearby ranch.

Those men and their crude flattery were among the reasons she wanted to leave that ranch as fast as she could, and she was always grateful to her ma's side of the family for the opportunity.

Becky had only met her mother's parents once when she was six, when her ma took the long journey to Omaha to meet Grandma and Grandpa Steinhauser. They'd been wonderful to her. Two years later, her ma was dead and her grandparents' contact had been nothing more than letters and birthday and Christmas gifts. Becky had always endured harsh words from her pa whenever something had arrived from Omaha.

And then she received word they'd passed away and she'd inherited money from them. A surprising amount. And it'd been left to her very shrewdly in a way her pa couldn't get his hands on. It was only after she'd received news of the inheritance and told Pa she was moving out and using the money to start up her own ranch that she'd realized her pa expected the inheritance and had plans for it.

Money from those nice people he'd repeatedly bad-mouthed and never let her visit.

And now Nate had said her nightgown was pretty. He

hadn't even said *she* was pretty. And here she stood gaping. Shaking her head, she turned away from the window, wondering how Nate was going to feel when he heard Roscoe Grable was going to lead the cattle drive. Because Becky wasn't letting anyone take over her ranch without her watching them closely.

Nate wasn't going to like it.

Again, too bad.

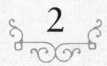

2

Why had he said that about her nightgown last night? Why? Why? Why?

Not right. Not the way a man should talk to the lady of the house—to any woman. Not the way a man should talk to his *boss*.

Not smart. Not a good way to get her cooperation, and they *needed* Becky to cooperate.

Why had he done it? Every time he challenged himself about it, he pictured her there at the window, feisty, with that long, dark braid shot through with pale streaks burned in by long hours in the Wyoming sun. The white nightgown covered her from neck to wrist to toes. But kneeling there, glaring at him, refusing to just make it easy on him and cooperate, well, she'd looked mighty pretty, and he'd been frustrated with her, so he'd said it.

He needed to apologize.

To do that he needed to face her, find a moment alone with her, and figure out what to say when he couldn't even figure out why he'd said it. He was tempted to go bang his head on the barn wall just to give himself a nice headache to think about.

The cattle had to be separated for the drive, with the oldest steers cut out and put on the best pastures to fatten up. Plenty of work to do.

But today, Becky came out of the house dressed for town.

She didn't dress that much differently for town, not even on Sundays for church, but some of her riding skirts were cleaner than others, less faded. Some of her blouses had a bit of ruffle around the collars.

Today she had on a black riding skirt that showed no sign of wear and a red plaid blouse with white lace around a stand-up collar. She wore her best black Stetson, too.

Becky walked toward the barn, and since Nate couldn't let her ride off alone, what with killers possibly riding the range, he dropped his plans for the day and hurried over there to join her.

She scowled at him. He wasn't sure if the scowl was for his ridiculous remark about her nightgown being pretty or for his request that she abandon the ranch to him and a bunch of strangers. Finally, she quit burning him with her eyes and strode into the barn while pulling on a pair of buckskin gloves. Even those were her Sunday go-to-meeting gloves. The woman was headed for town for a fact.

Nate picked up the pace, figuring she'd ride off without an escort without a pang of conscience. Which meant he'd just have to keep up with her.

In the barn stood Becky's golden stallion, one of the most beautiful critters Nate had ever seen. A palomino with a stunning white mane and tail. And beyond the glossy color, the stallion was tall and muscled, regal, and as strong and intelligent as any horse Nate had ever known.

Except his own.

He had to grab a rope and lasso his black stallion and do it quick. But because the black was a well-trained animal, the horse came when Nate whistled. Nate slid a rope around its neck and then saddled so he was only a few minutes behind Becky, who'd ridden off without him, Brutus at the palomino's side.

"What's going on?" Roscoe Grable came out of the barn, which explained why Becky's stallion had already been brought in. Becky must've asked him to handle that before he left the house this morning.

"No idea." Nate mounted up. "Looks like she's headed to town. I'm not letting her ride alone, not with that gang of outlaws roaming far and wide."

Roscoe gave Nate a firm nod of approval. "Feisty woman, our boss."

Roscoe said it with a smile and none too loud. They all respected Becky and were a little afraid of her.

Nate kicked his horse into a trot until he caught up beside the boss.

"Feisty, huh?" Becky must also have excellent hearing. "I'd say that about covers it."

Nate stayed quiet, half afraid of what might come out of his mouth. Then he thought of something harmless.

"I reckon these two stallions are about the most beautiful horses in Wyoming. It's a joy to watch your horse walk along."

"I'm going to get some fine colts out of both of these horses."

"And for every one that comes out black I'm going to expect a twenty-dollar stud fee."

Becky grinned at that. "So you noticed I've been moving your horse in with some of my best mares?"

Nate hoped that meant they were past the moment when he needed to speak of last night's folly. It also occurred to him they could talk about whatever secrets he needed to share with her right now. They were alone after all. Maybe if she'd told him her plans ahead of time and asked for someone—Nate—to ride along with her the stretch of miles to town, he wouldn't have to sneak up to her bedroom window in the middle of the night.

"Are you saying you were trying to sneak? Because if you were, you did a poor job of it."

"I've been getting colts and fillies out of my palomino for three years. I sell them except for the ones that resemble their sire. I just can't part with those beautiful golden horses. I've got six of them now that I've kept. I'd find good buyers for all six, but so far I can't stand to part with them. I reckon I'll be able to handle taking the money for any black foals that emerge."

Nate had been here a couple of years, so he knew how she prized those perfect golden babies. Some were born with darker golden hair, some with a darker mane. Those she'd sell. But not the ones that came out as a match to their pa.

"You'll have no trouble earning back the stud fee." Nate decided they'd talked enough on this topic, too. "What are you doing in town today? You usually take the wagon if you're going to the store."

"The general store isn't open. I'm meeting with Nell and Mariah to plan for when Mrs. Mussel comes to Pine Valley." She gave Nate a serious look. "I'd hoped with those low-down sneaks the Wainwrights dead, the territory might enjoy a stretch of peace. But if the Deadeye Gang struck again, so soon after the last time, Mrs. Mussel isn't safe. We have to do something to ensure she makes the trip from the train up to Pine Valley without coming to any harm. But to protect her and not pay any mind to the other stagecoaches, well, that's just pure wrong."

"When is she coming?"

"About a week and a half. Nell and the sheriff have been in contact with Fort Bridger, pushing for a cavalry escort for Mrs. Mussel, and we'd like those troops to stay around here, make a big fuss over hunting up that gang.

"You can talk about there being another holdup—word of it is already out. Sal talked of it when we met in town and didn't keep his voice down or ask me to stay quiet. But you best not mention the Marshals getting involved. You can say you want that to happen, and even telegraph the nearest Marshal's office, but you must act as if you don't know the Marshals are already coming."

He shook his head. "The Marshals will be arriving in one week. Sal rode away to contact them and say it's all right for them to come."

Becky whipped her head around so hard that her single braid whacked her in the face. "You told him that they could all come before you talked to me?"

Nate held up one hand as if he could surrender and keep his horse under control at the same time. He smiled as he said, "I didn't tell him that. I said I'd ask. I told him when the cattle drive would start. I told him if you objected, then that would be the end of it. But for now they're coming. They may have to turn aside, but they'll be hitting the trail to the Idee and will be arriving when Mrs. Mussel comes."

Becky nodded. "Don't worry, I'll keep quiet. But to not trust Mariah, whose pa and brother were killed by the gang, and Nell, whose whole family was attacked by the Wainwrights, is just plumb stupid."

With a shrug, Nate replied, "I agree, but word has a way of getting around. If Nell knows, it figures she'd tell Brand."

"Well, sure, a woman doesn't keep secrets from her husband."

"And two of Brand's children go to work with Nell every day."

Nell wasn't only the justice of the peace; she was also a seamstress and the owner of a strong business, mainly in providing chaps for the area's cowboys. Two of her stepdaughters helped her with the very successful and very boring job. Nate was thinking of having her make him a pair of new chaps, but he knew just how much she loathed making them, so he was afraid to ask.

"If those girls overheard Nell talking to Brand, they might repeat what they'd heard in all innocence. No, too many people already know this secret. Let's don't make it worse."

"Or we could make it better," Becky said, "by including people we trust who have helped and can help. Mariah would tell Clint, but he'd keep it quiet. What about the sheriff? Seems strange keeping the secret from him."

Nate glared at her.

Shaking her head, Becky said, "I know you're right. But that doesn't mean it isn't stupid."

Nate shrugged and nodded.

Brutus abandoned them at the turnoff that led to Brand Nolte's homestead, where he lived with Nell. Nate knew the dog's habits and had expected Brutus to leave. He had a son living with the Noltes, and Brutus always stopped to visit. He'd eventually catch back up to Becky and Nate.

Becky's other best friend, Mariah, also had a dog from a litter of Brutus and Lobo's. A year older than the Noltes' pup. Brutus would gather his two sons together and bring them along to town.

"You want to come to our planning meeting for Mrs. Mussel? We're meeting for lunch in Clint's Diner. You can sit with us."

Nate shook his head. "I think I'll see if the sheriff and Doc Preston need to eat. You ladies can plot and plan all on your own."

Since he knew that was exactly how Becky wanted it, Nate wasn't surprised when she nodded in agreement.

Still, he wasn't duped into believing that made her an agreeable, cooperative woman. He knew her too well for that.

Nell slapped a stack of papers on the table. Becky jumped. And Becky's nerves were normally rock-steady, so Nell was applying some serious strength when she handled those papers.

"The cavalry isn't riding to the rescue. They say they're spreading out far and wide to make the West safe for men, women, and children. They might possibly include this area, but no promises have been made. They can't just take orders from some female justice of the peace with shattered nerves."

Becky picked up the papers. "They actually said that?"

Nell almost growled. "No, but I read between the lines."

Mariah came out of the kitchen carrying three plates. One rested on her elbow, somewhat supported by her rounded belly.

"You're getting good at that." Becky smiled at her friend. No more red-hot iron until the baby came. Not a good job for a pregnant woman. Mariah had trained Deputy Willie to do most of the blacksmithing and horseshoeing. Mariah still did the cooper work. She could make wooden pails and buckets and such without getting near a burning forge.

She came straight for them, set the plates down, and took a seat. Clint was a few paces behind her with a heavy coffeepot and three tin cups.

"You ladies need any help with your plans, let me know." He poured coffee, then headed for the next table.

"Chicken parmesan. It's my favorite." Becky attacked the luscious dish Clint made so well. "And he made biscuits. How does he make them so delicious?"

Mariah tore open a hot biscuit and spread butter onto it. "He uses spices I've never heard of before. He grows them out at the homestead. Garlic and sage, peppercorns and basil. I don't know what they all are, but they make things special when Clint turns his hand to using them."

Fried chicken with tomato sauce and cheese on top was definitely special.

"We'll do the best we can to pressure the cavalry." Becky tapped her plate with her fork as she considered things. "Do you think my pa would have any influence?"

Nell arched both brows most of the way to her hairline.

Mariah swallowed at just the wrong moment and started choking. Nell reached around to pat her firmly on the back, and when Mariah decided to survive, she wiped her mouth and said, "Your pa hates women's suffrage. Hates it like poison. Do you really think he'd help us?"

Becky knew what they meant. "I doubt he would. But he's back from his cattle drive and he's got plenty of hired men. I thought, well, I thought maybe just this once he'd do it because I asked him to."

Her words had come out so bleak, she wished she'd never said anything. She looked from Mariah to Nell and saw sympathy in their eyes. Maybe pity.

"Don't feel sorry for me unless you want to pity me for even suggesting such a thing."

Mariah reached over, patted Becky's hand, and they both got back to eating.

Becky knew both her friends were tempted to hug her. She wasn't good at accepting hugs. She hadn't had much practice at it. Neither had Nell or Mariah honestly, but thanks to being married to men who loved them, they were learning.

And they drew Becky close occasionally, and she tolerated it.

Nate chose that moment to come in. No sheriff. No Doc Preston. Instead, he had Cassie and Michaela Nolte with him. Through the open door, Becky caught sight of Spike, Brutus's son who lived with Mariah, and the puppy named Hero who lived with the Nolte family.

Nell smiled and stood. "You found a handsome man to escort you to lunch? Nice work, girls."

She went to both girls and hugged them. They giggled and quietly chattered a bit to her.

Nate came over to the table where Becky sat by Mariah. "I caught up to the girls as they were leaving Nell's shop. I asked if I could join them for lunch. They told me very seriously they were not allowed to join your planning group unless they were fully ready to talk about the suffrage meeting. They have chosen to sit away from your table." His eyes sparked with humor.

Did he think women's suffrage was funny? Foolish? Becky decided she'd tell him a few hard truths on the ride home.

"Nell needs to talk to them." Mariah frowned at Nell as she walked with the girls to a nearby table. "They should be more enthused about suffrage."

"I will." Nell came back to join them, then looked back fondly at her two half-grown daughters, Cassie thirteen and Michaela seven. "But not today. We've got work to do."

Nate took his hat off and tipped it at them, then carried it to the girls' table and sat down, just as Clint glanced out of the kitchen, then ducked back in to fetch meals.

Clint made only one thing every day for breakfast, and another thing for the noon meal. He was closed after his noon crowd thinned out. So it saved a lot of time on ordering. He figured if you came in, you wanted what was available. And he was right.

Nell sat down again. "Now, we've got to find somewhere larger than the church to hold this meeting. I think we'll have to have it outside."

The three of them enjoyed planning what would happen when Mrs. Mussel arrived, and they made sure all the details were in good order. It was only her safety that nagged at them.

"I've contacted Esther Morris. She's no longer the justice of the peace in South Pass City. Her term is over, so she's not particularly tied down and will come. That makes two travelers coming from two different directions, and we must ensure the safety of both."

"You've talked to her?" Becky grabbed Nell's wrist. "She's coming?"

"We've been writing since Mrs. Mussel said she was coming. You knew I'd heard from her. But the mail slowed to a crawl over the winter, so I've had a small stack of letters all come at once just recently."

"Last I heard, she wasn't sure if she'd come."

"In the most recent letter, she committed. And she's got a crowd riding over with her. A big enough crowd she should be safe. And she said she's contacted the territorial governor, a man she knows well, to ask for special protection for Mrs. Mussel and those coming with her."

Becky wondered if the recent robbery by the Deadeye Gang, combined with the formidable voice of Esther Morris, sparked the decision for Nate's brother to visit with his Marshal friends. They'd get here in time to protect Mrs. Mussel and Mrs. Morris.

Nell pulled out a piece of paper covered front and back with her neat handwriting. "I've written a story for the newspaper. And I've already mailed off a copy to all the nearest towns."

The nearest towns weren't all that near, but the word needed to be spread.

"Is Mr. Kintzinger going to put it in the *Gazette*?"

"He said to bring it in for him to see." Nell scowled at the paper. "It's probably a little too long."

"Maybe he could split it in half and put an article in this week and next week," Mariah suggested.

"Or run a special edition of the paper." Becky itched to take Nell's article and read it right now. Nell was a decent writer. Becky had never attended school, and her education had ended early. "This is pretty big news."

As they finished up the details of their plans, the crowd grew in the diner.

Mariah said, "I'd better go help Clint. I think we're done, aren't we?"

The diner door crashed open and Samantha, Nell's oldest stepdaughter, a very newly married, very young woman, came rushing in. She was crying. "I want to move home."

The marriage wasn't quite a month old. And this wasn't her first bout of tears.

To be fair, to hear Nell tell it, Leland was a bit of a lunkhead. But he wasn't a bad husband to her; they were both just so young and had gotten married too quickly. No amount of common sense could slow their wedding down.

All three women sighed.

Becky thought Samantha's sisters sighed, too. Maybe everyone in the diner sighed.

Mariah got up eagerly and headed for the kitchen as Samantha threw herself into Nell's arms.

Leland came rushing into the diner just a few paces behind his runaway wife.

It was a sad testimony to how badly and loudly and publicly these two lived out their newlywed conflicts that everyone just kept eating the chicken parmesan.

Although Becky had to admit, most everyone ate a lot faster—herself included.

3

Becky rose from the table to leave, hoping Nate would come along soon. Then Pa came in.

Her stomach sank. Usually any talk between them was tense, though she'd had a meal with him recently that had gone well.

Joshua Pruitt owned the biggest ranch in the area. He was a hard man. His eyes went straight to her. She noticed he was alone. Often enough he came in with a group of cowhands, but Becky didn't see anyone else with him.

"Pa, how are you?"

He grunted.

She went to him, no hug, no handshake. Pa wasn't one for making a fuss—unless the fuss was complaining.

"I'm here for lunch. You done eating?"

"Yes." She glanced at Nate, who was watching her close. The girls were watching their big sister bicker with her husband. "But Nate isn't." She waved a hand at Nate. Pa knew her foreman. "He joined the two younger Nolte girls for lunch so I could visit with Mariah and Nell."

Pa gave Nell a sour look. He didn't approve of women's suffrage. He certainly didn't think a woman should fill the job of justice of the peace. Honestly, Pa didn't approve of much of anything, his daughter included.

Becky had mostly given up on him ever showing any interest in her or anything that mattered to her. But occasionally she tried to talk to him.

"Are you in town alone?"

"Yep, rode to town to talk to the blacksmith. I need a few things from the general store, too. Forgot it was closed. I saw that brute of a dog of yours and your yellow horse outside."

"His name is Brutus, Pa. And my palomino is making me a lot of money in stud fees. He's not just beautiful to look at, he's a strong, healthy animal that a lot of people want in their bloodlines."

"Should've let me breed him to a few of my mares."

Becky had made it clear she'd do that. For the usual stud fee, and Pa had to bring his mares to her place—the same rules for everyone. She didn't trust others to treat her golden beauty with the care Becky did. And that absolutely included her pa.

"If'n you're done eating," Pa said, "walk with me over to the blacksmith. I haven't seen you in a while."

Which was exactly how Pa seemed to want it. But Becky was curious why he'd ask her to walk with him, enough so that she nodded and told Nell what she was doing.

Over the caterwauling of Samantha and Leland, Nell heard Becky and nodded.

They stepped outside, and Brutus, his two sons tagging

along, came to her side. Brutus laid his ears back when Pa reached a hand to pet him. There was no snarling on the part of either of them, but Pa drew his hand back all the same.

"Stay here, Brutus." Becky was relieved when the big black dog settled onto the porch, where his sons climbed over him, wrestling.

Becky feared that if Pa so much as raised his voice, Brutus might take exception, and there was no need to add an overprotective dog to her conversation with Pa.

Clint's Diner was the farthermost building on the south side of town. To the west rose the Cirque of the Towers, the majestic mountains that guarded over Pine Valley. Their image reflected in a lake that lay between the town and the glorious beginnings of the Wind River Mountains.

Becky remembered her ma talking about how they'd seen those mountains and knew right away they'd found their home. Gazing at them always uplifted Becky's heart.

Pa's Circle J Ranch was a long ride to the northeast of Pine Valley, Becky's Idee much closer, mostly straight east of town. They'd count as next-door neighbors, but it was a neighborhood made up of thousands of acres.

The town had about ten men for every woman. There was a very small group of children, especially since Parson Blodgett and his wife had moved away with four of their large brood.

Despite those beautiful towering peaks, the town was usually a quiet little place. There was a wide street in front of the diner. To the south the blacksmith made a dead end of the main street. There was a corral behind it, and set back to the east stood the house Mariah had lived in with her pa and her brother, Theo, before they'd been shot and killed by the Deadeye Gang and Mariah left for dead. To this day, Mariah was the only person who'd ever survived an attack by the gang. She'd seen only one of the gang members, who was dead now. Mariah had been allowed to live in peace.

Now Becky and her pa walked the short vacant stretch toward the blacksmith shop.

"We haven't talked of this for a time, Becky, but you need to . . . um, that is, I'd like for you to come home. Move home."

Becky and Pa had gone round and round about this. At least he had moved past his harsh tirades. At least he was asking instead of ordering. Acting unsure of himself. He couldn't quite bring himself to act like he wanted her home because he loved and missed her.

"If we combined our two ranches, we'd really have a name in this territory. We'd make the Circle J Ranch double the size and we'd double the herd." As they drew near the smithy, Pa stopped in the middle of the main street, a very quiet spot over the noon hour. He turned to face her. "Doesn't that appeal to you, Becky girl? We'd be a team. The ranch would be a family operation. That's how it should be. Family should stick together."

Becky studied him for a moment. There was something in his eyes. Not the love a daughter longed for from her father. But something. He was sincere in his wish that she come home in a way he never had been before. But that sincerity, the wish that she'd partner with him, was rooted in something else altogether. He covered it well. But it was so strong, something peeked through. Perhaps, deep inside, lurked a desperate need, a need for her to come home. Not a *want* like before or gouged pride that had always seemed his main motivation, but a *need*. Why would he all of a sudden need her?

She couldn't figure out what she had that he needed. It wasn't money. He'd never shown any sign of needing her money.

Wanting it, oh yes, very definitely. But he didn't need it. Pa was rich. And no one bothered him or squatted on his land or tried to homestead the vast stretches between water holes that he controlled but didn't own.

So why would Pa need her? Maybe Nate would have some ideas.

She found herself wishing she could give Pa what he needed. But she knew it would be a terrible mistake. She tried to explain as gently as possible for about the fiftieth time. "Pa, you know I didn't like how things were at your ranch. I didn't get the respect the daughter of the house should from your cowhands. And you wouldn't stand up for me. The Circle J was a place I didn't feel safe. So I used my money to find a safe place for myself."

"I'd change things around."

Pa never changed anything. Becky doubted he was capable of changing.

"I'd get a married couple out to my place. Maybe the Grables would come and live with us. You were right. I shouldn't have had you, one poor little female, living amongst all those men."

Poor little female didn't suit her. Not when she ran a prosperous ranch in a wild land and did it well.

She lived mostly among men now, with Jan Grable being the exception. Becky lived and worked all day with men, and she never felt unsafe.

"You still have Skleen working for you." Becky felt her temper rise. She tried to keep her voice steady and calm, but it wasn't easy. "He was the worst of the bunch, Pa, and he's been working with you for years. You have no intention of sending him down the road if I move home. And there's a dozen of them just as bad. They come and go, but you have a knack for bringing in the same kind of character. Rough and rude. Not just disrespectful to me but at times frightening, and you take their side over me. I don't trust you to take my side when there's trouble. A girl should be able to trust her own father to keep her safe. That kind of man suits you, and they might not be a problem when it's an all-male ranch, but it didn't suit me. Now you have your place and run it the way you want to, and I have my place, run my way. We're better off separate, Pa."

Pa raised a hand as if to rest it on her wrist. He'd inflicted a lot of pain to her as a child, but he'd never offered a single gentle touch. Now, as he faced her, wanting her—no, *needing* her—at home, he still couldn't touch her gently. Instead, he lowered his hand to his side.

"Let's take some time and talk about it. If you come home, I'll listen to you, take your side. Protect you from others' rough talk. We could really have something to take pride in at the Circle J if we teamed up."

Trust.

He hadn't heard that word from her, or if he'd heard it, he just didn't understand what she'd meant by it.

Her heart ached in a way it rarely did when dealing with Pa. She'd given up on trusting him long ago. But right now she found that hurting little girl inside. The little girl who would go to her pa, the man she loved most in the world, for help or understanding or protection, and she was confused and hurt when she couldn't find what she needed.

The Circle J, Pa's brand. There would be no partnership if she went home. The ranch would be solely *his*. Her inheritance, the money left to her that he coveted, would all be in his hands.

She'd been struck by Pa's coveting her money. A sin listed right there in the Ten Commandments. Of course, honor your father and mother was in there, too. She didn't know how to honor Pa.

The day would never come when she'd go home. Honoring Pa, did that mean letting him hope? It didn't seem right to do that.

She could push him back without much trouble. She knew several ways to set him off, make him show his temper and display how weak his control was.

Honor had the same root word as *honesty*, so she decided to be honest with him. "I'd like us to be a family, Pa." She saw his eyes light up with hope and again with need. Desperate need. "But I'm never giving up the Idee and joining up with you. I've decided I won't go back, and you need to accept that."

The need was no longer well hidden. It flared to life in his eyes, quickly chased by anger. Yes, there was need.

Could Pa possibly have money problems? But how? He was one of the biggest landowners in the territory. Pa's hand closed like a vise on her wrist, and in just a few steps more he had her around the corner of the smithy. They stood on the west side of the shop so they were blocked from view.

His eyes blazed, and she took a step back to the length she could with him holding her wrist.

"Let me go, Pa. Now." She knew Pa well and had felt his fist before, though not as an adult.

Well, not often as an adult.

"You're coming home, girl. And that's that. I'm done waiting for you to come to your senses. I'm done waiting for you to quit shaming me."

"Get your hand off me." Fear traced a trail up her spine from what she saw in his eyes. She kept her voice steady and calm. Becky didn't reach for her gun, but it was there. And she wasn't going to let him slap her around, not anymore.

"Don't tell me what do to." He shook her once, hard.

"The last time you hit me"—Becky shoved her face right up to Pa's, no longer trying to put distance between herself and his fists—"I told you never again. Are you such a fool you think threatening me, maybe even beating me, will have me crawling home?"

Out of the corner of her eye she saw his fist pull back. She drew her gun, flipped it around so the butt end was facing Pa, and jammed it into his belly.

Pa roared and staggered back against the smithy wall, dragging her with him. She pulled the gun back to slam it into his gut again just as Pa's fist swung.

It smacked, flesh on flesh, inches from her face. Her vision was blocked by something . . .

Blinking, startled when no blow landed, breathing in heaving gasps, she saw a strong hand gripping Pa's left fist. Pa's right hand still held Becky's wrist.

A fist swung again, not at her, and hit Pa in the face. Pa's head snapped back and struck the smithy wall, hard. His hand lost its grip on her wrist, and she staggered back to see that the hand on Pa's fist and that blow to his chin had come from Nate.

A growl from behind her told her Brutus had joined the fray. So far he hadn't needed to step in with tooth and claw. Yet he was there if she needed him. Just like her ranch foreman.

Nate stepped between Becky and Pa, leaned close, and said with quiet intensity, "Are you really such a fool you think you can punch a woman on the streets of Pine Valley and no one will put a stop to it?"

Nate glanced over his shoulder to see Becky fumble her gun into its holster, her hands shaking hard enough she almost missed. "It looks, Pruitt, like I saved you from your own child."

Becky knew Nate thought she'd prepared to shoot Pa. And maybe she would have if that was the only way to stop him from hurting her.

"I won't put up with it," Nate said. "Many people in this town won't put up with it. And your daughter sure as certain won't put up with it. And she's strong enough to stop you."

Then Nate leaned closer. Becky did too, not wanting to miss a word.

"That you would put her in such a spot that she might've had to shoot her own father, that you might've forced her to put that kind of scar on her soul, well, that's the worst thing I've ever witnessed a parent do to a child. You are shameful, and if I ever heard Becky was thinking of teaming up with you, I'd grab her and force her into hiding until she came to her senses."

For some reason that made Becky grin for about one second before she came up beside Nate. She rested one hand on his shoulder and felt him trembling with rage.

Was that what she was doing? Trembling with rage? She was sorely afraid it wasn't rage. It was exactly what Nate had spoken of.

Fear of what she might be forced to do, looking into her heart and soul and knowing she'd do what had to be done. Because she wasn't going to allow Pa to beat her—not here, not anywhere, not ever. She'd fight him and she'd win. But at what cost to her soul?

"Don't try and convince me to partner up with you. Don't bother to speak the words to me." She pushed her face up to Pa's again and thought she saw a flicker of fear there. One hand clutched his belly where she'd shoved the gun into his gut. His eye was beginning to swell shut where Nate had punched him.

Pa looked small and cornered, like a trapped rat.

It was probably fear of Nate, but it might well be fear of what she'd've done to him if he'd hit her. Whatever its roots, the fear was there. The vicious pleasure she felt was so deep, so wide, she knew it for a sin.

She'd pray for forgiveness later, but right now she couldn't rein in her anger enough to approach God with a repentant heart.

Silence stretched between the three of them. Nate and Becky facing Pa. All of them locked in a circle of terrible rage.

Finally, Nate let go of Pa's fist and stepped back. Pa sank to the ground, holding his belly.

"Ready to head home, Miss Pruitt?"

"I am beyond ready."

Two years since she'd inherited that money and moved out. Bought her own land. Built her own house. Hired her own crew.

She decided to say one more thing just to drive home the kind of woman she was. "I had this meeting today with Nell and Mariah to help plan the speaker Mrs. Mussel's visit. She's coming to talk about women's suffrage and what an inspiration Wyoming is in fighting for that cause."

Pa growled. He took pride in being openly furious about women voting.

Down there, sitting on the ground and clutching his stomach, he snarled, "Weak-minded women, critters run by their emotions, need to be sheltered from the ugliness in this world."

"Like you sheltered me from Skleen and all the rest of your men? Is that what I need a man for? I needed someone to shelter me from you. And since there was no one, I found a way to shelter myself."

Pa's eyes narrowed and shone with hate. His eyes then shifted to Nate, then Brutus.

Becky heard a wolfish snarl and hoped it was Brutus, not Nate. Not her.

She turned from Pa to look at Nate. The gratitude she felt for his stepping in was beyond what she had words to speak of. At least now when she was so twisted up inside. She patted Brutus's head and gave Nate a good-natured slap on the back, a bit startled to see her hand was still shaking. She said, "Let's go home."

4

As they rode out of town, Nate's jaw was clenched so tight that he couldn't have spoken even if he'd been able to think of any words.

Becky didn't seem that upset, which made Nate wonder how often she'd had to put up with her father's cruel abuse.

While they rode along, Brutus left them for a while, then came back with only one pup. He must've taken his son home to Mariah and Clint's place.

That pup had apparently been born with one leg that wasn't quite straight and was a year old when Becky gave him to her friend. No one else had wanted him except Becky, who had loved him so much she would have kept him for herself if Mariah hadn't begged for the mostly grown dog they'd named Spike.

Brutus's other son, Hero, was still with Brutus, this one from a spring litter, about five months old now. This puppy was growing so fast that he tended to trip over his legs, roll to the ground, then leap up and keep moving.

When they passed the turnoff to the Nolte homestead, Brutus left them again.

The wind blew gently. Though the day was warm, a cold chill wouldn't leave Nate alone.

As if Becky's being abandoned by the dogs made her feel as if they were alone enough to talk, she said, "He'd've done it. He was ready to punch me. I should know Pa by now, but I'm shocked all the same."

"Has he hit you before?"

"When I was a child. He called it 'discipline.' I knew he was an unkind, unloving father, but I didn't quite figure out how harsh he was until I was twelve."

"What happened when you were twelve?" Nate imagined something so shockingly cruel, even a daughter couldn't lie to herself about her father anymore.

"I met Mariah." Becky glanced at him and managed a smile.

"She moved here when you were twelve?"

"Yes, her and her family. Her ma was alive then. Her Pa took on the job of town blacksmith. I never went to school or church. Pa thought both were nonsense, so I didn't meet her right away. Then one day when I was in town, I saw her working by her father's side at the smithy. A girl my age. We just fell right into being friends."

"You and Mariah are the same age?"

Becky nodded. "We're both twenty-two now. Nell's about thirty, and she didn't come to Pine Valley until about three years ago, a widow lady. But she fit right in with us. Three single, independent women. They're my best friends in the world."

Nate smiled. "You're a good team, the three of you."

Except they weren't quite such a good team anymore. Mariah and Nell were both married. That left Becky to be less important in their lives.

"Did having Mariah for a friend make you see your pa differently?"

"Mariah's father, John Stover—you've met him?"

"I did. Shortly after I started working for you."

"As you know, he was a huge man. Strong with the iron muscles of a blacksmith. And he could be grouchy. Mighty fierce when he was wielding that sledgehammer of his."

"That he was." The two of them rode on toward the Idee. Brutus would catch up eventually.

"I saw the way he was with Mariah and Theo. I knew then that a man didn't have to be so ugly about discipline. A truly strong man knows how to control himself. Oh, John Stover ruled if he needed to, and his words could make Mariah tremble." Becky smiled as she remembered it. "He was always on about Mariah and the blacksmithing. He wanted her in school, then when she refused, he wanted her at home. He was no modern thinker excited about suffrage."

"So why the smile?"

"Because Mariah saw how busy they were at the smithy and just refused to back down. She wanted to learn, to help the family earn money faster. For all his grouchy ways, John Stover let her come to work. Taught her how to be a blacksmith. And let me tell you that man was a strict teacher. He rode both those children of his to do the work right. But there was no cruelty to it. Not like my pa. Mariah had a father who loved her. And that's when I knew I didn't. That's the year I figured out what

43

Pa acted like wasn't how it should be. It wasn't a father's love. I started to defy him more. I came to town to church by myself. It was late in the game for school, and we were just too far out to ride in every day. Besides, I was working hard on the ranch by then, but Mariah helped me learn to read. She taught me the basics and sent her schoolbooks home with me. Later she started sending books I could read for fun. She taught me to cipher, and about history and science. Being her friend expanded my world. And she was passionate about suffrage. She read newspaper articles and shared them with me and gave me an appetite for a woman to have more power."

Becky shrugged. "I realized I'd need to get away from Pa. I didn't have any money, but Mariah said I could come to town as soon as I was old enough to be out of Pa's control and live with her." Her smile widened. "She said her pa would teach me blacksmithing."

"Let's get down and walk for a while. Give Brutus time to say a proper goodbye to his son and catch up to us."

Becky looked at him and nodded. As if Brutus couldn't outrun them all. Even these two magnificent stallions of theirs. But she got down anyway.

Nate couldn't quite let her tell her story and just brush off what her pa had just done in town. He stepped to the front of his black stallion as Becky moved to the front of her golden palomino. Her reached for her arm and stopped her, gently turned her.

"If your pa had punched anyone else in that town, the sheriff might well have locked him up. But because you're his daughter, somehow it's all right. I don't like that. And I think you're accepting it because you're used to it."

Becky studied him in silence with her dark eyes that could flash lightning when she was angry. Wisps escaped from the braid she had coiled at the nape of her neck. By this point in the summer, she had golden streaks in it. This was his second summer here, so he knew how pretty her hair got.

"That's a mighty pretty nightgown, Miss Pruitt."

Nate thought now that it wasn't just the nightgown that was pretty.

"You seem like you've gotten over what your pa did, but you can't have. It's too upsetting to be threatened like that. Are you all right?"

She didn't just jump in and assure him she was fine. Instead, her expression somber, she seemed to think it all through.

"Pa's dangerous, isn't he? I can't ever let myself be alone with him." Becky swallowed hard, and her throat felt jagged, as though she were swallowing broken glass. "While he was first asking me to partner up with him, then demanding I do, then threatening me if I refused, I saw something. Pa doesn't give much away of what he's feeling. But under all his usual cold desire to wield power, I saw *need* in his eyes."

Nate was stumped. It was well known how wealthy Joshua Pruitt was. "Need? You're sure?"

"It might have even been *desperate* need. Up until now I'd thought he wanted my money. Greed is nothing un-usual for Pa, and I know it stung his pride to have me move out. Those were his motives for trying to keep me on the Circle J, or at least I thought they were. But today there was that need. He couldn't hide it. But I can't imagine what he needs—my pa's a rich man. Anyway, I think that's what I saw." She shuddered. "And prideful or not, he doesn't want me around, not really. You've been with the Idee for a year. You know how Pa is. What do you think is behind what happened today? What does he need me for?"

Nate ran his right hand up and down her arm. He felt the shudders deepen. Then those hazel eyes glistened with tears and a sob tore out of her throat. She dropped her head until it rested against his chest. Unable to resist, he wrapped his arms around her, the strongest woman he'd ever known, crying because of the way she'd been treated by her cruel father.

Her arms came around his waist. He rested his lips on the top of her head. Then he heard himself crooning to her. He had a big family back in California. He had little sisters and a kindhearted ma. He'd held women before and knew how they could use a strong shoulder from time to time.

Not Becky Pruitt, though. Her pa had brought her low, and all Nate could do was wish he'd've pounded the coyote all the way into the ground. Now he stood here and wondered what the right thing was to say. How to help her. For now, just holding her was all he could think of.

Finally, as they stood there in the warm summer breeze, her sobs died away, replaced by sniffles. Her shudders steadied. When the last of the tears ended, he tugged his red neckerchief loose and leaned away just enough to offer it to her.

She stepped back and mopped her face, blew her nose, then crumpled the kerchief into a tight ball. "Pa shouldn't have the right to make me cry."

"I'm not sure you'd react differently no matter who attacked you like that. It's worse, I reckon, when it's your pa, but anyone would be upset by it. You kept your head, showed only strength while it was going on. You fought back, too. But now that it's over, letting go of some of the tension with a few tears is no sign of weakness."

"It's shameful."

"It's human."

"I don't see you crying." She looked up sharply at him. Those dark eyes could indeed flash.

"Maybe I could wring out a few tears if it'd make you feel better."

That made her smile. He noticed her nose was shining so bright that he wondered if he could see his own reflection.

And her tear-soaked eyes were glowing with grief and hurt. She really was mighty pretty. And he couldn't think of the last time he'd felt this close to a woman. Emotionally close, but he was *standing* really close, too. He felt drawn to her like a wildflower was drawn to the sun. He leaned down and kissed her.

Becky jerked away. Their eyes met.

Nate realized he had his arms around her waist, and he probably oughta let her go.

Then she wrapped her arms around his neck and kissed him back, long and deep. They might've stood there all day if Brutus hadn't run up and jumped, standing on his hind legs, leaning on the two of them.

Becky squeaked and leapt backward. She almost pulled Nate over because she forgot she had her arms wrapped around his neck.

When she fought her way free, he saw the red creeping up her neck. Tears and blushes. Not Becky's usual thing.

Then that flash in her eyes was back, and she jabbed a finger so hard at him, she almost poked him in the nose. He took a couple of quick steps back to get out of poking distance.

"You took advantage of me when I was so upset about my father."

"I did not!" Had he? Not consciously, but—

"You keep your hands to yourself, Nate Paxton. You put your hands on me again, be ready to pull back stumps." She whirled away from him, almost tripping over poor Brutus, and stormed toward her stallion.

"Becky, wait. I—"

She most certainly did not wait. Soon she was down the trail and out of earshot. Unless he started hollering.

And that seemed stupid.

Brutus stood there next to Nate. If it were possible for a dog to show such a thing, Brutus looked confused. Nate suspected the expression on his own face was similar. He hadn't deserved Becky's accusations. They made him mad. But she *had* been upset. She *had* turned to him and let him hold her through her tears.

And he'd returned that trust by kissing her.

And she'd kissed him back, with considerable abandon. But that could be caused by her upset, too.

Nate was also upset. Watching Pruitt rage at his daughter. Stepping in to stop the fool from hitting Becky—those things had left him angry and feeling like a warrior and like a protector when Becky had needed one most.

That all counted as upset.

48

One thing he knew, however. He'd taken the first kiss, and he shouldn't have. But Becky had taken the second, so she was just as much in the wrong as he was. He was no kind of genius, but he knew as sure as the sunrise that saying just that to Becky might get him fired, if not horsewhipped.

He watched the fast-moving palomino until it rounded a corner and disappeared. Nate remembered he didn't like her riding out there alone and mounted up. He went after her at a good clip until she came into view. Riding hard but safe enough, he made no attempt to close the distance between them.

He wished himself back to simpler times, like this morning when he was beating on himself for saying her nightgown was pretty.

He stayed well back until the ranch was about to come into view around a curve in the trail. Then, because he thought it might look strange to the men and he didn't want to answer any questions, he picked up the pace and was soon riding beside her.

They didn't talk. Nate was busy contemplating how warm he felt from kissing his boss and wondering whether she intended to kick him off her ranch and send him job hunting.

Whatever Becky was thinking, she kept it to herself, and he appreciated that.

5

Becky was thinking that she was out of her ever-loving mind.

She'd kissed Nate. She had never been a woman given to thinking much about men and here she'd found herself kissing one.

He'd kissed her.

She'd kissed him back.

Then her head cleared . . . somewhat—it wasn't completely clear even now—and she'd started yelling and accusing and blaming. Like the worst kind of weakling who didn't take responsibility for her own actions.

Nate caught up to her as she rounded the last bend in the trail and her ranch yard came into view. All she could think of was to run inside and hide for the rest of the day. And that would never do. But maybe she could go in for a while. Change out of her going-to-town clothes. Yes, that'd work. She needed to do that. Then she'd have a few quiet moments before getting back to work.

Becky turned to face Nate as they rode toward her

ranch. "Nate, I'm sorry I attacked you like that." She forced honesty from her overly warm lips. Lips that felt slightly swollen.

Nate looked puzzled. "You didn't attack me."

She kept talking, fast, because she didn't want to hear what he had to say. "You shouldn't have kissed me. But you were upset. So was I." Becky felt her heart speed up, and she looked forward again. She didn't quite have the courage to look him in the eyes. "We were both stirred up. You kissed me, and I kissed you back. We were behaving as we shouldn't."

Nate removed his hat, swiped his forearm across his brow. "You're right that your pa stirred us both up."

"It shouldn't have happened," she went on, "but it did. You rode to town to protect me in a rugged, sometimes dangerous countryside. You stepped between me and my father so he couldn't deal out any pain. Then you held me while I cried. Both of us were . . . well, we weren't ourselves."

"I wonder if we weren't more ourselves right at that minute than we've ever been before."

Becky had no idea what that meant. "It happened. It shouldn't have, but it did. Kissing you . . . uh, that is, us kissing . . . I mean kissing *each other* was a mistake. And it won't happen again. I apologize for my part in it." Desperate to end this awkward conversation and sorely afraid she was blushing, judging by the heat in her face, she looked anywhere but at Nate and saw Roscoe coming out of the barn. She rode straight for him.

"Been a long day already, Roscoe, and plenty more to do. Can I leave my horse for you to tend?"

Roscoe's eyes sharpened as he studied her. She had no idea what she looked like. But she did know that she always handled her own horse and most especially she handled her palomino. Every day but today.

Roscoe didn't comment. He took the reins as she swung down and headed for the house. She glanced back once to see Roscoe look between her and Nate.

She headed inside at a fast walk. Not a run. No, not even close. Well, maybe close. But she definitely wasn't running away from Nate and what he'd made her feel and want.

"You're out of order, Mr. Burke." Nell whacked her gavel on the table. Sitting there wearing her black robe, she felt very official. And very irritated by this squabble.

"I don't see why. I've got just as much claim on the general store as Mr. Betancourt. You can't just hand something so valuable off to him because he asked first."

Nell kept a very bland expression on her face, while inside she had to admit, Jim Burke, the town undertaker, had a point.

"It was decided that Mr. Betancourt's claim was legitimate. He paid bills owed by the Wainwrights." Using the Wainwrights' money, but Nell didn't tell Jim that. "And this town needs an undertaker. Don't leave the job you've trained for."

Honestly, *trained* was a strong word for what Jim did. Build a box, stick a body in it, and dig a hole. No great training to be seen anywhere. "And besides, we already gave Mr. Betancourt's job to someone else, so he can't have it back."

Joy Blodgett had stepped in as teacher even though at sixteen she wasn't really old enough. But the girl had been raised by a fierce parson and a fiercer ma, and she had four little brothers she handled very well. She handled her two *older* brothers well, too. And she'd finished all her books and taken a stiff exam to qualify. Joy had insisted on facing that challenge, and she'd done quite well indeed.

Joy at the school. Steven Betancourt at the general store. Jim Burke preparing bodies for burial. The town really needed him, though Nell couldn't blame the man for not liking this job.

"I'd've paid those bills if I'd known there was such a situation. Betancourt just swooped in, found out about the outstanding bills, paid them, and moved right into the store. One of those bills was money owed to Mariah Roberts for her house. And one of those bills, well, two of them were to me for burying the scoundrels."

Nell looked the man in the eye for a long time. For a while he met her eyes, defiant, ready to fight all the way to the Supreme Court. Then his gaze dropped.

"I don't want to be an undertaker anymore. Burying strangers is a sad business, with no one to come to their funerals. No one to care if they live or die. Worse, to imagine someone, somewhere might care, but we can't find them to notify them."

Then Jim's eyes came back up. Almost beseeching Nell to save him from what seemed to her like a grisly, thankless job.

Jim was no youngster, though. He'd been the town undertaker since he showed up here. Before she came. Just after Mariah. Jim Burke had buried her ma.

Quietly, Nell said, "Would you really want to be a store-keeper, Mr. Burke? It's a demanding job, isn't it, Mr. Betancourt?"

"It's more demanding than I thought it would be." Steven Betancourt turned to look at Jim. "Long hours. A constant shortage of supplies. I don't have a partner like the Wainwrights did. Henry would run the freight wagon and go for supplies. Pete kept the store running."

"He did go for supplies," Nell said sharply. "But he also lied about needing supply runs when he was, in fact, robbing stagecoaches and murdering people. Including the Stovers, men this town respected and loved."

Mariah's father and brother had died under Henry Wainwright's guns. And there'd been enough proof in the books kept by Pete Wainwright to show unexplained income that matched up with the dates of the robberies.

Nell looked between the two men. At last she said, "Mr. Betancourt, would you consider taking on a partner?" Without waiting for an answer, she shifted her attention to Jim. "And would you be interested in running a supply wagon? There's not much that's enjoyable about driving a slow wagon down rutted trails for long days. Or would you be willing to work in the general store while Mr. Betancourt runs for supplies? Or perhaps the two of you could share the responsibilities?"

She let her questions hang in the air, wondering what Solomon had felt like when he'd asked the women if he could cut a baby in half. He might've earned a moment of silence with that one.

Jim looked at Steven. "What do you think? Could you use a partner?" Jim's voice echoed with hope. He stood taller. "Maybe not a full partner. Maybe I could still handle the job of mortician. It's certainly not full-time work."

Steven studied the other man. "I honestly could use some help. What about supplies? Would you want to do the runs, or at least take a turn? Right now, I'm working to get a freight wagon to come through Pine Valley more often and bring more when they do come. Henry did a lot of the hauling himself as a guise for his filthy robberies."

Steven glanced at Nell. She gave him a firm nod of approval.

"They've said they'll come more often," Steven went on, "but so far they haven't. Twice I've driven to Green River—the closest town to us with the Union Pacific Railroad station. I can get all the supplies I need shipped in there, but the train only passes through once a week. I mail an order to the general store in Green River and ask them to forward it to wherever they get their supplies." Steven threw his arms wide. "I'm figuring it out, but it's slow and it's over a hundred miles. I'm on the trail for days and days. I've only gone twice in two months, and I've had to shut the store down for two weeks both times. That's half the time since I started up that the store's been closed."

Betancourt sighed and said rather sadly, "I sort of miss teaching school."

The two men stood looking each other in the eye.

"We'll talk about it." Jim gave a firm nod. "Maybe I could take a turn with the supply run. And maybe instead of being a partner, you might consider hiring me to run the store and keep it open when you're gone."

Smiles bloomed on both men's faces.

Steven turned to Nell. "I think we can settle this without

forcing you to rule on it, Your Honor. Thank you for helping us find a solution."

"Thank you, Judge Nolte," Jim added with a smile.

Nell rapped her gavel again. "Case dismissed."

The two men walked out, talking rapidly.

Solomon would've been proud.

The door burst open, and Samantha came running in. Through broken sobs, she said, "I want to come home."

Leland came storming in right behind her. "Now you just settle down, Samantha. No sense throwing a fit just because . . ."

Nell tuned them both out while they squabbled on.

Samantha, the oldest of three sisters, had run her family's household for quite a few years after her ma died and was used to being in control. And Leland was the oldest of seven children. He was used to thinking things should go as he saw fit. Their differences weren't overly serious in Nell's opinion.

They'd simply gotten married too suddenly. And for a fact, Samantha, at sixteen and traumatized by a wolf attack, had been in no condition, physically or emotionally, to get married. She'd been badly scarred and had feared what the future held for her with those terrible bites on her face.

Leland and his proposal must have seemed like a true white knight riding to her rescue. Leland, for his part, was a farmer without much of an idea of how to handle a wife. Neither shield nor any armor to be seen.

And Samantha, raised in a motherless home, had basic cooking skills, very few sewing skills, had hair almost as short as Leland's, and on most occasions preferred wearing britches to dresses.

Leland found that outrageous.

Samantha found him overbearing and had no interest in putting up with it.

It all amounted to a couple of youngsters who probably should still be living with their parents instead of being declared full adults and standing on their own.

Now they all had to cope with the results.

About once a week they'd have a big fight and then Samantha would ask to come home.

Nell ignored the bickering and went straight to God with a heartfelt prayer. She was pretty sure it was beyond anything Solomon, and most certainly she, could handle.

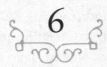

6

Nate's brother rode into the ranch yard, and it drove out the tangle in his head.

Days. He'd been avoiding his boss for days. Talking strictly business when they absolutely had to talk about the other matter. The kiss.

Lately he'd been ridiculously polite to her, speaking in one-syllable words when he could. Thank the good Lord God in heaven, Sal had showed up. Nate's brother would be a distraction, a barrier between Nate and Becky and that kiss.

And her apology still made him want to punch the barn wall.

She thought he was upset before? She didn't know what upset was.

Both dogs ran over to stand at Nate's side, watching Sal approach them wearing a smile. "Nate! Good to see you again." Two men rode with Sal. The promised Marshals for a fact, only they'd come to work as cowpokes and not lawmen.

They'd decided not to pretend they didn't know one

another or to try to hide their meeting in town a week ago. Too many people might've seen them, and word got around in a little settlement like Pine Valley.

Nate and Sal decided to tell the truth just as much as possible. It kept a person from having to remember what he'd said. Of course, they'd have to leave out a few big details.

"Sal. Welcome. Glad to see you decided to stop by." And that was the honest truth. Nate had never been so glad to see anyone in his life.

Roscoe came out of the barn to the sound of hooves. The rest of the men were getting five hundred head of Angus cattle settled on lush grass to fatten up a bit before the long drive to Denver.

"Roscoe, come and meet my brother," Nate called.

Roscoe Grable had been the foreman when Nate rode in. A tough, smart, decent man Nate had respected as his boss. Nate had signed on as a simple cowhand, his first job after leaving the U.S. Marshals Service. He'd handled cows before, enjoyed the work, and moved up quickly to ramrod when a few cowhands had drifted after the first cattle drive, including Becky's ramrod, the second-in-command. Well, third, since Becky was first, then Roscoe.

Then Roscoe had been bucked off a mean mustang and come up with a badly battered knee. He'd requested a move to cook, at least temporarily, and advised Becky to hire Nate to replace him. Roscoe lived in the house with his wife, Becky's housekeeper. He'd told Nate he might be taking his job back once his leg was healed. But Roscoe was an old-timer and seemed to settle in well as bunkhouse cook. The leg was fine now or as close to fine as it was going to get. And it'd been fine for most of a year. Even so, Roscoe hadn't demanded his job back, and Nate hadn't been demoted back to ramrod.

Nate made quick introductions. Afterward Sal introduced his saddle partners, Owen Riley and Tex Mitchel.

"We're hunting work, Nate. You said you've got a drive coming up and might be shorthanded."

"Let's go talk to Miss Pruitt. I told her I suggested you come around, and only Miss Pruitt takes on hands. She's the boss and has the final say on such matters." Nate called her Becky mostly, as did the hands. But they didn't start that at first—his brother and the two newcomers had to earn that right.

Nate wondered if he'd lost any rights after that kiss. Mentally shaking the notion away, he led the way to Becky's back door and knocked.

The dogs stayed close. It gave Nate cool satisfaction to know the critters were so protective of Becky and everyone else on the ranch.

Jan Grable came to the door and opened it with her usual friendly smile. "Nate, come on in. Becky's doing bookwork, but she'll be ready for a break. I just finished making doughnuts and was about to bring a platter of them out to the bunkhouse. You and these men can have some while they're still hot."

"Thanks, Jan. Sounds terrific. I've got some men here hunting work. One of them is my brother, Sal." Nate pointed at Sal, then introduced the others.

Jan Grable was a savvy woman. Nate wondered if she could tell they were lawmen. Nate thought it was obvious, but then he'd been told.

"Sal, welcome." She nodded at Nate's brother and gave the other two men a wide smile.

"It smells like a slice of heaven in here, Mrs. Grable," Sal said as he followed Nate inside.

Nate dragged his Stetson off his head, running his gloved fingers through his hair to push it off his forehead. He hung his hat on a peg in the entryway near the door, then tugged off his gloves and dropped them onto a bench Becky kept there.

Sal copied his actions, and the two newcomers did the same. They headed for the kitchen table just as Becky came in.

"I heard about your doughnuts being ready, Jan. I've been smelling them for an hour. Thank you so much." Becky gave Sal, Owen, and Tex a long look, which was something she would've done for any stranger entering her house.

Jan poured coffee for everyone and put out a plate of the fresh doughnuts. She was a hand with the baking. Nate knew it personally.

Brutus slipped under the table to lie at Becky's feet.

Lobo stayed outside.

"Mrs. Grable's married to Roscoe, who came out of the barn to meet you." Nate sat and drew his heavy ceramic coffee cup close. "He was foreman here before he got his knee banged up getting thrown from a horse. I got the job until he healed up."

Becky said, "Join us." She looked at Sal. "You must be Nate's brother. I see the resemblance."

They were both dark-haired and brown-eyed. On the lean side. But Nate had never thought they looked overly alike. Was this Becky ruining their sly plan already?

"I'm Sal Paxton, miss, and these are my saddle partners, Tex Mitchel and Owen Riley. Nate didn't meet them the other day in town, but he said you might take on more hands with the cattle drive coming up."

Becky asked a few very astute questions while they drank their coffee and feasted on the doughnuts. Nate remembered her asking him these exact questions. They carried on a very businesslike conversation until Mrs. Grable left the kitchen with a platter filled with doughnuts, covered by a white kitchen towel.

Becky stopped with her questions and said curtly, "It seems you're hired."

Tex, a short, stocky blond, replied in a Texas drawl, "Thank you, miss. Me and Owen are good cowhands. We intend to work for you fair and square. And any pay you feel you need to hand over for appearances' sake will be returned to you quietly. We've got urgent business that, as we understand, has come close to you through your friends in town. We want to put an end to the Deadeye Gang, and quick-like. Then we'll be on the trail and out of your lives."

Owen, a quieter man with straggly blond hair, sprawled in a chair by the table, looking on the lazy side. He nodded. "Obliged for putting up with us, Miss Pruitt."

Sal smiled and added, "Nate speaks highly of you, Miss Pruitt. It's a pleasure to finally meet you."

"I'll show the men around the place, get them settled in the bunkhouse. Thanks." Nate met her eyes, and it wasn't easy. "You're an honest woman, Miss Becky. We all appreciate your allowing us to set up here."

7

There was a tap on her window again that night.
She'd been expecting it.

Becky did much less leaping this time. She was in fact asleep on top of her covers, still fully dressed except for her boots. She'd dozed for a bit, which was a good thing because morning came real early.

They had things to talk about after today. She hadn't gotten ready for bed, which would have meant putting on that nightgown he'd called pretty.

She swung the shutters open and saw Nate standing there. She heard the soft padding of Brutus and Lobo outside. Brutus leapt through the window while Lobo settled below it. He should not be in here—Nate, not Brutus. Brutus was always welcome.

Becky would have insisted Nate stay outside while he talked to her, but she wasn't sure just how deeply asleep the Grables were. And she very much needed to talk to Nate. Certainly not about that kiss. They'd done all the talking about that they were going to.

"Just come in. I'm not whispering to you through the window again."

Nate hesitated, then clambered inside.

"Owen is the senior U.S. Marshal in Colorado," Nate began, whispering fast. No nonsense.

Becky appreciated that.

"Though he's a quiet man, we answer to him. Tex is a former Texas Ranger. He wanted to wander farther than one state, so he signed on to be a Marshal. Sal spends his time mostly in Colorado—he's the one who connected us with the Marshals. Nell's letters demanding protection for the stagecoaches Mrs. Mussel and Mrs. Morris are riding in on caught Sal's attention because he knew I lived near Pine Valley. She's up in arms about Mrs. Mussel coming. She wants protection for such an important visitor. Marshals see a bigger problem, but those letters from Nell, combined with letters from Esther Morris and others, are what brought the Marshals in. It's high time they provide us with some protection."

"Tell me what you're planning."

Nate shook his head. "I can't, Becky. And it's not that I don't trust you. But they're keeping this so quiet, I don't know what's going on myself. I think the other seven Marshals are out in the hills already, sneaking around, studying the trails and where the stagecoaches will run. They know the schedules.

"Big territory. The outlaws have no pattern, though they've hit twice mighty close to Pine Valley. Otherwise they've struck both near and far. Henry Wainwright seemed to be the leader of the holdups, Pete the money manager. Were the rest of the men from around here, or do they plan to rendezvous somewhere we can't figure out?"

Becky wondered how they picked their targets. "Do the Marshals know when big payrolls come through? Seems someone is feeding them information. You might be able to backtrack, find out who all knew about gold and payroll shipments. Maybe they can use that information to predict where and when the next attack will take place."

Nate nodded. "Makes sense. I'll ask Owen if he's doing that." He looked at her uncertainly. "I'm not sure I'm supposed to tell you what I have already. I might present this sensible idea as . . . well, as my own." He winced a bit, watching her.

"It's wise to do it that way." She smiled at him. "But I appreciate that you don't *want* to take credit for it."

He perked up a bit. Good, he was having a happy moment. She hoped he was enjoying it because it was about to end.

"I'm sending Roscoe on the cattle drive. He'll take charge of it, and Jan will go along. He's done it plenty. I'm staying here with you and your Marshal friends."

"What?" Nate yelped, then slapped a hand over his mouth.

Which gave Becky a chance to finish. "I am *not* letting a bunch of men I don't know have free rein over my land and my herd while I'm away. I'll agree to let you all work from here but not without my being home. That's final."

Nate glared at her from over the hand he'd clamped over his mouth.

"Glare all you want. It's my way or you can find yourself another place to work."

From behind Nate, a quiet voice said, "It's your way then, Miss Pruitt."

They spun around and saw Owen Riley standing outside her window.

Becky noticed the dogs hadn't growled at his approach. Brutus hadn't even gone to the window to look. Owen must be smart enough to have befriended the dogs.

He had none of the lazy look she'd wondered about earlier. Instead, he looked sharp and keenly intelligent, on edge for any kind of trouble anytime. She could look at him now and well imagine him to be their leader.

"So long as we understand each other, Mr. Riley."

"We do. I want to add that there are things you don't know. Things Nate doesn't know. Reasons we chose your ranch. A lot of the planning we need to do will begin after your men leave for the drive and you'll be informed of more then. If you're insisting on staying, is there another woman, someone trustworthy who could come out here and stay? It's not fitting that you be here alone."

Becky thought of Nell, but she came with a husband and children and duties as the town's justice of the peace.

There was Mariah, but Clint would be unhappy about her leaving him, not to mention her expectant state. And Clint would be sorely missed if he closed the diner for weeks. So sorely missed that the townsfolk might kick up a big enough fuss that the secretive planning done out here at Becky's might come to light.

Finally, there was Pa. Two weeks ago she might have even considered it because he would make a likely chaperone. But recent events had taught Becky all over again that her pa wasn't to be trusted.

"I'll have to give it some thought," she said, then added, "A lot of newcomers make up this state, Owen, but I'm not one of them. My pa came here early and started his ranch when there weren't many folks around. I was born out here, and I've ridden this range more than most anyone alive, except for Pa. When you go to making plans, I'd recommend you involve me in them. I know the terrain, the hideouts, the dangerous trails, the overlooks to those trails where those filthy Deadeye Gang members might stake out an oncoming stage. I can help you. Keep that in mind."

Owen arched one brow and studied her long and slow. Then, not looking all that happy about it, he replied, "I'll let you know if I decide I need you. I appreciate your willingness."

"Also," Becky continued, "there's a woman coming to Pine Valley, Mrs. Mussel, who's to give a speech here in the middle of August. That's a week away. We'll have our rally, and just days later all my men will head for Denver. That will leave you Marshals, Nate, and me behind. I've contacted the U.S. Marshals and the cavalry—as has Nell Nolte, our justice of the peace—demanding Mrs. Mussel's safety be assured. I've been given reason to hope our requests will be honored."

"I'm aware of those letters and telegraphs, Miss Pruitt. It's part of the reason we're here."

"To protect Mrs. Mussel?" Becky had become increasingly sure her letters had fallen on deaf ears, but now hope awakened.

"No."

Her eyes narrowed, and she exchanged a glance with Nate.

Owen raised both hands as if he were surrendering there at the window. "Not solely to protect her, Miss Pruitt, but your efforts, along with Judge Nolte's, drew our attention to this ranch, and we realized then how perfectly situated it is."

"Perfectly situated? Why in the world is that?"

Owen ignored the question and said, "Protecting Mrs. Mussel is a need that *will* be met. In fact, there are already outriders planning to accompany her."

Becky shook her head. "Those outriders were all killed when the Deadeye Gang struck last."

"And there were enough men that it shouldn't have happened." Owen's expression turned grim, causing Becky to wonder if he knew some of the men who'd died.

"We'll see to that stage of hers. And to all future stages until this gang is caught. The lawlessness has been allowed to go on for too long."

He sounded very confident, but Becky remained skeptical. The Deadeye Gang was ruthless and seemed to be more reckless and deadly than ever.

As Owen stood there in the window, Becky realized he was much older than she'd thought when she met him earlier. Cowhands tended to be young. It wasn't a job for men with aching joints and reflexes slowed by age. With the single lantern flickering, it deepened the wrinkles in Owen's face. She suspected he had joint pain to deal with for a fact.

"Come on out of her bedroom now, Nate," Owen said. "You've got no business being in there this late at night."

A light flush tinted Nate's cheeks. "Some things need to be said in secret, Owen. We're usually working surrounded by a crowd. But what needed to be said has been said. Leaving is a wise idea. Good night, Miss Becky."

Nate's eyes, recently so angry, sparked now with something else. Something that made her wonder.

Yes, he'd wanted her to ride off with the cattle drive. But maybe he liked her being here, too.

He was soon gone out the window. No parting remark about her nightgown tonight. Brutus licked her fingertips, then leapt out the window after Nate.

Becky closed and locked the shutters with a bit too much force, got into her pretty nightgown, thought of Nate's blush, and wondered some more.

"We need another stage." Bernard Skleen started talking before Randall Kingston could say hello. But Randall smiled and gestured broadly for him to come in.

Bern went into this blamed fool house, built so grand it was as if Randall wanted the sheriff to come snooping around.

And he hadn't gotten the money to build it from Bern and the Deadeye Gang. Still, everything about Kingston shouted *thief.* Wherever the money had come from, it hadn't been gotten honestly.

Bern could respect that.

"When I heard Henry and Pete were dead, I figured you'd be back. Those two didn't have a lick of sense, stretching the jobs out so far. You need to hit and hit fast when you're working an area like you are." Kingston led the way to his office. A law office with shelves full of lawbooks, all of them coated in dust.

And Kingston didn't do his own cleaning, so whoever did it for him didn't pay these books any more mind than Kingston did.

Kingston was a tall one, good enough looking, though Bern couldn't judge that. But plenty of hair still on his head. All his teeth. He dressed up, too. A black suit and a white shirt, polished black books and a string tie with what looked like a gold nugget for a pendent. Next to him, Bern felt small and homely, and yet being on the small side had served him well. Bern had learned at a very young age how to slip in and out of homes at night. On the streets of St. Louis, he'd been a hand at relieving folks of their valuables. Getting in and out of houses without being noticed.

Bern was a wiry one hundred and forty pounds. Five-foot-four in his stocking feet. No hair worth mentioning left on his head. He and Kingston made a laughable pair, but it didn't matter, as they were careful not to be seen together any more than necessary.

Kingston said, "I got word of a gold shipment coming out of South Pass City in about two weeks. They're heading for the train but are taking a different route."

"Has South Pass found a new gold strike?" Bern's attention was sharply focused now.

"Nope, but I guess a few have been hoarding so that now, with the mines drying up, they plan to make a run for a new spot. They know they'll need a lot of good luck and skill to get that gold out. They're sending outriders with the gold shipment, and I've heard they hired some tough men."

Bern waved a hand at Kingston and smiled. "Last bunch

was tough, too. And with two weeks to scout around, we'll find a place to waylay them. In rugged country like this, there's usually plenty to pick from. The boss likes to ride out from time to time, see what's to be seen. Pick a spot. Thinks he's a trailblazer or some such."

"He still won't do the holdups with you, though? Same as Pete?"

Bern shook his head. "Nope, and he's got the right of it. He stays to the house, but he provides us with cover, and that's worth a lot. With the Wainwrights out of it, we don't have an ear to the ground in Pine Valley. The boss is working on that but hasn't picked out anyone as yet."

"Are all of your boss's men involved?"

"The last two who didn't want in on the gang rode off a month ago. Some stay out of the robbery, but they keep the boss's business running."

"So they know to cover for you when you're gone?"

"Yep, they understand what's at stake, and they know a share is coming to them. There is always work to be done. But they keep their mouths shut, and so do we. We've had a couple of big strikes lately, Randall. You're getting us good information."

Randall nodded but didn't offer an explanation as to how he got the information. And Bern knew better, after working on this for two years, not to press for anything Randall didn't want to give.

"How's Oliver?"

Randall's eyes went tense around the corners. "My brother's a man best avoided. Best let be. Key Larson was a friend of his, but Key didn't know how we ran things. Losing him was a good step forward."

"Henry did for him after he kidnapped that girl who survived the stagecoach. He knew good and well that killing her would bring fire raining down on our heads." Bern settled into a chair but only after Randall gestured to it.

Then, morning or not, Randall went to a sideboard in his law office and poured a whiskey for each of them. He handed Bern a half-filled glass and waited while Bern took a sip.

Liquid fire. Bern had no taste for it and considered a drinker to be a fool. Yet he knew better than to not act delighted when Kingston offered a glass of his best whiskey.

Bern had to wonder what kind of man Oliver was that the thought of him made Kingston tense up like he'd done. Because Kingston was no angel, and it looked like he carried around some dark thoughts about Oliver Hawkins.

As they sipped the whiskey, Kingston shared the rest of the details of the gold shipment coming out of South Pass City. Many men were cashing in their life's work.

Bern intended to put the men right back in the mine, having to build from scratch.

"Clint?" Mariah reached for her husband in the night.

He shot straight up, then spun to look down at her. "Is it time? Is the baby coming?"

Mariah had to fight not to laugh. Her husband had very sharp eyes, even in the dark, so she did her best not to even smile. Running a hand over her rounded stomach, she said, "No. I just, well, I know how early you get up.

72

I'm sorry." And she was. It was pure selfishness to want to talk to him in the night sometimes. She mostly controlled herself, but this time . . .

He lay back, slid one arm under her shoulders, and pulled her close so her head rested on his shoulder. Their baby, still inside her but very much theirs and fully loved, was pressed between them.

"Having trouble sleeping?"

She laid her hand over his heart, beating too fast. "I'm sorry. Yes. I shouldn't have awakened you." If he only knew how many times she'd controlled herself, she might be given some credit for her weak moments.

"What's on your mind?"

"A couple of things." Or three, or five. She knew very little about what lay ahead as far as having a baby. At the root of everything was that she wanted her mother. She should've talked to Parson Blodgett's wife before they moved away. But that worry would upset Clint, so she didn't mention it. There were other women in town. Mariah needed to pick one of them.

"I'm not doing any blacksmithing these days, and Willie is very capable." He'd learned blacksmithing well. Underpaid for the job of deputy, he'd been a hard worker and quick learner. "Did I tell you that he's teaching Kate how to run the forge? And I've been working with her on making wooden pails. She'll make a fine cooper one day."

Kate and Willie Minton had their children raised, and Kate seemed to like being a partner in the smithy.

"So that's where you sneaked off to today," he said. "I figured you were shoeing horses or some such—even though I ordered you not to."

That made her grin, and she caught a few of his chest hairs and yanked. They both knew Clint didn't *order* her to do things, or in this case, not do things. He talked to her. She talked to him. They came to agreements. He was teasing her.

"Ouch!" He pressed her hand flat on his chest. His heart was slowing to a normal pace.

"I'm thinking of selling the smithy to Willie. He can't afford much. We talked about price, and he wondered if he could just rent it. He offered me fifteen dollars a month. He'd take on the cost of iron and collect any money he generated beyond rent and materials."

"Does the smithy make that much profit a month? Can Willie afford it?"

"I did some figuring, and it seems fair. I told him if he kept it up, fifteen dollars a month for a few years, maybe five, and he'd own it. But if things went bad for him, he could just walk away and I'd take the smithy back."

Clint's hand came up to rest on her head. She felt his strength and protection surrounding her and loved it.

"I know it's not easy to give up your pa's business. That blacksmith shop is more than your work; it holds memories you cherish. It's been a big part of your life."

"I won't be able to work there, though, not with a new baby and maybe a few more ahead for us."

Clint kissed her on the top of her head. "A few more would be a wonderful thing."

They rested together for a while, then Clint said, "What else is worrying you? You said a couple of things."

The next one was a bit embarrassing. She'd've talked with Nell about it, but she knew exactly how Clint would act. Still, it was better than telling him she wanted her mother. "I'm worried about Becky."

She felt Clint's chest rise and fall in a quiet chuckle. "Thinking of matchmaking, Mrs. Roberts?"

"Nell and Becky and I used to talk together all the time about how independent we were and how proud we were to live in a land where women had the right to vote. How none of us needed a man; we could take care of ourselves."

"And yet somehow you and Nell ended up married."

Mariah nodded, knowing Clint could feel it. "And it's wonderful to be married to a good, decent man. Looking back now on all we said, well, we poisoned each other against marriage. Of course, Nell and I have survived that poison and cast it aside. But we've left Becky behind. It wouldn't matter so much if she had family, but things are likely never to improve between her and her pa."

"Joshua Pruitt is a hard man." Clint pulled her close. "Here we both are, lonely for our fathers, and there Becky is with a living father right near her and there's only un-happiness between them. Do you think we should help them heal their relationship?"

"Good heavens, no." Mariah shot upward just as Clint had before. Yet Clint had his arms around her and kept her close. "Joshua is dreadful."

"He is for a fact."

"That leaves Becky without her pa's love, and with Nell and me so busy being married . . ."

Clint ran a hand over her, outlining the baby. He kissed her forehead.

"I want someone for her. Someone of her very own. She's so alone."

"Now, honey, she's surrounded all day by cowhands. She's got the Grables in the house with her. She's not alone."

"To be surrounded by people and still feel alone is worse than if she was completely by herself."

"Probably not worse."

"Becky usually sends her cowhands off to Denver, driving her herd. She gets the best money there. The workload is light once they leave, and she always comes into town for church. I was wondering if we could invite her to Sunday dinner along with Nell's family?"

"Of course we can."

"And invite Mr. Betancourt."

Clint groaned, then laughed. "So you *are* matchmaking."

"I'm just giving two intelligent, lonely people a chance to spend a little time together."

Clint kissed her nose. "No."

Mariah pulled away from him and propped herself up on her elbow. "Why not?"

Clint laughed. "I'll tell you why not."

And he whispered something to her that made her want to kick her own backside because she hadn't thought of it herself.

8

Sal, Tex, and Owen were good cowhands.

Becky was glad to see it because she didn't like looking like a fool to her men, and if she'd hired three useless drovers, they'd have thought she was going soft.

Tex was the best. He handled cattle with such skill, Becky wondered if she could get him to leave off being a Marshal and sign on with her permanently. Sal was a solid hand. Owen wasn't as skilled, but he made up for it by taking the worst, dirtiest jobs and sticking with them until they were done.

She wondered about their lives before they joined the Marshals Service. And Tex, a former Texas Ranger?

Sal, Nate's brother, made Becky realize she'd never heard much about Nate's past. It was the kind of thing that was rude to ask about because a lot of men came out west to start over. If Nate offered to talk of his childhood and his earlier jobs, they'd all listen. But no one would ask.

Owen kept up a mild, almost lazy attitude when he

wasn't working. If she hadn't been told and hadn't talked to him that night when he stood at her window, Becky would never have guessed him to be the leader of this pack of Marshals.

Becky wasn't sure how devious the Marshals were. There was little chance to talk, but it burned in Becky's mind that Owen had said there was a very specific reason why they were using her ranch.

As they drove a small herd of older cattle to pasture to fatten them up one last time before the cattle drive, she narrowed her eyes as she tried to remember what exactly Owen had said. Something about how her ranch was "perfectly situated." She'd drawn their attention because of the letters she'd written demanding the cavalry or the Marshals protect Mrs. Mussel. And they'd realized how perfectly situated her ranch was.

What did the Marshals have planned exactly? And why did they think of her ranch as the perfect spot? Was it because her place wasn't near any major trails or near any of the stagecoach robberies?

Becky could tell that Nate wondered what Owen meant just as much as she did. She grumbled as she hazed a three-year-old steer that tried to get out of line.

She'd been herding cattle since the day she learned to ride a horse. There'd been two younger brothers who'd died when a fever swept through the ranch. Two years later, when Becky was eight, her ma died birthing a baby. The baby died with her. That left Becky alone with her pa, and Pa didn't have much time to fuss with her. She grew up fast, worked hard, and never complained. Now here she was, still at it.

She saw the first of the older herd wade into the belly-deep grass ahead. The other cattle smelled it and picked up their pace. Soon there was nothing left to herd as the cattle went along exactly to where they were supposed to go.

Becky, riding drag, reined her horse over to Nate, who'd slowed to watch the cattle speed up until a few of them were running. With a few minutes to spare before the other men rode up to discuss what was next, Becky asked him, "What do you think Owen meant when he said my ranch was 'perfectly situated' for the Marshals?"

Nate turned away from the cattle to meet her gaze. "I'm wondering that, too. One of the reasons I got out of the Marshals was that they were often plotting things but not telling me what the real plot was. It made me feel like they didn't trust me. They didn't tell me secrets unless I absolutely needed to know them. Truth was, they just didn't trust anyone, and probably for good reason. But I found myself in a couple of tight spots because I didn't know what my leader was plotting. I got fed up by it all, tried to talk Sal into quitting and wandering with me. Turned out he liked being a lawman more than he disliked being mistrusted. So I quit and drifted and ended up here. This suits me way better."

"That's the most you've ever talked about yourself." Becky knew a man's past could be private, but she asked anyway. "Where did you and Sal grow up?"

Nate knew the ways of the West. Her asking him such a thing wasn't idle talk. He didn't treat her question as such.

"Sal is four years older than me. He was born on a wagon train on the way to California. My folks took the Santa Fe Trail and settled into ranching around Los Angeles. When that didn't pay the bills, Pa took a job as a lawman. The job fed the family while we got the cattle business up and running. That's what made Sal and me become Marshals. It was a decent life, though Pa got busted up a few times. But he recovered, while plenty who broke the law near him didn't. My folks still live out there. There was a sister between Sal and me. Then two younger brothers and one sister, the youngest of us all."

"Your ma had six children and survived it all?" Becky had lost her ma when she was bringing a baby. Mariah had lost her ma the same way. It was a dangerous business giving birth, and yet that danger stopped no one.

"She was a strong woman, my ma, and a blessed one. I had several friends whose pa was a widower or on his second wife. All six of us grew into adults, too."

"I had two little brothers die of fever. Then my ma died when she couldn't deliver a third little one. Left me the only child with my cranky old pa."

"Having children is the most natural thing in the world." Nate turned to face her as they rode side by side. "I never could figure why God doesn't make it a whole lot safer. It might've been about Adam and Eve, but it seems like a man oughta get a chance to die in childbirth, too."

"And yet the world just keeps getting more and more people in it."

They rode in silence for a while, each holding back from the other drovers. No one was pushing hard. Rather, they were letting the cattle make their way along. Pushing them was a good way to have a herd break up and scatter.

Becky thought she and Nate were almost back to a solid working relationship. Not quite, though. That kiss they'd shared wouldn't be fading from her mind anytime soon.

"Is Owen keeping you in the dark about what he's got planned just as much as me?" Becky could guess the answer to that, but maybe if Nate got to thinking about it, he might find a way to convince Owen to give them more details.

"Sal doesn't know a thing, or if he does, I can't read it when he lies. Tex probably doesn't know either. Owen's got something more than what he says is going on. But I can't get a single word out of him. Of course, it's hard to talk to him without us being overheard. And I don't want the men to think there's more to the Marshals getting hired other than as cowhands. In fact, I don't spend much time talking to them other than Sal. So, yes, I'm in the dark. I reckon that's how Owen wants it. That's why I left the Marshals Service—I had a few close calls that could've been avoided if I'd known what all was going on."

"Close calls? Like what?" Becky asked.

The last cow headed into the narrow mouth of the canyon ahead. One of her cowhands swung off his horse to close and latch the gate. The rest of them turned to head back to the ranch.

"Like my trusting the wrong man," Nate answered, "a man my superiors suspected of a crime."

"Can't they see the risk you're taking?"

"All they'll say is that I shouldn't have trusted anyone. And I reckon they'd be right. But I finally decided I didn't want to learn the skill of always being suspicious of everyone. It's not natural to me, and I don't want any part of becoming so untrusting. It's why I quit."

"And that doesn't bother Sal?"

Becky and Nate began leading the procession back toward the ranch house and were far enough ahead to keep talking.

"It likely does. I think he's coming to the end of his career." Nate locked eyes with her. "I'm thinking we could use another steady hand. And once we clean out this rat's nest of killers who haunt the territory, Sal just might be interested in hiring on for good at the Idee."

"I've watched him work. There'd be a place for him here."

Nate smiled and tipped his hat to her.

"Now that we've got all the cattle settled, starting tomorrow I'm riding into town every day to work on the rally we're holding for Mrs. Mussel. She'll be here Friday. Her speech is Saturday. She'll join us for church and a noon meal on Sunday, then she'll be off."

"And she's got guards? Enough of them?"

Becky frowned and glanced over her shoulder at Owen. "So I've been told. If they're guarding against an attack by the Deadeye Gang, there's still one other thing to worry about."

"What's that?"

"My pa is always on a tear against suffrage. I know he'll come to town and cause trouble."

Nate nodded, fire flashing in his eyes. "I reckon Mrs. Mussel is used to troublemakers in her crowd. But I'll ask your cowhands to join me in controlling your pa and his men."

Becky felt some of the pressure come off her chest. "That's a good idea."

"It's dangerous country. Both the Deadeye Gang and your pa make it so. You can plan on my riding in with you."

"I hate putting Pa's name in with those evil outlaws. But for now, I reckon I need protection from him more than that gang." Becky's eyes shifted so they met Nate's once more. "Thank you, Nate."

In that moment, Becky remembered her last ride home from town. It was there in Nate's expression, too. Becky decided that Mrs. Grable should ride in with them and get involved in the women's suffrage cause, also to act as chaperone between Becky and her troublesome ranch foreman.

Then one of the hands who'd driven the herd to the canyon pasture caught up to Becky and asked a question about what was next. She looked away from Nate fast, glad this rare chance to talk with Nate privately was over.

Joshua Pruitt seethed and raged, unable to see a way out. Trapped, a man of his power and reach, trapped like a rat. He wouldn't stand for it.

He reached for a crystal decanter and poured himself a glass of whiskey and a second for Bernard Skleen. As he handed the whiskey over, he fought for control before he talked to Skleen.

He clenched a fist, the one not holding the whiskey glass, and thought about his daughter and how satisfying it would've been to dole out some much-deserved punishment. She'd betrayed him. Stolen from him. He'd made financial moves counting on that inheritance of hers. And now he was in a mess, thanks to her.

His men were back from the cattle drive. That was all the honest money he was going to make this year, and it wasn't enough. He went earlier in the year than Becky. It was as if she'd figured out how he ranched and deliberately chose another way—as though she were better than him. She flirted with oncoming winter to get a couple of more weeks of weight on her herd.

He pushed his cows to Fort Bridger in August. Becky took hers to Denver a month later. He couldn't make it all the way to Denver because he had work that needed doing here. And that would have to continue now because of Becky's greed.

Wouldn't have mattered anyway, for Denver wasn't enough money, either.

He still raised longhorns, with Becky using money that should've been his to bring in Angus. They earned a little more, and she'd spent most of her inheritance to acquire them. She'd be years earning that investment back. It was easy if there was money enough and a person didn't need to borrow a penny. It irked him that she'd kept the money that should be his, money left to her by arrogant grandparents who'd always thought their daughter had married beneath her.

With Becky's disloyalty, he couldn't straighten things out, not without more strikes. Robberies. He hadn't set out to be a dishonest man, but he needed to survive and so had done a few things that led him down a path until there was no turning back.

He realized he was close to crushing his glass. He had to fight for control or he'd throw it against the wall.

Heaven knew the money was easy, but they'd hit too

many times and too close together. They were risking exposure. He'd agreed with the Wainwrights on taking it slow. But now they were dead, and he found out they'd sold his debt to someone who had no patience. In fact, he'd made it clear he would collect in blood if necessary.

"What did you find out?" Joshua turned from the whiskey decanter. He'd almost forgotten Skleen was there.

Skleen took a sip of the whiskey, smiled, and settled into the leather chair in front of Joshua's desk. He stretched his legs out and held the whiskey with both hands, resting it on his belly.

Skleen sure enough made himself at home. Not a cowhand on the place would have settled in quite as comfortably. Yet Skleen knew things no one else did. Joshua had to put up with the arrogant little banty rooster of a man.

At least for now.

"I got us one. It'll be two weeks, which gives us time to get organized. I've got all the details. Should be a big payday." He told Joshua every detail save one. Skleen never did tell where he got his information. The man was sharp enough to know he held power in his hands by being the one connected to an informant. Didn't matter. When Joshua closed down this crooked operation, he wasn't going to need information anymore. And if this strike was as big as Skleen claimed, it might be the last robbery.

The two men discussed the job in more detail—the approach, the trail where they'd lie in wait. It wasn't far away. They'd struck too close to home too many times. So long as no witnesses survived, it didn't matter. But they'd been forced to take bigger risks without the Wainwrights.

The risks gave Joshua a vicious satisfaction.

With the next strike in shape, Joshua had a little something extra to arrange.

"Hold up, Skleen. I've got another job for you, and it's going to take all the men."

Skleen swallowed the last of his drink and lowered the glass, his eyes wary. He didn't take jobs from Joshua. He brought jobs here for the gang. His jaw tightened. "What is it?"

Joshua found that he enjoyed giving orders to this arrogant man. It occurred to him that when this was all over and the gang went their separate ways, Skleen shouldn't just ride away. He was too dangerous. Joshua could feel the itch between his shoulder blades when he looked into Skleen's watery blue eyes.

"I've taken a strong dislike to this speechifying that's coming to Pine Valley," Joshua began.

Skleen snorted. "Women voting? End of the country, I'd say. Hope the rest of the states hold out against it."

"My daughter is a big supporter, and she's pushed me about as hard as a man can be pushed. I intend to strike a blow."

Skleen's eyes narrowed, yet he didn't ask any questions.

"Two women are coming—a Mrs. Mussel and a Mrs. Morris. One's getting off the train in Fort Bridger and taking the stagecoach from there. The other, Esther Morris, is taking the stage from South Pass City. I want the men to split into two groups and kill everyone on those stages."

Skleen's brows lifted. "We've got enough men, but we've never just struck at a stagecoach to kill, Boss. We've always been after a payroll. We'll raise some mighty big suspicions if we change our ways."

Joshua thought of how terrible Becky would feel if these two women she looked at as heroes died on the journey to Pine Valley. He could taste the triumph in his plot.

"Changing our ways might be the best thing we could do. Up to now we've done everything too much the same. This might throw off any lawmen paying attention. Cast doubts on any information they think they've gathered on us."

Skleen nodded, his expression thoughtful as if in consideration. "It'd suit me to strike out at those women. Not sure it's wise, though. Doubt they'd have much money with them. They're the type who come to collect money, not spend it."

Joshua thought a better thing for Skleen to have said would've been, Yes, sir. I'll get to planning it right away. "I'm not asking, Skleen. I'm telling."

Skleen had been looking into the middle distance, mulling over whether this was a good idea. Now his eyes lifted, met Joshua's, turned ice-cold.

Their gazes clashed for too long.

Skleen would have to die for sure when they parted ways. Joshua had no doubt of it.

Then with a jerk of his chin, in what was a nod of agreement, Skleen said, "Do you know when they're coming to town and by what routes?"

Joshua relaxed a little. "I know all that."

They settled in to planning murder, only this time Joshua knew it was all his idea and none of it was for money.

Once Skleen had left, Joshua's thoughts turned to next year and the train carrying the cattle farther west. Prices were high enough it'd pay. He just needed to settle one last debt—an ugly one—and then he'd be back on top.

He pondered his troublesome daughter. She'd ruined him or come close to it. He still dreamed some nights about storming onto her ranch and dragging her back home. He'd counted on that money she inherited.

His sons would have stuck by him. Three sons, all of them dead. All he was left with was one worthless daughter. With sons he'd've built something. Instead, his daughter had struck out on her own.

Joshua had a moment close to amusement when he thought of how he'd been treated by his own pa. Joshua hadn't stuck by him, either. But then his pa hadn't asked. Had as good as kicked Joshua out. Since then, Joshua had spent his life trying to prove his pa was wrong.

Pa was long dead now, but Joshua still had bitter memories of how worthless his pa had made him feel. And Joshua had never done that to Becky. He'd trained her at his side, and now she ran a decent ranch—all with the skills he'd taught her.

He hadn't kicked her out. She'd left on her own.

Disloyal, selfish, weak—that's what she was. A few cowhands had said the wrong word to her, made the wrong joke, and she'd stabbed her own pa in the back.

If his mother-in-law had lived just a bit longer, Joshua would've figured out a marriage between her and one of his cowhands and there'd have been no nonsense about her leaving. He'd've had the son he always wanted, even if it was a son-in-law.

He should've married again after Claudette, his weakling wife, died. But women were scarce out here, and he'd never gotten around to it. Never wanted to bring another woman onto the ranch. He'd put it off, figuring instead to see that Becky married wisely, letting go of the idea of another wife and more children.

Then Becky had inherited a fortune and run off.

It had cornered Joshua at just the wrong time. He felt a wave of desperation when he thought about just how wrong of a time it had been. It near to choked him. And he didn't like it. Instead, he let his fury soar.

He had dreams of making Becky very sorry she'd betrayed him.

He did think now and then that if she died, all she owned would be his. He hadn't quite worked up the will to kill his only living child, though he'd been tempted more than once.

Hurting her, well, he'd been mighty tempted to do that. His desire to hurt her as much as she'd hurt him with her disloyalty never quite faded.

9

Becky rode into town, the hoofbeats of her palomino keeping time to the sound of music. Nate and Sal were just a pace behind her.

She saw Mr. Betancourt standing in front of the general store, playing a rousing version of "The Battle Hymn of the Republic" on his fiddle. He was accompanied by Joy Blodgett, who played a fife. Deputy Willie held a drum that looked old enough to have come through the Civil War, while out of the saloon came the tinny sound of an out-of-tune piano, no doubt being played by the saloon keeper.

Nell must have found the musicians in town and gotten them together.

She'd gotten everyone together.

The whole of the main street was bustling. Nearly a dozen people were hard at work, the pounding of their hammers matching the beat of the music. Nell appeared to be overseeing the builders, which was something Becky highly approved of.

The crew was busy erecting a small platform for Mrs.

Mussel in the middle of the wide street out front of Clint's Diner. It was high enough that Mrs. Mussel would stand slightly overhead of the crowd that was expected to gather to hear her speech.

Becky was a little worried about the crowd. Not that there wouldn't be one. The frontier was a quiet place, not counting the stampedes and thunderstorms and blizzards. And wolves and robbers and murderers. All right, fine—the frontier was a potentially riotous place in the normal course of things, but that wasn't the same as a town gathering like this one.

Every man, woman, and child within riding distance of Pine Valley would be present for the speech.

Becky saw Nell stretching out some pretty fabric across the front of the platform, likely for a bunting. Mariah was sifting through boards and handing out nails she'd made herself. But she was getting really pregnant, so everyone tried to protect her from any heavy lifting.

Hard to slow her down, though.

Both Sheriff Mast and Doc Preston were there. Mr. Kintzinger had come, but he ran the town newspaper and was busily taking notes, so he wasn't that much help.

James Burke, the undertaker, was the one who'd brought the boards, most of which he'd scavenged from a collapsed building outside of town. He used them to build coffins, and once the speech was over and the platform torn down, he'd said he wanted his boards back. But thanks to his years of building coffins, he was a fast builder, his work solid. Becky had to wonder how well-made a coffin needed to be, but regardless, Jim's carpentry skills were excellent.

Leland and Samantha were also there, along with Warren Blodgett and some strangers who must be new homesteaders. Nell had a nice group working hard.

Becky let her palomino loose in the corral behind Mariah's blacksmith shop. Nate did the same with his black stallion. Sal had a buckskin gelding he favored. That critter went in, too.

While Mariah wouldn't charge them, Becky would ask Willie to give them hay and water and a bait of grain—later, after the rehearsal was over. He'd gladly take her coins.

She saw Mariah wielding a hammer and left Nate and Sal behind to go wrestle the tool away from her friend.

Mariah let go after only a token struggle and grinned at Becky. "You think I'm too fragile to help knock this stage together?"

"No, I don't. But there's a shortage of tools and an abundance of help. It makes good sense for you to let someone take over for you."

Mariah looked around, then leaned close. "There are a couple of slackers here. I hoped if I set to building, it'd bump Percy Kintzinger off his writing."

"Maybe he'll come out with a special edition of the paper today."

"Oh, I hope so. He's already done one edition this week, and Mrs. Mussel will be here tomorrow. Having a newspaper with a story about this event will be an excellent surprise." Mariah clutched her hands under her chin and almost giggled. "I am looking forward to meeting her."

"It's all very exciting." Becky looked around at the activity. The chatter and music, the fresh mountain breeze cutting the heat of the August day. The scent of pine freshening the air. The Cirque of the Towers standing guard over them all.

It was beautiful. Mrs. Mussel would arrive on Friday, give her speech on Saturday, stay one more day to visit with everyone in town who wished it, then head out on Monday. She was traveling all over the western frontier, speaking for the cause of women's suffrage. They were lucky to have her for a few days.

"And Esther Morris will come, too?" Becky glanced at Nell, who was hammering a nail home. Nate and Sal had requested the hammers Nell's two younger girls were using.

Michaela gave hers up to Sal, yet Cassie shook her head and kept on working. Nate looked at Becky, then came and took the hammer away that she'd confiscated from Mariah.

He moved close and whispered, "You think Nell knows what she's doing? I've done some building before."

Mariah overheard him and said, "Nell amazes me with all she knows. Go ahead and let her run things—you're used to taking orders from a woman."

Nate smiled and gave his head a little tilt. "So true," he said and went to work.

"It's an inspiring sight, isn't it?" Becky said, and she knew Mariah understood all that those words meant. The town coming together, working for a cause that was dear to their hearts. Yet she had her doubts about others in town.

The musicians switched over to "The Battle Cry of

Freedom." Willie especially seemed to enjoy the drumming.

"Not a grouchy face to be seen." Mariah crossed her arms and smiled wide.

"If Pa were here, you'd see one."

"He's never going to change, Becky. Your pa is set in his ways, and those ways include not letting women vote."

"Yep. Stubborn old goat."

"He'll come in, though, won't he? It's hard to believe a single person for miles around would miss a chance to listen to a new speaker."

Becky turned slightly away from Mariah so her expression didn't show. Becky very much doubted she could hide what her pa had almost done to her. And she didn't want to talk about it. For some reason she felt ashamed to have a pa so cruel and greedy.

"If he comes, I'm afraid he'll shout Mrs. Mussel down, say ugly things deliberately to disrupt the day. Yes, I think he'll come. He and his men are back from their cattle drive, so they'll all come in most likely. And his men think a lot like he does. It'd be for the best if they stayed out at the Circle J."

Becky dreaded seeing her father again, though she almost certainly would. And soon. With the herds settled to their fall grazing, there'd be little at the ranch to do.

Bernard Skleen and half of his gang picked a spot high above the trail that ran from South Pass City to Pine Valley. He looked down over the narrow pass, the spot he'd scouted out a long time ago just as he'd located similar narrow trails all over Wyoming.

He heard the distant sound of pounding hooves and rolling wheels. He didn't signal his men. They were all listening, just as ready as he was. Instead, he aimed his rifle down at the trail. A curve at the beginning of the stretch kept him from seeing the stage. Because he expected outriders, he'd brought a bigger group than usual with him.

There used to be four, sometimes five men who'd rob a stage in a holdup. But Pruitt's men were all in the gang now. It'd been a slow steady change over in the cowpokes at the Circle J.

Skleen didn't like it because the money now needed to be split more ways. But it took too much explaining to the men not in the gang why a group rode away and was gone for a week or more, then came back and took right up with the ranching with no objection from the boss. Once or twice, sure, a man took off and no one said much. But they'd been hitting the trail real regular lately. Skleen liked it that way. And as he was the one who knew about the best shipments, he was mostly in charge of where and when they rode out.

With his gun trained on the trail below, trusting the six men who'd ridden with him not to shoot until everyone was in the bottleneck, Skleen waited. Tense with excitement. He liked thieving, but he'd also found a taste for killing. He was always ready for another chance at it.

A lone figure came into view. Skleen narrowed his eyes as a man wearing a cavalry uniform rounded the trail and rode into the canyon neck. Two more were right behind him, then three, followed by a string of ten men before the stagecoach appeared. The coach bearing Esther Morris, that fool woman who'd been appointed as the first female justice of the peace in the whole of the country.

Skleen had eagerly volunteered to lead the group to stop her from reaching Pine Valley alive. He drew his finger away from the trigger as more men poured into the canyon. There seemed to be an entire cavalry unit riding with Esther Morris. They couldn't win a fight against so many soldiers. Skleen pulled back, afraid the others wouldn't realize it. And being scared of anything was infuriating.

The troops kept coming. His men held their fire, obviously aware that they were outmanned and outgunned.

Soon those leading the stagecoach vanished out of the narrow trail before the last ones came through. Esther Morris moved on unharmed, not that Skleen could see her inside the coach.

Dust drifted up from the trail below as hooves battered the dirt into powder.

The hooves rumbled.

No gunshots sounded.

Skleen had with him experienced, cold-blooded men. They kept their powder dry. He knew, even as he watched the last man ride out of sight, that a similar crowd would be riding with Josette Mussel.

Skleen withdrew to his horse and reached for the saddle just a bit after the rest of the men.

"This was always a foolhardy idea, Bern."

Skleen didn't even look up to see who'd said it. "Yep,

but the boss wanted it. I was willing. Now we've got to get back, and fast. I don't want anyone noticing the boss is at the ranch alone. No one much rides up there, but best to be seen back home in case one of those troopers noticed anything amiss when they rode through the canyon. They were mighty watchful. And men who ride wary like that notice things others wouldn't. Let's head out."

They were riding within minutes, staying clear of the trail to avoid being followed by anyone.

Skleen's neck itched the whole long ride home. He hoped the other half of their gang didn't find themselves cut down, with a bunch of faces, not to mention branded horses, linked to the Circle J. When Key Larson had died last year, he'd been working for the Circle J, but Joshua had claimed ignorance of what Larson was up to and the sheriff let it alone. But a gang of men all linked to Joshua Pruitt couldn't be so easily explained away.

Joshua wanted those two suffragettes dead, mainly just to spite his daughter who was a big supporter of women getting the right to vote. For some reason Skleen didn't understand, Pruitt was in a rage over his daughter, and that had fed some hunger in him to hurt her.

But there was no money in it. The boss would have to find another way to do Miss Becky harm.

It suited Skleen to cooperate with the boss. He'd had his eye on Miss Becky and had even approached her. She'd spurned him, then gone so far as to take a big old fistful of money she'd come into from her ma's parents and move out.

It left Skleen licking a few wounds to have her hate the idea of a marriage to him quite so much.

Yes, that woman needed to be humbled for a fact.

The boss would have to find another way. And Skleen would be glad to help when the time came.

The time wasn't now.

10

Mrs. Esther Morris got to town first.

Becky stood side by side with Nell, who was wearing her black robe, and Mariah, heavily pregnant. The rest of the town had turned out to greet Mrs. Morris's stage.

There was a crowd of possibly fifty people. Becky was no judge of such things, but it was a decent turnout just to welcome the stagecoach. They milled about on the main street, enjoying the music, the warm sunshine, and the chance to see their neighbors as they waited for the big event. The stage platform looked quite festive with its bright blue bunting.

The town band struck up "When Johnny Comes Marching Home Again" as the stagecoach neared the crowd gathered there to receive Mrs. Morris. Mrs. Preston had confided to Nell that she'd rewritten the popular song's words to suit the suffrage movement and intended to teach the whole town the lyrics after Mrs. Mussel's speech.

Becky had ridden into town again today, Nate with her. Nearly all her cowhands intended to come tomorrow to hear the speechmaking. Owen and Tex thought they should stay back. While their presence here was no secret, they didn't want to draw any attention.

A seemingly unending line of uniformed riders galloped alongside the coach. Becky realized the cavalry had indeed come. This might well be why Owen didn't want to come. He might know some of the men who served in the U.S. Army.

The stagecoach driver shouted "Whoa!"

A smile bloomed on Becky's face. She glanced at her friends and saw their pleasure and relief. Dust kicked up a long plume behind the stage. The riders dismounted and tied their horses to the hitching posts along the main street. Becky had initially thought there were fifty people there to welcome Mrs. Morris, but now with this band of outriders, that number was close to one hundred.

The brakes were drawn, and the stage slowed to a stop, unscathed. Becky realized she'd been wound up with fear, even after Owen had sworn the two women traveling to Pine Valley would be safe.

The cavalry riders swarmed the town.

The door to the stage swung open, revealing a tall, robust-looking woman. As she stepped lightly to the ground, Becky could tell she was a seasoned traveler. Becky walked toward her along with her friends. They'd agreed Nell would give the woman a formal greeting before the others started in with their hellos.

Before Nell could say a word of welcome, Mrs. Morris caught Nell's hands in hers. "Another woman judge!" A huge smile broke out on Mrs. Morris's craggy face as she pulled her into her arms.

Nell clung to her like a lost child who'd just found her mother.

"Can you believe we've lived to see the day?" Mrs. Morris rocked Nell for a long minute.

At last, Nell stepped back and swept a hand toward Mariah and Becky. "My very best friends in the world."

Nell did a fine job with the introductions. At least they seemed fine to Becky, who knew little of polite manners.

Waving a hand gracefully to her right, Nell said, "My friend Becky who owns and runs her own ranch."

Mrs. Morris beamed, and when Becky reached out to shake the woman's hand, Mrs. Morris took her hand in both of hers and as good as hugged Becky's hand. It touched something in Becky's heart. A lonely place deep inside someone who missed her mother. "So wonderful to meet you, Mrs. Morris."

Mrs. Morris spoke of the pride she felt to see a woman being fearless, taking on any work she felt able to do.

Nell gestured to her left. "And my friend Mariah Roberts, the town blacksmith. Lately, though, she's hired on an assistant and is staying clear of the forge until her baby arrives."

Mrs. Morris seemed to glow. "A woman judge, a rancher, and a blacksmith. Oh, Wyoming is the most magnificent land. To see you women doing such work lifts my heart. I should send all three of you along with Mrs. Mussel and let you speak with her, encourage other women to be as fearless, and encourage men to respect women and their abilities.

The crowd surrounded Mrs. Morris, and they were all treated to a wise and kindly conversation about Pine Valley and the Cirque of the Towers, which Mrs. Morris had never seen before and admired greatly.

She launched into talk of suffrage and how proud she was of Wyoming. Though Mrs. Morris didn't boast of it, it seemed she knew the territorial governor, who'd ordered the cavalry to ride guard for Mrs. Morris. And Mrs. Mussel's coach would have the same protection.

The townspeople spent time visiting with Mrs. Morris and weren't nearly done with her when a rumbling sound told Becky the next stagecoach was approaching, this time from the south.

Soon a cavalry rider appeared, and Becky hooked an arm through Mariah's and Nell's elbows. Both their husbands were at their sides. Becky saw that Nate stood close behind her.

The stage slowed and then came to a stop. Dust filled the air again, scenting the summer day.

Mrs. Mussel emerged from the stage, her husband and three half-grown children following her.

Becky smiled at the petite woman, who looked to be a contrast in every way to Mrs. Morris. They embraced and began talking immediately, sisters in the cause of suffrage.

The two women included everyone in their talk but most especially Becky, Nell, and Mariah. And that made them Becky's sisters, too.

The following day, Nate saw Joshua Pruitt ride into town, leading a sizable group of his cowpokes. It looked to Nate like he'd brought with him every man working his place to listen to the speech.

Becky had brought most everyone too, or rather she'd given leave for them to come. A few had stayed behind, as it wasn't wise to completely desert the ranch. Owen and Tex had wanted an excuse, so it had been easy to pick them to stand guard of the place.

Nate thought they'd been subtle about it. He sure hoped the men weren't too suspicious about the new cowhands. It helped that Sal had come along. A little.

The band started up their playing. Dave Westcott had dragged his piano out of the saloon to join them.

Nell climbed the three steps at the front of the platform stage to introduce Mrs. Mussel, who stood waiting at the bottom of the steps. Mrs. Morris sat beside the band.

Nate braced himself for trouble. He'd had a word with the cavalry officers concerning Joshua's men, so they were ready. The cavalry soldiers were wearing their uniforms and had formed a phalanx around the back of crowd. If any trouble started, they'd be close at hand.

Nate watched Joshua closely. He saw the man's eyes go straight to Becky, who stood in the front row, smiling with delight. Nate had rarely seen Becky shine with such happiness as she'd been doing since these two suffragettes had arrived in town.

He watched her, beaming and eager for Nell to talk, and he hated that Joshua was going to ruin everything. Oh, they'd squelch any trouble he started, and Nate had no doubt the speech would go on. He even suspected Mrs. Mussel had faced trouble before and could handle it just fine.

But Becky would be so angry and so ashamed of her father's contempt for these women. Nate rested his eyes on Becky, and his heart sped up as he realized how important she was becoming to him.

A cowhand didn't come to a wealthy woman like Becky Pruitt unless he had something of his own. Wyoming had a lot more to figure out if it really wanted to be the equality state.

For now, all Nate could do was be ready because Joshua *would* say something offensive. The man couldn't keep his mouth shut.

Nate's brother Sal stood nearby. Nate sidled over to Sal while Nell gave her little introduction speech and whispered, "That's him. Joshua Pruitt."

"Becky's pa?"

"Yep. He'll be looking to make trouble."

Sal said under his breath, "I'll handle it."

Nate went back to listening but stayed on edge. Sure, Sal said he'd handle it, but Nate wasn't the type of man who left things to others. Certainly not something as important to him as this was.

Becky hardly heard Nell's speech for worrying about Pa. And that made her furious.

She saw Nell glance up at the pounding hooves. Nell knew exactly what Pa was capable of. Nevertheless, Nell continued to speak, even though she knew full well that her pa was going to do his worst.

It hardened Becky's heart toward her father in a way that surprised her because she'd long ago given up on the man ever being a decent pa or even a decent man. Her expectations were already in the dirt, but right now they dipped even lower. What she felt for her own father was as close to true hatred as Becky had ever felt for anyone.

And it shamed her, for the Bible spoke of dishonoring your father as a sin. Plenty of prayers for forgiveness loomed in Becky's future. She decided to hold off on the praying because she was sorely afraid not honoring Pa would figure heavily in her behavior today.

Nell finished her introduction, and the crowd applauded with great vigor. Their very own justice of the peace—many people in Pine Valley took great pride in that.

Pa wasn't one of them.

Mrs. Mussel took to the stage and began a speech that roused the crowd. She was a fiery speaker who made the case for women being granted full rights as American citizens.

Becky had read plenty of articles in *The Revolution*, the newspaper published by Susan B. Anthony and Elizabeth Cady Stanton. But to listen to this woman, so courageously speaking truth to all who'd come, lifted Becky's heart. Her whole spirit soared.

Just then a shout rang out from the back of the crowd.

"We're done listening to the female yammering." A gunshot blasted.

Becky whirled around to see her pa, shouting and raising his six-gun. The men with him whooped and hollered. Their guns began firing, too.

As she dreaded what might come next, she saw the cavalry troops make a sudden move. They'd been ready for this. At least two soldiers set upon each of the men causing the ruckus.

Swift and brutal, the cavalry attacked without drawing their pistols, even knowing they were running into the teeth of armed men. But they moved quickly and quietly. Just five minutes after Pa had first disrupted Mrs. Mussel, silence reigned. Pa's men were either bound and gagged or unconscious on the ground. Not a single shot had been fired by the cavalry. And yet there was no reason to believe the men wouldn't recover from being silenced.

The crowd, used to the raucous ways of the West, turned back to the platform stage.

Mrs. Mussel spoke for well over an hour. After she finished, she introduced Mrs. Morris, which was unexpected. Becky wondered if the two women had planned it to go this way.

The people were lacking in public entertainments and speeches, so the idea of more to come roused them to applause for Mrs. Morris.

Mrs. Morris gave a short but wise and intelligent speech. When she was done, she spent time saying her goodbyes before climbing into her stagecoach and dashing away.

Mrs. Mussel, too, was the soul of congenial friendliness, but long before the sun set, she and her husband and children were gone. And the cavalry riders who'd accompanied them, after untying Pa's men, all left town as well.

Becky had expected the two women to stay another night and day. All in all, though, she thought it best they leave town before Pa thought of more awful things to say. Or he thought to do something worse.

Becky hugged Mariah and Nell goodbye, promising to

see them at church the next day. They all set out for home, as did most of the townsfolk. Pa, helped by his men who hadn't been knocked cold, had a big job loading up his cowhands. They were still hard at work on that as Becky and Nate and her men were heading out of town.

Honor your father . . .

Becky had some praying to do, and some thinking. Inside, when she set aside her contempt and anger at her father, she felt the fiery words Mrs. Mussel and Mrs. Morris had spoken, stirring her to heights she'd never before reached.

Nate rode up beside her. He'd been avoiding her very thoroughly since that kiss.

"Those women were inspiring. Their message wasn't just for women's rights, either. It was for all of us to treat each other more decently. A strongly pro-American speech. Speaking of freedom and how to use our freedom to make the world a better place."

Becky turned to Nate and smiled at him for the first time in a while. "It *was* for everyone, wasn't it?" Her smile shrank. "Including for Pa, but he didn't hear a word those women said."

Her pa hadn't been among those who'd been knocked cold. He'd been hog-tied and gagged and tossed onto the ground for the duration. A humiliation her pa wouldn't soon forget. Becky had to wonder in what way he'd move to retaliate for his embarrassment.

She was afraid he'd strike back in a way that was a scourge. She was glad those women had ridden off today. "I wonder how often Mrs. Mussel feels she has to run after giving a speech."

Nate said, "I heard she'll be in Fort Bridger by nightfall. The cavalry couldn't be gone any longer than that."

"Yes, then on to Laramie and a meeting with the governor next week. She's a busy woman."

Nate grinned. "It seems to me that all women are busy, although she certainly leads a different kind of life."

They discussed the speeches as they rode home. Sal came up and rode beside them on the wider stretches. All her cowhands who'd attended, Jan Grable among them, made their way back to the Idee. The excitement Becky had been feeling for nearly a year was now over.

But she was left feeling as if she'd been changed by the two women's high-minded words. *Inspiring*. Nate's word. That just about covered it.

She rode into her ranch yard before dark, and they all split up to do a few last things necessary because her men were leaving for the roundup at first light.

11

Roscoe Grable squared his shoulders and looked over the cattle being hazed out of three canyons. The lush grass remained, only there was much less of it than before the cattle had settled in.

Becky could see that Roscoe liked being in charge. She'd asked him if he was interested in returning to the job of foreman, and he hadn't committed to it. "Let's see how worn out I am when I get back from Denver, Miss Becky. Let's just see."

Jan, his wife, had charge of the chuckwagon, and both seemed younger lately. As they rode off, Becky stood outside her back door, waving goodbye. She hadn't gone along on the cattle drives from the beginning.

Nell stood beside her. That was what they'd settled on for the proprieties. Jan Grable had accepted it, or she might've balked about going. What Becky hadn't told Jan was that Nell wasn't staying. She'd head back for town as soon as the dust settled behind the herd.

None of the Marshals seemed overly worried about what was proper. Nate was a different story, but then he didn't know how soon Nell was leaving . . . or that she wasn't coming back. Becky and four men. It wasn't right, but it was going to happen anyway. And the four men would soon grow to ten.

Nell moved into the house and stayed for lunch. Later when she rode off, it wasn't long before Owen led Nate, Sal, and Tex inside to finally tell her all that was going on. Brutus followed on Sal's heels. Her fearsome guard dog treated them as if they were pack mates.

Becky hadn't told the men that Nell wasn't coming back. She'd see what the men thought.

Owen settled in at the kitchen table. "Here's the thing I've not been telling you, Miss Pruitt."

His tone made the hair stand up on the back of Becky's neck. Something bad was coming. Becky didn't ask him to go on; she knew he would anyway. Her gut reaction was to tell him to stop.

"First," Owen began, "I want to know if you intend to keep secret what I'm telling you? Because this is a matter of life and death, and I'm afraid it won't be easy for you to remain silent."

Becky hesitated. Her word was good, she knew that, and anyone who knew her would agree. For that reason, she didn't give her word casually. "What you tell me will remain a secret," she promised.

Owen studied her for a long moment. Finally he nodded and glanced at Tex, who nodded in return.

Becky noticed he didn't look at Sal or Nate, which said to Becky they didn't know this secret either.

Quietly, Owen continued, "We believe the center of the Deadeye Gang is on your father's ranch."

Becky drew in a sharp breath. After her mind rabbited around for a while, she asked, "Because of Key Larson?"

Key had been part of the stagecoach robbery that saw Mariah's pa and brother both killed. Key was the one Mariah had seen. He'd made several attempts on Mariah's life even though her memory of the robbery had been lost due to her injuries. There also seemed to be some qualms among the gang about killing a woman, and about killing the town's only blacksmith. They'd had no inkling really as to the gang's identity, so their thinking was only speculation. But with Key Larson dead now, it appeared the gang no longer believed Mariah needed to die.

"Not just because of Larson." Owen hesitated again. "But that made us start asking questions."

Becky marveled at the sharp intelligence in his eyes. So different from the quiet, soft-spoken, somewhat lazy-sounding man he was when with her cowhands. Not that he wasn't hardworking, he just feigned a lazy tone that was in direct contrast to this savvy, ruthless Marshal.

It was a fine disguise.

"Then with the Wainwrights being discovered as part of the gang, we considered that the whole gang might well be rooted to this area. It's not that easy to send messages over long distances. It stood to reason that the men all lived in the same general area."

"That alone isn't enough." Becky narrowed her eyes at the Marshal. "There could be men at other ranches involved."

"I'm not sure how much you know about this investigation, miss, but Sheriff Mast from Pine Valley asked a lot of questions around here about men who'd rode off from their jobs. Those who'd been gone for a stretch that co-incided with the times of the robberies. The ranchers as well as anyone else Mast questioned were all cooperative. They want these ugly robberies stopped just as badly as anyone. All of them except Joshua Pruitt. Your pa."

Becky swallowed hard. "That's not enough either. Pa doesn't like being pushed. He'd see it as insulting. He's arrogant and hardheaded, and his refusing to answer questions isn't an admission of guilt."

Yet Becky could see how Pa's stubbornness had drawn the attention of the Marshals. The mulish old coot had brought this on himself.

"It's enough to focus our attention on his ranch, but there's more."

Becky waited. She'd batted two clues right back in Owen's face. She saw the glint in his eyes and knew he'd saved the best for last.

"We've had a man riding with your pa since Key Larson was killed."

That'd happened last fall. Which meant Owen's man had been with Pa the better part of a year. "What man?"

Owen shook his head. "You don't need to know that."

Nate grunted. Becky remembered Nate hadn't liked not knowing the details of the cases he was assigned to. This was a good example of that.

"He's been reporting on the men being absent," Owen went on. "Of course, cowhands are known for their wandering ways. Some wander during the winter season and return come spring. But this was different. Your pa has five cowhands who left together during calving season—the same time as one of the robberies." Owen paused, then sounded more human than usual. "We haven't heard from our man in a while. I'm afraid he's been found out. I'm afraid he may be dead."

Becky recalled Mrs. Mussel's speech and how her heart had hardened toward Pa as she listened. The way he drew back his fist when she'd refused to return to the Circle J Ranch and hand her money over to him.

"Men rode off at a busy time of year, and Pa hired them back?" Becky knew she'd never put up with that from her own men. No good rancher would.

"Yes, he hired them back, no questions. What's more, your pa didn't even dock their pay. Our man was there on payday. We think Joshua Pruitt is likely in on the robberies. In fact, he might be the mastermind behind the Deadeye Gang."

Owen locked eyes with her. She felt dizzy, as if possibly every drop of blood had drained from her face.

"That makes your pa directly involved in fifteen murders in the last two and a half years. The gang wasn't pulling that many jobs at first. Two the first year, two the second. After the fourth robbery, the stagecoach lines started sending outriders, and the robberies stopped for a time. When the outriders were suspended, the robberies started up again. Two more in fast succession. That's when we caught the Wainwrights and hoped it was over. Then they robbed another stage, and the coach company hired the outriders again. It didn't stop the gang, though. The last robbery, they killed four men riding guard plus the driver and two passengers." Owen raised his voice a notch and added, "They *must* be stopped. And if we're right about this, your pa will hang for certain."

Becky felt her throat grow tight. She coughed, then looked back up at him.

"We want to use your ranch to catch him. It's our understanding that you and your pa are on bad terms. We realize it's an ugly thing to ask of a daughter, Miss Pruitt, but we're asking all the same. We're asking you to take a hand in sentencing your pa to death."

Nate erupted from his chair and rushed to Becky's side. Her face had gone white, and he thought she might pass out any second. He stood behind her and rested both of his hands on her shoulders. "I didn't take you for a fool, Riley."

Becky stayed awake, but Nate didn't let go.

A lot of men might've taken offense at being called a fool. Owen just watched with sharp eyes and cool calculation. As if reading every word, every expression, Becky's ashen face, Nate's movements—he even studied Sal and Tex.

"You might ride on the side of the law," Nate said, "and I guess we should be thankful for that. But that cruel streak of yours matches the men you hunt down." He loosened his grip on Becky, as she remained steady.

Owen arched his brows as if this were all part of his job.

Nate sank down on his haunches beside Becky, who was still pale, shaken. And Becky Pruitt was the strongest woman Nate had ever known.

The fact that she hadn't erupted into screaming proved just how strong.

"You don't have to do this, Becky. No decent lawman

would ask a daughter to have a hand in pursuing her own father."

Becky's gaze locked with Nate's. She looked deeply into his eyes. He felt as if she were drawing strength from him. And he hoped she used that strength to kick Owen and his men, even Nate's brother, off her ranch.

Finally, she blinked, shook her head a bit violently, then straightened. "Did you know about this?"

"I knew exactly what you knew, and when you knew it. I told you everything Sal told me that day I met him in town."

Color seeped into her face again. Not enough, but it was better.

"Would you do it? Would you take part in a plan to betray your father?"

It wasn't fair to ask that of him. What's more, he was sure she knew it.

"My pa was a good lawman. It's impossible to imagine him other than completely honorable. It was a cornerstone of his life. I-I can't . . ." Nate looked at Sal. "Would you?"

Sal had the same confused look on his face that Nate was sure was on his.

"The difference is, I've always known my pa to be a harsh man, who surrounded himself with other harsh men. His heart is dark and cruel."

Becky snuck a look at Owen, and her expression seemed to shout, Like you! She drew a long, deep breath. "I need time to think about this. I will keep my promise not to tell your secret, but to actively help with my pa's downfall . . ." She shook her head and repeated, "I need time."

"In the end," Owen said, "it's the same, Miss Pruitt. You can kick us off this ranch, but we're looking very carefully at your pa and the Circle J. He may not be the mastermind. He may just be looking the other way, letting his men ride off and come back without asking questions. He may not be profiting from the holdups at all. We'll uncover the truth of that, and we'll do it with or without your help. Whether or not you cooperate with us doesn't change the outcome. I know I'm asking a hard thing of you, and one of the reasons I stated it in such a severe way was because I want you to be clearheaded when you decide how to handle things. But—"

"No, stop now. Don't say any more," Nate said, standing tall beside Becky.

"One last thing." Owen was a hard man. Becky had signed on for much more than she'd bargained for when she agreed to let him use the Idee Ranch to base his investigation.

"Let's hear it." Becky sounded exhausted.

Nate stepped a bit closer to her.

"We would've never come up with this plan if you didn't have a reputation for honesty." Owen's eyes on Becky held a fire that burned straight into her soul. "We wouldn't have risked telling you the truth if you weren't known far and wide for being a decent, trustworthy woman." His eyes narrowed. "The kind of woman who would step forward if she saw a chance to put an end to a murdering band of outlaws."

Owen stood, Tex just a pace behind him. Sal stayed put, his arms crossed. Owen and Tex headed out the back door.

When they were gone, Becky said, "Well, that was a sharply made comment. If I don't help him, I'm not a decent, trustworthy woman—that was his point, right?"

"Right." Nate had a notion to go clear those men off the ranch right now.

"That was his point, Miss Becky." Sal's voice was as kind as Owen's was cold. "But what he said is also true. We're relentless when it comes to catching outlaws, but we don't harm honest men. If your pa and his cowpokes are behind this, they need to be stopped. If we're on the wrong track, then we'll know it soon enough. If you can't believe your pa would be party to such a thing as the robberies, don't think of helping us as betraying him. Think of it as clearing his name."

Sal got up and left.

"Another sharply made comment." Becky turned to Nate. "Your brother was as decent as Owen was ruthless. I suppose they practice that and take turns being the good Marshal and the bad Marshal."

Nate stood there silent, watching her. Then, instead of following the other men outside, he sat down at the table in a chair right around the corner from hers. He said, "Tell me about your pa, Becky. I know you left his ranch and started this one because you didn't like the men he hired or the way he ran things. And I saw the way he treated you in Pine Valley the other day. Was he always violent with you? Buying your own ranch, building your own house and barn, bringing in your own herd—those are all steps beyond not liking him. It reaches the level of hating him, or possibly worse, fearing him. Tell me what he's like."

Becky's expression turned grim. Nate saw her turning things over in her head and expected any minute for her to order him back to work so she could be alone to think.

Instead, she started talking. Nate noticed it wasn't about her pa.

12

I don't have many memories of my ma. I was by no means a baby when she died, but I was young, eight years old. I remember my two little brothers dying more than my ma because they were my playmates, my best friends, my tormentors. All the things two young boys can be. I loved them."

She smiled thinking of a few of their antics. Because she couldn't sit still, she stood and got coffee for Nate and herself. The coffee was still hot, left for her by Jan before she rode away.

There were cookies too, and a stew ready for supper. Jan didn't like leaving Becky on her own. But with Roscoe working as foreman, someone needed to be camp cook.

Becky returned to her chair and held the pottery coffee cup with both hands to absorb its warmth. Owen had left her feeling cold to the bone.

"Ma was a hardworking woman. Pa was always after her about everything. He had a mean tongue, and he used it on her, me, Frank and Buddy. I felt the back of his hand plenty of times. Ma could hand out a whoopin' too, but her heart was never in it. If we broke something or made a mess, she just cleaned it up, swept up the pieces, whatever needed doing. It wasn't long before I caught on to that and learned to clean up after myself and my brothers."

"Why do you talk about your ma and brothers when I asked about your pa?"

"Nell told me her first husband used to slap her. He was a lawman. She learned he wanted to talk all about himself. He wanted her to listen, but if she had an idea about some crime he was trying to arrest someone for, he didn't want to hear Nell's ideas. She learned to listen without talking. I-I think now, looking back, my ma learned that. I think she taught me and the boys not to sass pa. To give him a peaceful house when he came home. I never saw him hit her, but he hit me and the boys plenty. He was quick with a backhand. But like I said, it was so long ago. Then the fever went through the family. Both boys died from it. Ma got real sick but survived. Pa and I didn't even have a sniffle.

"The shock of it, well, I just remember crying and visiting their graves and not quite understanding that they were gone forever. Ma tried to talk to me about heaven and about seeing the boys again. It was all part of that muddled time. Before I'd begun to adjust to not having them around, Ma was bringing another baby into the world. I don't remember much about it. She certainly didn't talk much about being in a hopeful condition, as I've heard it called."

"And she died."

"My brothers weren't two years dead and then Ma was

gone. It was just me and Pa. I was old enough to ride, but not old enough to be left by myself in the house alone. I remember Pa saying he wished I was old enough to cook, that then I'd be good for something."

"He said that?" Nate reached across the corner of the table and took her hand in his.

"Pa never much watched his mouth." Becky curled her free hand around her waist, her belly hurting from long-ignored pain. Right now a swallow of coffee was beyond her. "His sons had died, and he'd been left with a useless girl. Ma was a weakling who'd left him with the chore of watching over me."

Becky frowned, and she clutched her belly tighter. "He cursed God for the hard life he'd been left with. And I rode with him, all day every day. I learned to ranch from watching him. I learned not to say much and for certain not ever to sass him. I was as good a roper as him by the time I was twelve. I could throw a calf for branding by the time I was fourteen and hog-tie a thousand-pound steer by the time I was sixteen. I learned to ignore the crude remarks his men made about work, about life, about me. Pa didn't let the ugly things said in front of me upset him."

"Are any of those men still working for him?" Nate's sharp tone drew her attention, and she wondered if he was considering riding to the Circle J and slamming a fist into a few mouths—including her pa's.

"I think a few are. I should have asked Owen which men he suspected of being the outlaws. I know who works for Pa mostly. Some hire on for a season, then wander off somewhere, but I know a lot of them."

"How bad was it?" Nate asked.

Becky had changed the subject, hoping they could speculate about Pa's men instead of Pa. "When I was eighteen, we had three newcomers among the cowhands. One of them dragged me into the barn, where the other two were waiting. Someone else came along and I got away, but I was scared. I told Pa about it, and he said something about leaving his men alone. Not flaunting myself. And then less than a month later, I inherited close to one hundred thousand dollars from my ma's parents. They'd been gone awhile, but the money wouldn't come to me until I turned eighteen. There were all kinds of rules attached to it so Pa couldn't take it from me.

"He'd known both my grandparents were dead, but he'd never mentioned it to me. A lawyer came to the ranch with the will and careful instructions. He didn't trust Pa to even tell me about the inheritance if he got word. He'd've taken the money and cut me out, and I'd've never known about it. But my grandparents didn't trust Pa and so found a way to go around him legally. I needed to be old enough, and living in Wyoming, where women had more rights than usual, didn't hurt.

"I gathered that money and bought this land, far enough away from Pa and his men to feel safe. I hired decent cowhands. I hired the Grables so I wouldn't be a woman alone with so many men. And I've had almost nothing to do with Pa since except when we cross paths in town." Becky gasped.

"What is it?" Nate looked concerned.

"The last time I ate a meal with Pa, I asked him to help guard that wounded man who'd been shot by the Deadeye Gang and survived the robbery."

"The man Henry killed?"

Becky nodded. "It's a wonder Pa didn't arrange to guard him and then kill him, if Pa's really involved with the gang."

Nate didn't respond. Becky had to wonder what he was thinking.

"I've never gone back to his place since I left. Not for Christmas or Thanksgiving. And I sure as certain have never been invited to Sunday dinner. Pa let me know plain and simple—long before he braced me with it in town the other day—that he'd counted on that money I inherited to help him expand his ranch. If I'd been a boy, I'd've stayed and been a partner."

"Maybe if he'd managed to raise a son to be a polecat like him."

Becky thought of her little brothers and how sweet they'd been. She hoped they'd've been made of sterner stuff. "Even with all his uncaring and tolerance for men being bad around me, and toward me, I've never thought he'd murder anyone."

Becky had said enough. There were dozens of stories, but Nate didn't need to hear them.

"I started out this talk wanting to go run those men off the ranch, including my own brother. Now I kind of hope they hang your father."

Becky didn't say anything.

"Well, are you going to let Owen and the other Marshals use your ranch?"

Becky stared at the wall in front of her. Looked through it, in fact. Sorting through all she'd endured from Pa, studying what loyalty she felt for him.

At last she made her decision and was surprised that

the ache in her belly eased. "If Pa's innocent, they'll soon find out and start investigating somewhere else. If he's guilty, he and his outlaws have to be stopped. Yes. Owen and his men can stay."

Becky stood from the table and walked toward the back door. She plucked her tan Stetson off its peg and pulled on her buckskin gloves. She walked out without paying attention to what Nate did, but she heard the door close behind her.

The two of them got back to work.

"What are we going to do about Samantha and Leland?" Nell rolled to her side and stared at her husband. She'd been so determined to never marry again. And living in Wyoming with so many men for each woman, it wasn't that easy to stay single.

Nell had managed nicely.

But then Brand and his three girls had come along. Marrying Brand Nolte was such a great thing that she hadn't regretted it for one single moment.

She loved his girls, too. All three of them. Samantha, the now-married oldest. Cassie, thirteen, and little Michaela, seven. Samantha and Cassandra were dark-haired and blue-eyed. A match for Brand. Michaela was a blonde. Brand said she looked like Pamela, his first wife. Nell found herself thinking Michaela also looked a little like Brand's second wife. Nell decided she could pretend Michaela looked like her if she wanted to. The two older girls looked like Brand, while Michaela was fine-boned and blond like Nell, so they made a likely family.

Except their oldest child had married in haste and was repenting at the top of her lungs to anyone who'd listen.

And Leland wasn't acting with any great sign of maturity either.

Brand sighed. Talking over problems was usually done when they got to bed. They slept in a new bedroom they'd built to straddle Nell's recently claimed homestead and the one Brand had owned for nearly a year.

Brand slept on his property, and Nell slept on hers. This arrangement satisfied the government's requirement that a homestead had to be improved upon, which meant the settler and owner was to build a house on the land homesteaded and then sleep in that house at least six months of the year. Nell thought if they were ever feeling reckless, they could just switch sides of the bed and dare the government to come in and prove it.

"Samantha's scars are healing, don't you think?"

Nell didn't want to talk about those terrible scars. Yes, they were healing. No, they were never going away. The scars weren't the problem, but she knew Brand worried about his daughter feeling bad about herself.

"They are healed enough they can't be used as an excuse for Samantha and Leland to carry on the way they do. Samantha is used to running things inside and out. You worked alongside her but gave her a lot of responsibility and freedom. Leland's ma was a fireball. He should be used to a woman being a handful. In fact, I think the source of a lot of their problems is that Leland is determined not to give Samantha as much freedom as Parson Blodgett gave his wife."

"So, Leland scolding and insulting Samantha is his idea

of protecting her?" Brand propped his head up on his fist. "That sounds stupid. Is Leland a stupid man?"

"It's possible. And Samantha has the bit in her teeth. They're both the oldest in the family and used to running things their way. They just need to start talking to each other instead of bickering. But I blame that on them being young and not spending any time at all courting. They just ran wild and straight to the preacher."

It wasn't quite that bad but close enough.

"What are we going to do about Samantha and Leland?" Brand rolled forward so he was looming over her.

"I asked first."

"I have an idea." Brand leaned down and kissed her.

"You do? That's wonderful. Tell me, and we can plot out how to teach them to get along."

Brand smiled. It was September. Though autumn was coming, the days were still long. Dusk had just settled in. She could see his expression with no trouble.

"My idea—" he paused and kissed her again, longer, deeper—"has nothing to do with those two half-wit children and everything to do with being alone in the night with my beautiful new wife."

Nell circled his neck with her arms and decided that for now, she'd just let those two problem children learn to get along on their own. "I am married to a very wise man." She pulled him close, then closer.

13

Something itched on the back of Becky's neck, and she spun around, her hand on her pistol.

Nothing.

But there was something.

She studied the land before her. Rocks and grass, dirt and trees and cattle.

Nothing else.

Until a man stood from the ground only a few yards in front of her to the left.

She whipped her gun out as the man held up both hands in a stop motion, or in surrender, Becky wasn't sure. "Don't shoot, Miss Pruitt. I'm with the Marshals." He held a badge that did indeed look like the badge she'd been shown.

"He's with us, Miss Pruitt." Owen came riding in from behind her.

The man before her stood dressed in brown leather from head to foot—the kind of clothes an Indian might wear. A jerkin and loose britches. He had brown hair, brown skin, moccasins, and he was scuffed with dirt. He didn't pull the gun she saw on his hip.

She didn't shoot, but it annoyed her. Scared her a little, too. To be snuck up on like this. She'd've bet it couldn't happen.

Where was Brutus anyway? He usually stuck by her side. Today she couldn't remember seeing him or Lobo, not once.

Still, it was fascinating. "How did you just appear? How did you get so close when there's no cover?"

"Why, I am Morgan Sawyer, miss. The fastest, smartest, toughest, sneakiest man in the entire Marshals Service."

Owen snorted. "Bragging-est more like."

Morgan grinned, then thrust out a hand as Owen dismounted and shook it. The two slapped each other on the back.

"About time you got here, Morg. You're the last."

"The last?" Becky was confused. "You're waiting for seven men, and this is the first one I've seen."

Owen turned to her. "They've been slipping in all night, setting up in the bunkhouse. Not even Nate knows they're here."

"I always come in last when we do jobs like this. I like to make sure everyone else gets in okay."

Becky thought again of Brutus and Lobo. "How did you get past my dogs? No one gets past them. They better not be harmed."

"I've been real busy gentling them since I got here. I walked out with the dogs all through last night. Each man slipped in and told me how far behind him the next was.

So Brutus and Lobo weren't surprised. I expected Morgan here would surprise them, coming in full daylight like he done. But we'll get them to accept Morg, too. They'll likely recognize a wolf man when they see one and claim him as their own."

Morg laughed. "I can show you how to sneak around if you've a mind to learn, Miss Becky."

"I know how to sneak around just fine."

Sawyer smiled. "I know how good Nate is, and word is he's spoken of your skill."

At the mention of his name, Nate came galloping up, Brutus on his heels. Brutus gave out a vicious snarl and charged at Sawyer.

"Hold, Brutus. Here, boy."

Lobo came into sight a second later, up to Becky's side and opposite Brutus, the two of them guarding her. Becky wasn't impressed. They'd been seduced by these newcomers—all but this one they hadn't met. Men smart enough to know they needed to befriend two dangerous dogs before they could take over her ranch.

She rubbed the thick fur on top of her dogs' heads. She, too, had let the newcomers invade, so she knew how her companions felt.

"We're all here. Miss Pruitt. We'll have our meeting in the bunkhouse, unless you'd let us in your house. We want you to hear our plans."

"I don't have a room big enough for so many men. I'll come to the bunkhouse and attend your meeting."

It gave her pause to go into that bunkhouse with all the men, most of them complete strangers. A woman alone shouldn't behave so, but she didn't have a choice.

Then Nate stepped up beside her, Brutus between them, and she realized she wasn't alone. It eased her mind some.

"Let's go," Owen said, taking charge. The man was as good as running her ranch now.

And that didn't suit her at all.

Clint finished serving up the noon meal at the diner.

Mariah, who'd spent time today doing some fine decorative work at the smithy, shut down her forge.

Nell filled out her last homestead claim acknowledgment form and hung her robe on a wall peg.

Brand rode into town so the trip would be safer—four people instead of three. His two girls, Cassie and Michaela, still of school age, were at Samantha's until their ma and pa came to fetch them.

Nell hoped it kept the newlyweds from scrapping for a day. They were going, unannounced, to see Becky.

Mariah had a campaign to wage, and Nell was all in favorite of it. The two of them rode ahead of the men because the trail was too narrow for four abreast.

"She's out there alone with Nate and three men you've never seen before? That doesn't sound like Becky." Mariah frowned as she considered just how strange it was. Becky was a woman who worked hard every day at a man's job, yet she was conscious of proprieties. Her worthless oaf of a pa had made her more than conscious. She wouldn't like being alone out there. So why had she done it? Why send Jan Grable on the drive, who usually stayed home with Becky? A few hands had stayed behind, but they were men Becky knew well and trusted. Not Nate and three strangers.

"It's a mystery." Nell knew investigating techniques and the law. Besides that, with her keen and suspicious and judging mind, she could read people. "And Becky was acting strange."

"Strange how?" Mariah asked.

Nell shook her head. "I only know something was bothering her."

"I'm surprised she kept Nate home. One of them should be on the drive."

"She explained that away, said Roscoe Grable might be taking up the job of foreman again. She said it right in front of Nate. He nodded when she said it, so he didn't seem upset."

The two of them rode along, turning things over in their minds without talking them out.

Finally, Mariah said, "At least Nate is there."

Then the two of them giggled like a pair of little girls. They were still grinning when they rode into Becky's ranch.

14

"Someone's coming." Sawyer jerked his gun free.

"Stop. Those are friends of mine. Owen, Nell was here when the drovers rode off with the herd, remember?"

Owen went to the window of the bunkhouse, nodded, and said, "Get out there, Miss Pruitt. See why they're here."

He sounded suspicious, like a man who made a living the way he did was supposed to be.

"Mariah Roberts, the one on the gray mustang, had her father killed by the Deadeye Gang." Becky looked away from her friends to Owen. "Beside her is Nell Nolte. It was her house that was attacked when the Wainwrights were shot. Brand, her husband, had his oldest daughter attacked by a wolf. The whole thing staged by Henry Wainwright. All four of those people are above suspicion. You might not want word to get out about what you're up to, and I won't tell them. But if you need folks who live in town for any reason, Clint, the man who pulled up to ride by Mariah, his wife, runs the diner. He sees most everyone sooner or later. He's got a good view of the goings-on in town."

Becky headed for the door.

Owen caught her arm, and her eyes narrowed as she glared at his hand on her.

He opened his hand but held her gaze. "Four of us—Nate, Tex, Sal and I—are going to head out and ride herd. The others of us will stay inside, out of sight. Don't tell your visitors we're here."

"I gave you my word." Becky said it with ice in her voice.

Owen nodded, and Becky hurried out.

"I'm coming with you, Becky." Nate was right behind her.

She was glad to have him at hand. The two dogs ran ahead to greet the visitors.

"I'm going to rip his hand off if he puts it on you again."

Becky gave him a smile that felt a bit savage. "How about you hold my hat while I rip it off."

Nate jerked his chin down. "Then we agree."

"We do indeed."

Becky walked up to her friends as they were dismounting. There was a hitching post by her back door.

"Good to see you folks." Becky thought she sounded just a little overly hearty, and her friends knew her too well. She tried to subtly draw in a calming breath and shake off the tension of what was going on around her. "Come on in. I've got coffee ready. Jan left a pile of cookies behind, as if I'd starve with her gone on the drive."

Nell came up to her and slung an arm around her waist. "How are you managing alone out here? I should've offered to stay with you."

"Oh, I'm fine." Becky swung the back door open and stood back to let everyone go inside the house.

"I won't let her ride out here alone," Brand said. "I'd come out and stay too, but then I'd have to bring both of my girls. And ride everyone into town every day, which means we wouldn't end up being here much at all."

"Thanks for even considering such a thing." Becky waved a hand to get Brand to walk on through.

Mariah was next. A very round woman.

"How much longer before our little friend makes his appearance?" Becky smiled at Mariah, who absolutely glowed from impending motherhood and a loving marriage. Becky didn't know much about that.

"It's getting close. Before the end of September, Doc says."

"It's the first part of September now. Should you be out riding?"

Mariah shrugged. "I'd better do my visiting now. I might be staying close to home when Junior arrives." She patted her belly.

"I'm keeping a close eye on her." Clint gave her a cranky look. "Not counting that she was working at the smithy today."

"It was just a little job, Clint. Fine details on a hinge for Mr. Kintzinger."

"He can live without fine details. We wouldn't have come if you lived much farther out." Clint stepped behind Mariah and guided her inside.

Nate sidled up next to her. He arched a brow, though Becky couldn't read much from it. Her own thoughts were centered on what in the world these folks were there for. Maybe Nate was thinking the same thing.

She went in ahead of Nate, who closed the door behind her.

Her two best friends in the world sat at her kitchen table. Nell had found the cookies, and Mariah was pouring coffee. It looked as though they were planning to sit a spell.

Then Mariah launched into the visit of Mrs. Mussel and the reason for their presence became clear. Her friends wanted to discuss every little detail.

Becky was excited to talk about it, too.

Becky settled in to talk seriously about how well they thought Mrs. Mussel and Mrs. Morris had done, and how the people of Pine Valley were encouraged by the speeches. At least those who believed in the cause of women's suffrage.

They left after a pleasant hour together.

Becky stood at her back door waving as they rode off. Nate stood beside her. Brutus walked along beside the visitors for a while. Becky didn't worry about it. He'd come back. Probably to get treats from the men in the bunkhouse. Lobo lingered at Becky's side.

Becky watched as they rode off. Nell and Mariah were side by side, chattering. Mariah looked back, saw Becky watching them, and waved as if she were leaving on a journey to lands far off. So chipper. It made no sense.

"Mariah and Nell aren't ones to drop by in the middle of a workday. I wonder what they were up to. I expected Nell to kick up a fuss about my being out here with no other women. Instead, she explained why she couldn't be here and then started talking about her work as justice of the peace."

"And Mariah's selling the smithy to Deputy Willie." Nate shoved his hat back a bit and folded his arms. "A forge and a baby are a hard mix, I suppose. Tyke's gonna get burned unless everyone is real careful."

"The schoolteacher and the undertaker are running the general store. Joy Blodgett is the new schoolmarm. I suppose next Doc will start being the sheriff, and Sheriff Joe will start setting bones and delivering babies."

"Clint made his chicken parmesan for lunch today, and Brand's got a new calf."

"It was nice of them to catch us up on town news. We didn't have time to hear all this while Mrs. Mussel and Mrs. Morris were here. But even so, it was the kind of talk we usually do after church on Sunday." Nate nodded thoughtfully.

Becky watched him to see if he had any inspiration.

All he said was, "They were definitely up to something."

"Can you step back inside for just a minute, Nate? I want to know what's being said out there in the bunkhouse when I'm not around."

They moved inside but stayed near the closed back door. "I can't tell you much because they don't tell me much. I'm in the foreman's cabin so any discussion in the night leaves me out."

"I don't like it at all. My ranch is being taken over. My dogs too."

Nate rested a hand on her shoulder. "They won't be here for long."

"No, but if they find what they suspect is true, they'll ride away from here with my pa in shackles, heading for the gallows." Becky swallowed hard and looked up into Nate's eyes. She saw only kindness there.

Shaking his head, Nate leaned close. "They're asking something of you no one should ever have to give, Becky. If you want out of this, just say the word and I'll put a stop to it."

She was a confused woman when she let that comfort her. It should have made her mad. If this needed to stop, she was fully capable of stopping it herself. She didn't need her foreman to handle it. But it helped. A lot. Too much.

"I'm seeing it through, Nate." She leaned closer to him and felt his arms go around her and hold her. Her life was so lonely. She felt as if his arms were water poured out onto earth so parched it was cracked. She soaked up his kindness. "The worst part is that I can't say with any certainty that Pa isn't involved with the gang and their holdups. It sickens me to admit it, but Pa is capable of it."

She started to pull back from his embrace, relieved to have his strong arms as she set out on this dreadful course of action. Their gazes met. His arms tightened. Something that was wound very tight inside her released. She saw his eyes flicker down to her mouth, and that warmed her lips.

Then she stepped back fully and turned aside. Yet she couldn't tell him to keep his hands off her. She couldn't tell him his actions were improper because she'd allowed it, wanted it. To say she hadn't would make her a hypocrite. She had no idea how to get Nate to leave. It seemed her brain was too befuddled to make a solid decision.

A hard knock on the back door was their only warning.

Nate slipped into the kitchen. Becky was standing facing the door when it opened.

Sal. Nate's brother. "Where's Nate?"

Becky glanced over her shoulder, hoping she didn't look as mixed up as she felt. "Nate?"

She saw he'd ducked around the corner. Nate stepped back into the kitchen holding a coffee cup. "We got rid of Becky's friends," he stated, his tone even. "We have no idea why they came out here. They never do that." He looked at Becky. "Do they?"

Shaking her head, Becky said, "No. Never."

Sal nodded. "Well, we're going out tonight. Becky, you and Nate know this land better than any of us. We've gathered together our best Marshals for scouting the area. With their skills and your knowledge, we're going to watch all the trails leading to and from the Circle J. We'll be ready to follow if his men ride off, and there'll be enough of us that if a few of them scatter, we can dog them all. But anything we can learn beforehand will increase our chances for success. Can you come out to the bunkhouse, Miss Pruitt? It's high time we plan the opening campaign in this war."

15

Becky was in the lead of a silent column in the dark of night.

She'd chosen a dark gray mustang to ride instead of her beautiful palomino. She loved that horse, but it would shine like a beacon in the darkness.

Nate rode beside her on his huge black stallion.

She was more involved than she'd expected to be. Probably more involved than Owen had intended. But Becky knew some back trails that few if any of the men were familiar with. Hard trails to find in the dark. They'd talked about the possibility of waiting and her guiding them along the trails in the daylight, but after discussing it at length, they decided the wait wasn't a good idea. She'd agreed to lead them.

It was September, the days still warm usually, though the nights could drop below freezing. As they rode out among the foothills of the Wind River Mountains, Becky noted that all the men were properly dressed for the cold. They rode along quietly with only the sound of hoofbeats marking their steady progress. Even the horses seemed to be mindful of the need for silence.

Becky had on a buckskin coat, one she'd hand-dyed into a dark gray. This wasn't the first time she'd ridden out at night. Owen had protested, but at Becky's insistence, Brutus and Lobo padded alongside her. While Owen didn't trust the dogs to stay close and quiet, Becky knew them well. They could sense the tension and understood what Becky needed. Lobo wouldn't dash off rabbit hunting on a whim, and Brutus wouldn't attack unless she told him to.

The moon was full, the stars in full view. Not a cloud in the sky. Becky would have preferred an overcast night with a bit of wind. Any small sounds might be dismissed as the breeze rustling trees. To her knowledge, Pa didn't post sentries. But then a lot of what might be going on with Pa wasn't as she'd suspected, at least if these men were right about him.

The plan was for the ten men to spread out around Pa's ranch, to cover all trails away from his place. They'd stake out the Circle J with pairs of observing Marshals, and if any of Pa's men rode off in a manner that seemed suspicious, those men would have a shadow.

A puff of wind stirred the fringe on Becky's coat. A clink of metal behind her made her wince.

Pa's house lay ten miles to the north and east of Becky's. Pa had been out there before there was a town. By the time Becky started building her place, she'd decided to live closer to town with a good amount of space between her and Pa. She didn't much like the solitary life out at Pa's. She wanted to go to town for supplies without it taking the best part of a day. And she wanted to ride into town for church on Sunday.

Pa had never bothered with church, nor had any of his cowhands. Back then, Becky had made the ride when she had the gumption, but with the long miles, rugged terrain, and six months of winter, she wasn't a regular attender, though she had always been a woman of faith.

They rode on increasingly narrow trails, winding into dense woods and rugged climbs for half an hour or so. The trees towered overhead, forming a canopy that blocked out the moon and stars. The scent of pine, loamy soil, and the cool nighttime breeze surrounded them like a cocoon. Considering their grim mission, Becky had trouble enjoying the scents and sounds of the Wyoming wilderness like she usually did. But they were still there, and they helped to steady her.

Becky rode on for just a bit longer, then held up her hand. The others stopped instantly. They had sharp eyes and a knowing way about them. They were good men to ride with, despite her not liking how they'd invaded her ranch.

No one spoke.

She gestured for Owen to come closer and pointed to a trail leading up the side of a mountain that led to Pa's place. Owen nodded and gestured to two other men, one of them Morgan Sawyer. It was a decent lookout over Pa's ranch, so rugged and surrounded by pine trees and paved by stone that no cattle went up here.

As Owen turned to lead the way up the trail, Sawyer hissed.

Everyone froze.

In a voice so quiet it could have been the wind, Sawyer said, "Someone's coming. Get off the trail."

Their whole group leaving the trail wouldn't be easy.

As quick as she could, Becky made her way between two massive tree trunks and the scrub brush that filled in the space, the dogs following her. She heard someone behind her and glanced back to see Nate shadowing her into the woods.

She was grateful for the darkness provided by the towering trees and the night.

A full minute passed before Becky heard the hoofbeats approaching. Sawyer had ears like a bat. Waiting, conscious of her own breathing, she focused on what she could see of the trail.

Sure enough, she spotted faint shadows moving like ghosts along the trail. Without the quiet hooves and Sawyer's sharp hearing, Becky would have walked right into this group. In the dark, she didn't recognize a single one of them. She knew her pa's men by sight and knew most of their names, yet she couldn't identify anyone in this passage at night.

Becky's heart quickened. These men, riding away from Pa's place, had to be the Deadeye Gang. They were likely heading out to find another stagecoach to rob.

She noticed then a new shadow, someone from the Marshals' group coming out onto the trail. It was Sawyer. Then came another man, then another, falling in behind Sawyer and his horse.

They'd planned to surround the ranch, follow if a group rode off in any direction. They'd discussed how to notify each other. How they'd follow without being seen. They'd brought along supplies, preparing to wait for days, possibly even weeks if they had to.

Instead, the gang had ridden right past them. They'd almost missed their chance. If they'd waited one more day to post guards at Pa's, they'd have missed the outlaws.

Becky might be misjudging the situation, but she was bitterly afraid that these ghost riders in the night were proof of her pa's guilt. Maybe he wasn't part of the gang beyond his turning a blind eye, but he had to have noticed his men leaving the ranch. He had put up with it. And when innocent people were killed, he had kept silent about it.

Pa had, at the very least, done all of that. And that made him a party to murder.

Becky had just as good as slipped a noose around her own pa's neck.

As she fought back her anger at Pa, Becky saw Nate leave their hiding place, and she followed him. Where was he heading? All their plans had been thrown into disarray. How far would these men ride? Where were they going?

She should probably ride along for a time, then turn back for home, but she didn't want to be alone in the night or alone at her ranch. They'd intended for her to show them hiding places, then she'd go home. One of them would escort her, though she'd sensed that no one wanted to be left out of the chase. So it'd be Nate, the former Marshal. But Nate knew this land better than any of them. Better than most anyone around except Becky. So they needed him. She decided that staying with the Marshals was the best idea.

She was a bit surprised that the whole group of Marshals

followed the night riders rather than some staying to stake out Pa's place. Yet it was a sizable bunch of men they were after. Everyone set out, and there was no time for Becky to call a meeting.

While she rode along, she thought of her ranch. Her cattle were grazing. She hadn't known for sure if she'd get back home tonight so she'd given the chickens a few days' worth of feed just in case.

She was sticking with the lawmen. Which meant she was sticking with the outlaws.

She was riding toward justice, but as she followed the silent column of tough men, it struck Becky that she was moving away from her ranch. A ranch she'd broken all the rules of normal civilized behavior to possess.

With a vicious gang right ahead of them, she realized it was possible that if things went terribly wrong, she might never see her home again.

16

Nate had a reputation for being the best tracker in Wyoming.

For the next two days he was given a lesson in humility.

He'd never seen the likes of Morgan Sawyer on a trail. There were four others almost as good, and Nate got included in that number. But not a one of the four was a patch on Sawyer.

They had developed a system . . . or maybe not *developed* it. Maybe they did this all the time, but it was new to Nate. During the daylight hours, two of the best trackers with Sawyer leading would follow the gang. The rest of them settled in, ate, slept if they could, and waited.

Sawyer and two others would tail the gang. When the land formations were right to provide a hideout for the Marshals, Sawyer would pick a spot, post a watch, and send one man back to lead the group forward. By the time the Marshals reached the hideout Sawyer had chosen, the man who'd come back for them rode off again to catch up

with the pair who'd gone ahead. As the Deadeye Gang—
leastways that was Nate's belief as to who they were—
rode deep into the night, their little parade of Marshals
would hang back except for those few following. When the
gang broke off their forced march, the Marshals gathered,
posted a lookout, and got a chance to sleep a bit more.

It was a grim and silent march for a fact.

Nate didn't sleep next to Becky, but he positioned himself between her and the posse. Not a one of them ever
said a wrong word to Becky, and Nate hoped that meant
they were honorable in their dealings with women. Still,
he knew better than to leave much to chance.

On their third day on the trail, just before high noon
when they caught up to the hideout Sawyer had chosen,
he was there waiting for them.

"I want Becky and Nate to see them. We've got a good
overlook behind some shrubs. With field glasses I'm hoping Becky can point out the gang members by name. We
might recognize some of them as wanted men. And I have
to wonder if they're nearing the end of this trek. No reason to stop and just linger over a noon meal. I think they
know just how much farther they must go and how long
it'll take to get there. I'm guessing they've got a short ride
yet today to reach their destination, with a stagecoach
robbery planned for tomorrow morning."

Owen came along, and they set up just right so Nate
and Becky could look down on the men they followed.
There were six in all. Nate knew most of them. Becky
knew all of them.

Speaking barely above a whisper, even this far away,
Becky didn't need the binoculars. "Bernard Skleen is the

146

man riding the big lineback dun gelding. He's been with Pa a long time."

Sawyer said, "Skleen picks the times to stop, rides up front. The way he points and stands around watching the others tells me he's the leader."

"It would make sense if this was going on a while since he's been at the Circle J for years."

Owen looked through the spy glasses for a long spell. Morgan Sawyer was beside them, looking at the men.

Owen said, "I've seen Skleen before. He went by the name Utah Mike when I knew him. He's a wanted man in Colorado. We heard he lit out for the Indian Territory. He's a nasty, murderous desperado."

"You're sure that's Utah Mike?" Sawyer spoke, as did everyone, at a whisper. "I've heard of him but never run across him before. The one riding the red roan mustang is Clancy Bonneau. He was holding up stagecoaches in California when I knew him. Just a kid back then. I never figured he'd live to an old age. And he still might not."

Another was a known man. Owen and Sawyer put a name to him, and Becky told them the name he went by now. All of them studied the group. The ones they didn't know were given names by Becky, though Nate had to wonder if any of them was going by his real name.

They all memorized the names and faces and the horses they rode.

The outlaw gang broke camp and then loaded up their horses to continue on their way.

Sawyer said, "I'll give them a few minutes, then head out to follow.

Nate saw dark circles under Sawyer's eyes and wondered

when the man would have to get at least one good night's sleep. "Three of them are newcomers I've never seen before," Nate said. "Becky, you know their names, but if they just joined up at your pa's ranch and now they're out riding with this gang, they must've come in looking for outlaw work. Which means, on the outlaw trails, your pa's ranch is known. Word is getting passed along."

Becky nodded, her jaw clenched tight, her arms crossed over her chest.

Sal slipped up beside them. "Come away from the overlook. We'll talk where we're sure they can't hear us."

The four of them who'd been watching followed Sal.

Nate was glad they moved away. A man could sometimes feel that he was being watched. He didn't believe it was a special sense beyond explanation, but he did believe shadows could shift, and faint noises, maybe even breathing could affect someone being watched. They might not be able to explain what was making them jumpy, but men who survived for a long time in a hard land, especially those who rode the outlaw trail, learned to trust their instincts. It was best not to watch them for too long.

"We've been talking," Sal said as he led the group back to the campsite. When they reached the other Marshals, he continued, "Tex is familiar with Wyoming, and this trail we've been following is unknown, but considering the direction, he thinks we're going to end up just east of South Pass City."

Tex nodded. "There's a trail there that winds a bit. If these outlaws have inside information, they might be planning to waylay a gold shipment headed for some big bank in Denver. Or maybe one headed for the train. The trail to Denver crosses the tracks. That's the kind of news everyone tries hard to keep secret. And they don't always succeed."

Nate snapped his fingers. "There's a real rugged stretch along there, well before they reach the railroad tracks. It'd make a good place to strike. And these robbers might be thinking to get that gold before it reaches the train station. The trail runs through a narrow canyon. It'd be a perfect place to lie in wait to shoot down on a wagon, even one with guards and outriders. They could kill everyone without exposing themselves, then ride down and get away with the gold."

"It's too near Pine Valley." Becky shook her head. "They're fools to think they can keep up their murderous attacks so close to home."

"Especially," Nate said, "when they attack so often. The very few attacks, spaced out and far from home, must've been the Wainwrights' influence."

Nate thought of those two supposedly respectable businessmen in Pine Valley. They had owned the general store. Pete Wainwright had been mayor. They maintained respectability while being the worst kind of thieves and murderers. They'd died attacking Nell and her family only a couple of months ago.

Nate looked down at Brutus. Lobo had abandoned them. Becky said the dog had likely gone home to protect the ranch as much as a dog could do such a thing. Lobo might not feed the chickens, but she would drive off varmints and unwanted visitors. Yet Brutus had stuck with them. The dog stayed put and silent when Becky told him to.

Everyone around Pine Valley had hoped, with the men who seemed to be the leaders of the Deadeye Gang killed, the crime wave would end. Instead, it was worse than ever.

Becky said, "It almost seems like with this stepped-up string of robberies, they've got some goal. They intend to get their money and ride off. They know they can't keep up their crime spree at this rate."

Nate shook his head. "But if new men keep coming in, they can't *all* be aiming for that goal."

Everyone sat around the campsite while Sawyer went on with two others. They pondered all they knew but came up with few answers.

"How long until we reach this place?" Owen looked at Nate in a way that made him want to sit up straighter. A look that said what Nate knew might be enough to turn this whole mission around.

Nate realized that Owen, despite his being a haughty, sometimes cruel man, knew how to get the best out of people. Knew how to lead. Even letting Sawyer take charge of the tracking, recognizing the skill and using it, was a kind of leadership. Nate occasionally wanted to punch Owen in the mouth, but he had to admit, the man understood how to get a group of strong, independent men—and one woman—to work well together.

Nate stated with full assurance, "We'll reach that pass by the end of the day—in time to settle in before dark."

"They won't even set up camp. Instead, they'll filter out," Owen said, "find the best lookouts, sleep in place, and be ready at dawn tomorrow for whoever comes down that trail. I'm betting it's a gold shipment."

"They're a patient bunch," Sal added, "and they've done

this many times before. They'll wait there for however long it takes."

Owen turned somber eyes to Becky. "It's not too late for you to bow out, Miss Pruitt. If you stay with us, you might be in a danger. At the very least, you're likely to witness bloodshed. I'd spare you that if I could."

Nate turned to study Becky and saw from her grim expression that she had no doubts about what she might witness.

Instead of agreeing to hang back or even go home, she didn't answer Owen. "If we do it right, we can take these men out in the night."

Nate said quietly, "We can try to take the wanted ones, but we can't just slip up on a man who hasn't committed a crime and kill him."

"If you're riding with a pack of wanted men, the law's gonna take hard actions," Tex said. He drew his gun and aimed it at the ground, checking the load.

"If any among you thinks it's right to attack men before we know for sure if they've committed a crime, you're just flat-out wrong." Nate remembered part of why he was no longer a Marshal.

"Listen, Nate," Owen said, leaning back against a tree, "we have to—"

"We can stop them if we think they're setting up to waylay the stage, but I know how the Marshals think. You're planning to sneak up on those men in the night and pronounce them all guilty."

Owen glared at Nate. "So you're saying these men, acting as suspicious as all get-out and riding with wanted outlaws, can't be taken in, dead or alive?"

"You tell me, Owen Riley," Nate shot back at the so-called leader. A big part of being a leader was guiding the way toward what was right. "Should they be killed for a crime they might be going to commit? I remember a few too many Marshals who'd acted as judge, jury, and executioner when it wasn't necessary. Sure, if they set up with rifles overlooking a stagecoach or a shipment of gold, we can fight them. But if we follow them to where they camp tonight, even to where they set up to watch for the stage, we can try and stop them. But we can't just charge in shooting men who've done nothing wrong. If we do that, then we're as guilty as they are."

"You know this is the right gang, Nate," Tex said as he holstered his six-gun. "You know those men are the killers we've been seeking."

"I don't know that, not for certain, and neither do you. In a fight, yes, we can defend ourselves and defend a freight wagon, but we can't just attack. Let's slip down there in the night and pluck out the outlaws with wanted posters. If we're careful, we can thin the herd so much that they won't attack this shipment, and maybe we can break up their gang for good."

"And let half of them go free?" Tex rose to his feet, shaking his head in disgust. "There are six men in this gang. Every one of them is a stone-cold killer and you know it, Nate. Why let half go free? We can put a stop to their rampage once and for all."

Nate stood and squared off with Tex. He held Tex's gaze like he was getting ready for a shootout.

Finally, Owen ended the standoff. "You're right, Nate. We can't just kill men we haven't got proof are criminals, not for just riding with wanted men."

Nate replied quickly before he forced Owen—a proud, tough man—to back up any farther. "I understand the impulse too well. It's another reason why I left the Marshals. Now, let's talk about how we pick off the known bandits, quick and quiet-like. Thin the herd enough to stop the rampaging. If we can take them alive, we capture the others, too. Then we'll haul them all to jail."

"With your plan we've got another problem," Becky interjected.

All the men turned toward her.

Owen said, "What's that?"

"None of them can see me or Nate. You others are strangers to them, especially if you capture all the men and keep them locked up so they can't talk. But if a single one of them sees me or Nate, even the ones you arrest, if they get a chance to pass on what happened, they'll know exactly who was after them and where to find me. This is a gang who doesn't leave witnesses alive."

"You need to ride out of here, Miss Pruitt." Tex slid angry eyes between Becky and Nate. "You're right, we can't risk them seeing you. Nate needs to go along, too."

"And leave you even more shorthanded? Right now we've got eleven on our side and they've got six. That's a lot in our favor." Becky crossed her arms and stood. She moved to Nate's side.

Nate picked up what she meant. "If Becky and I ride out, it's nine to six. That puts you all in more danger. What's more, some folks saw me meeting up with Sal, and they might know we hired Owen and Tex. If they recognize any of you, they'll go straight to Becky's place."

Besides, though Nate didn't say it out loud, he didn't trust a single one of them, not even his brother, not to solve this crime by unloading guns into this gang.

If he left, he was as good as giving them permission to turn killer.

17

Mariah met Nell at high noon for a conference. They had a plan, but it needed polishing.

The town courthouse was closed over the noon hour. Town courthouse was a highfalutin name for the abandoned building next to Nell's dress shop. An abandoned building she'd bought, cleaned out, and now used for her justice-of-the-peace work. Nell had locked up, and they'd met at Clint's Diner. It was a little crowded, but they could speak quietly under the usual steady chatter of the men who frequented the place.

"Did you see any spark between them?" Nell asked.

"No." Mariah took a bite of Clint's delicious beef stew. He insisted on calling it blanquette de veau. He'd even told Mariah in confidence that he wasn't using veal. Since Mariah didn't know what veal was, and he was clearly using beef, she decided to humor him. It was a delicious beef stew, different from the one he called beef bourguignon, and he'd confessed that he changed his beef bourguignon recipe, too. It called for wine, only he didn't have

155

any. Instead, he'd seasoned up beef broth. Mariah had told him to start calling both Clint's beef stew.

She thought he might just do it. Both recipes were Clint's own, so he should just call them beef stew. That way folks had some idea as to what they were being served. It was only fair to be informed.

But since Clint made one thing and one thing only for each meal, it didn't really matter what he called it. People ate whatever they were served. And they were grateful because Clint was indeed a brilliant cook.

"What do we do now?" Nell ate her beef stew with gusto, as did everyone else in the place, while she waited for Mariah to come up with something.

The visit, inviting Nate to join them, was Nell's idea to get Becky and Nate to spend time together but not while working. It'd been a nice visit, though it didn't seem to change much.

Now it was Mariah's turn to think of something.

"We can invite them over for dinner after church on Sunday."

Parson Blodgett had moved back to Nebraska, so the Sunday service was simply prayer, hymn singing, Bible reading, and occasionally some talk of how God had made life better the previous week.

Still, even without a parson, they gathered for church. And yes, there was usually a meal afterward for their small group of friends, cooked by Clint, who seemed to enjoy preparing it. Mariah sometimes wondered if they shouldn't take turns.

"Come out to my place this Sunday," Nell said between bites. "I'll put a roast on before we leave for church. Then

I'll make potatoes when we get home. Our corn is ripe now, so we can eat that. I'll check in the general store. If I can find fruit, I'll bake a pie."

Clint chose that moment to bring out a custard he often made as a dessert. It was so delicious that Mariah liked to eat it in tiny bites just to make it last. And that was with Clint always giving her a double serving. *"One for the baby,"* he liked to say.

He set a custard down for Nell and a double portion for Mariah.

"Thank you, honey. My favorite custard." She'd seen Clint serving it to others so she knew it was coming.

"It's not custard. It's crème brûlée."

Sure it was.

"It's delicious. You're a genius."

"I'll call it anything you want," Nell said, "so long as you keep making it. But plan on coming out to my house for dinner on Sunday. I'll cook for a change, and you can have a break."

"That would be nice, Nell. I'll bring something to add to the meal."

"No, you won't." Nell waggled a finger at him. "You'll just sit and enjoy a day off for once."

"Yes, Your Honor."

Nell gave him a gentle swat on the arm.

Mariah smiled at her friend. "Clint loves cooking, but giving him a break from it is a good idea." She glanced up at her husband. "I hope you don't feel neglected."

"I'll manage somehow."

The door to the diner slammed open, and Samantha charged in. She scanned the room, spotted Nell, and rushed over to her. "I'm moving home." She plopped down in the chair next to Nell, buried her face against Nell's neck, and sobbed.

Good thing her face was buried—she couldn't see Nell and Mariah exchange looks and roll their eyes.

Clint rubbed a hand over his face. "Being married isn't all that hard, Sam."

She didn't respond, probably because she couldn't hear Clint over her weeping.

Samantha must've made a good escape this time because most of the crowd thinned before Leland crashed his way into the diner. Those remaining visibly picked up the pace of their eating.

"Samantha Blodgett, you git home." Leland jabbed his thumb toward their house at the edge of town. Didn't matter. Samantha was still crying. The big oaf could've pointed to the blazing sun and she wouldn't have noticed.

Everyone who was still eating—all of them men—well aware of the antics of the unhappily married couple, shot to their feet, dropped coins on their tables, and rushed out. No one left a bite of food behind, though. They might be uncomfortable with tears, but Clint's cooking stiffened their spines.

Clint came to Leland's side and said, "I need a hand. Come with me."

"I'm not helping in the kitchen. That's women's work."

Mariah saw the wave of annoyance cross Clint's face at the ridiculous insult. Then he grabbed the youngster by the back of his shirt collar and dragged him away.

Just as he shoved Leland through the kitchen door, Clint turned back to Mariah and grinned.

She thought that "women's work" comment might explain what was at the root of the constant trouble. Not the notion so much. Many men thought that way. But Leland's attitude, his criticism given at top volume and his tendency to generally nag, was unfortunate. And Samantha was just as bad. Instead of standing her ground, talking with her husband, reasoning with him, demanding that he treat her right, she'd burst into tears and run for Nell or her pa and demand her old room back. A room in the loft of Brand's cabin, shared with two little sisters. Not a welcoming spot for Leland. Usually, Nell was the lucky recipient of the weeping because she was closer—that is to say, right here in town.

Nell, as justice of the peace and owner of a seamstress shop, had strong opinions about what was women's work, but she had no practice at being a mother and few notions on how to help Samantha.

Mariah had no idea what to do either. But with Samantha in Nell's incapable hands, and Leland hauled away by Clint, Mariah could settle in and enjoy her custard. It never lasted as long as she'd like, though, and when she finished, Mariah stared at Samantha and thought about what Leland had said, and it came to her in a snap.

"Samantha!" She spoke sharply enough that it penetrated the weeping.

Samantha looked up. "Wh-what?"

"I've got an idea that might fix your marriage."

"But I don't want to fix it. I want to go home," Samantha wailed.

She probably did want to go home. Being lonely for her

family might explain more about all the fights and tears than not getting along with her husband.

Leland wasn't a stranger exactly, but Samantha had been part of a tight-knit family of younger sisters and a doting pa all her life. One of the favorite things for the Nolte family to do was to share a hug.

Samantha had moved in with a boy she'd known about the same length of time she'd known Nell. The girl was just plain homesick for her family. Mariah wondered if maybe Samantha should move to the Nolte homestead and take Leland with her. Mariah decided to think about that a bit longer. For now, the girl needed something to do that would occupy her mind. And Mariah had just the thing.

"We've just had a big event in Pine Valley."

With a sniffle, Samantha said, "You're talking about Mrs. Mussel?"

Mariah leaned close. Nell sat between them, but Mariah ignored her to speak directly to Samantha. "Yes, that's what I'm talking about. The speech went perfectly."

Mariah didn't mention that low-down coyote Joshua Pruitt. "We need your help."

Mariah thought fast because she wasn't sure if they needed even a speck of help. "Mr. Kintzinger from the land office publishes a newspaper in town now. There was one follow-up story in the paper last week, reporting on the speech. But we need more. Nell and I have some old copies of *The Revolution* that carry articles about Mrs. Mussel as well as Mrs. Morris."

"*The Revolution?*" Samantha pulled a handkerchief out of her sleeve. With as much crying as the girl did, it was good she always carried one.

Mariah looked sideways at Nell. "She doesn't know what *The Revolution* is?"

Nell opened her mouth, closed it, and shrugged. "Tell her."

Mariah turned back to Samantha. "It's a newspaper that talks about the cause of women's suffrage, published by Elizabeth Cady Stanton and Susan B. Anthony."

"B-but what cause?" Samantha blew her nose. "Women's suffrage is the right to vote, isn't it? In Wyoming, women already have the right to vote."

"Oh, but there's more, so much more." Mariah reached for Samantha's arm and squeezed. "Women in Wyoming had for nearly two years the right to sit on juries. Did you know that? That's been taken away by a governor who thinks he's protecting us. We're backsliding already, losing our rights.

"A woman named Elizabeth Packard just got the state of Illinois to pass a law that says a woman can't be locked up in an insane asylum without being declared insane. In other words, they can't lock her up just on the word of her husband. It was already illegal to do this to people generally, but there was one exception—wives."

Samantha squeaked and took a nervous glance at the kitchen, as if her husband might charge through the door and lock her up in an asylum.

"When a woman marries, she gives up all her rights as a citizen, or nearly all of them. When a woman marries, the married couple becomes one person, and that person is the husband. That woman becomes civilly dead. She can't sign legal documents, and any property she owns becomes her husband's. Any inheritance she receives or any money she earns is automatically her husband's. The job Nell has as justice of the peace for which she's paid, as well as the money she earns as a seamstress—"

"Making stupid chaps," Nell muttered.

Mariah, rolling along with her pep talk for Samantha, ignored Nell's remark. "That money, all your ma's money, is now your pa's."

"B-but Pa wouldn't do wrong by Ma."

Mariah thought it was sweet that Samantha called her ma of about a month *Ma*.

"Yes, that's right. Your pa is an honorable man, but not all husbands are. Why does a woman have to hope and pray that she doesn't marry a scoundrel? This country is filled with strange laws that deny women their full rights. Mrs. Mussel and many other women are fighting those unjust laws. Samantha, you're going through a hard time in this new marriage of yours, but I think it'll help you to think of bigger things. Leland isn't a bad man. You're just having trouble adjusting to marriage. I want you to get Nell's copies of *The Revolution* and start reading. Learn how to handle conflict with Leland as a strong woman would, not as an easily upset girl."

Samantha sat up straighter, squared her shoulders. She looked a little cranky, as if not liking being referred to as an *easily upset girl*. Well, good. Then she shouldn't be one.

"You go on and work with Mr. Kintzinger at the newspaper, get a story in the paper every week about women's suffrage. And while you're at it, write a story about the risk Mrs. Mussel faced by coming here at the height of the danger from the Deadeye Gang. A courageous woman faced danger to lift all women to a higher place. Her goals can lift men, too, if they'd only realize it. You need to capture all of that in your story. Go talk to Mr. Kintzinger about it. Nell can talk to him, too. Maybe in working on this, you'll find out you need to talk differently to Leland, as I'm sure he needs to talk differently to you. Instead of fighting and crying and running off, you can learn to stand up straight, look Leland in the eye, and tell him what you're thinking. Tell him how you'd like things to be between you two. I hope working on the stories for the newspaper and reading *The Revolution* will help you to do that."

"Y-you think Mr. Kintzinger will let me write stories for him?"

Mariah jabbed a finger right at Samantha's chest. "I think if he doesn't, then you need to start your own paper."

Samantha gasped, but then a rather military light gleamed in her eyes.

Mariah gave her an encouraging pat on the shoulder. "What do you say? Will you do it? Will you educate yourself about what Mrs. Mussel is doing, as well as your ma, and write about it? Will you use what you learn about a woman being strong to try to get along better with Leland? He's got things to learn, too. But you do your best, and we'll urge Leland to do his best, too."

Samantha listened.

Mariah figured that was all she'd do.

Then with a firm nod, Samantha said, "Nell, can I get your copies of *The Revolution*?"

Nell gave her an enthusiastic hug. "I have a whole stack of them at my dress shop, on the shelf under the counter. And Leland should read them too, and his brother and sister. This is everybody's fight, not just women's."

Leland came out of the kitchen carrying three cups of coffee, looking thoroughly chastened. Clint followed with the pot.

Sitting down beside his wife, Leland gave her a cup while Clint refilled Mariah's and Nell's and sat with a cup of his own. As Clint took a deep drink from his cup and without, as far as Mariah could tell, kicking Leland under the table, Leland slid an arm around Samantha.

"I'm sorry. I know I fuss at you and criticize you. I think I know exactly how you should behave, but I don't seem to know how I should behave. Let's go home, Samantha. I'm going to try and be a better husband to you."

"Can we stop by Nell's shop to pick up some newspapers she wants me to read? She thinks it'll help me, oh, I guess learn how to be a better wife to you."

Mariah clamped her mouth shut. In the big picture it was probably true that it would help her be a better wife. But that wasn't the real focus of *The Revolution*.

"I'll go with you both." Nell took a few quick bites of the custard, not licking the plate but close enough. Then she gulped down the coffee Clint had just poured her, got up, and left with the young couple. The young couple who walked with their arms around each other.

That was how most of their fights ended, though, so it wasn't all that good of a sign.

When they were out the door and out of sight past the window, Mariah looked at Clint. "What did you tell him?"

"I'll tell you while you help me clean up the kitchen, wife. That's women's work."

Since Clint would hardly let her do a thing in the kitchen, Mariah giggled.

Clint took her hand, and together they walked to the back of the diner to clean up what little was left to clean in Clint's usually tidy kitchen, and they compared notes on their efforts at making two youngsters grow up.

18

We'll be able to see them right over that ridge. From this point on, be quiet. Absolutely quiet." Morgan Sawyer didn't scold anyone, or order them, or even look at the group much. He was here for his expertise, and he expected them to appreciate anything he had to say.

The plan was for them to pair off, with each pair following one man. Becky was the exception. She'd join a pair, so they'd have three in their group.

Two men eased up to the ridgetop and peered down on a campfire. There around the fire were the same six men they'd been following for days.

Becky had been told they were eating and talking, hopefully too far away to hear any noise made by the Marshals.

A hiss came from the ridge—the sign that the group was breaking up. The two men watching slipped away silently into the darkness. Soon all the other groups would do the same. It meant one villain would be left untrailed. But they'd picked him carefully. The youngest. Not a known man.

Becky was sorely afraid the youngsters could be just as mean, just as deadly as the older ones, but they were determined to stay in pairs, so there was no other option.

The next pair of Marshals moved to the ridgetop, Sal among them. They waited a long time before they headed out. Becky wasn't sure who it was they were following.

They kept moving, the outlaws and the paired-up Marshals. Finally, it was Becky's turn. She eased up to the ridge with Nate and, she saw now, Tex.

Tex whispered to Nate, "Utah Mike, last to leave."

Who was Bernard Skleen. Utah Mike was the name the lawmen had said they knew Skleen by. The name on wanted posters. Skleen had been working for Becky's pa for a long time. She remembered him with a shudder. He'd been one of the worst of them at Pa's ranch. And Pa had been a lot more loyal to Skleen than he was to her.

One of the biggest reasons she'd taken Grandma's money and run.

Becky fell in behind Nate, who let Tex go ahead of them. Becky knew Nate was a fine tracker, but she'd seen how Tex could handle a trail, too. Tex led the way.

She'd come along with the hunting party rather than stay back in camp as Owen had urged. Not because she thought they needed her exactly, but because she was safer near them than anywhere alone. Even so, it didn't quite feel that way right now as they headed straight into danger.

Becky slid a hand over her six-gun. It was loaded and ready.

She'd lived in Wyoming her whole life. Things were much more settled now, murderous stagecoach robbers notwithstanding. She'd been born into a land of cougars, bears, and wolves. There were men who settled their disputes with guns. There were blizzards, avalanches, cliffs to navigate, wild horses to break, and cattle that were known to stampede.

And Becky had survived all of it. Danger came as no shock, and her gun was a tool she always carried.

She followed along with Nate, edging forward in the dark woods. Everyone was on foot now. They'd left their horses behind when they saw the outlaws stripping the leather off their mounts to let them rest, hopefully for the night.

They walked in silence, Becky bringing up the rear.

Nate had urged her to stay close enough so she could hold on to the back of his shirt or at least touch him every few minutes . . . or seconds. And she did. They were on rugged ground. Steep. Climbing toward some unknown spot the outlaws had selected earlier, which overlooked the trail where something was expected tomorrow. Becky didn't know much about stage lines, so it could be that. It was Nate who knew Wyoming the best. Sal had worked in the area plenty. Between them all, they were sure this wasn't the trail the main stages ran on. This was a back trail, the kind of slippery location men trying to sneak a freight wagon with a shipment of gold might take.

This trail was a tough one to climb, so steep in places it'd make a mountain goat faint, and so narrow it'd make a rabbit feel crowded.

Regardless of that, they kept moving—slowly since the

man they were after was moving slowly. Sometimes it was more climbing than walking, though they didn't need to find toeholds and scale a sheer cliff.

Becky heard the echoing hoot of a great horned owl. As she inched along, she felt the night breeze fluttering around them. The scent of pine hugged them close.

Becky loved Wyoming and yet she rarely got to explore the beautiful land of her birth. Despite the dangers, the scents and sounds soothed her. She remained on high alert, though, listening for any noise coming from ahead of them.

They trudged forward and upward and kept at it for a long time. Becky kept her eyes sharp, but on a narrow trail with tall trees on either side, it became so dark that she focused on two things only. Keeping silent, and not tumbling off the mountain.

Suddenly a hand closed over her wrist. It took her a second to realize it was Nate's hand. He wanted her to stop walking.

Whatever the other groups did, their job was to catch Skleen. He was one of the men who had a dead-or-alive poster on him. And Tex didn't seem overly inclined toward being gentle with the man.

Becky didn't like the idea of killing a man from cover, but then they'd agreed no gunfire—which would alert the other outlaws—unless it came down to a fight for their lives. So Tex would probably jump Skleen, try and take him down without letting him cry out a warning, and they'd haul him back to the camp alive.

If they were stopping now, Skleen was probably right ahead. Becky and Nate were supposed to stay out of sight.

Nate pressed down on Becky's shoulder, and she stepped off the trail to the extent that was possible and hunkered down. She didn't have her hand on her gun. It sickened her to think of pulling the trigger in the pitch-dark and maybe hitting Nate. It surprised her how terrible even thinking of it made her feel. Not just the thought of shooting anyone, which was bad. Not just the thought of accidentally shooting the wrong man. That was worse. For just that one second, she imagined shooting Nate and felt a burn of tears. And that was just the *thought* of it. Why?

Her reaction wasn't normal. Not for her. She rarely cried and was calm in times of trouble. Feeling severely aware of the seriousness of what Tex and Nate were about to do didn't explain the burn of tears. No, they were about feelings she shouldn't have. Feelings that went back to Nate stepping between her and Pa. Feelings connected to that kiss.

She'd seen Nate doing his tracking. He was as skilled as anyone she'd ever met, until she met Morgan Sawyer. And around here, a lot of men wandered in the mountains. She'd seen men with rare talent as woodsmen.

But Nate was a cut above them.

The threat of tears was foolish. She was no careless youngster. She'd never risk shooting what she couldn't see.

She pictured Nate slipping along and wished she'd demanded to go with him. Everything felt better when he was close by.

Shoving aside her strange emotions, she paid strict attention to the silent woods around her. She strained to hear what was going on. There were night sounds as before, but nothing that didn't belong.

A sudden thrashing up ahead brought her to her feet. Hidden behind a tree, she heard thundering footsteps coming down the treacherous path.

And she knew.

Somehow, Skleen had heard the pursuit. Somehow, he'd gotten past two skilled Marshals.

Neither Nate nor Tex would be running flat-out like this. They might be chasing Skleen, yet he was the one running.

With no wish to reveal herself or shoot anyone, she grasped a sapling beside her, timed it to the second, and as the footsteps came even with her, she used the young tree to swing herself out into the trail and land both feet hard in Skleen's belly.

Skleen slammed into her legs and staggered sideways straight across the narrow trail. His head smashed into a much larger tree. He staggered but didn't go down.

The impact sent Becky's legs whipping back and wrenched her whole body. Landing on her feet, Becky swept her gun out of its holster and slammed the butt end of it into Skleen's head. It sent him sliding and falling past her down that trail. She steadied herself and got out of the way of oncoming footsteps.

Quietly, but loud enough, she said to whoever came first, "I knocked him down."

There was no sound below them, no pounding boots, no man scrambling to his feet.

It was Nate who came first, then went on by. Tex was two paces behind him. Mainly because she didn't want to be left behind, she followed after Tex. She heard a rushing sound in the dense woods that lined the trail. It told her just where they were.

Then she heard the metallic snick of shackles being snapped closed.

Tex said, "Use his kerchief to gag him."

"He's out cold," Nate said.

"Keep quiet. Stay back. If he comes around, I don't want him making any noise that might warn the others. I'll take him back to camp."

Tex hoisted Skleen to his feet. The man staggered but stayed upright.

They'd gone a dozen yards down the steep, rocky slope when Skleen wrenched free. He got loose from Tex, then fell and skidded downward a dozen more yards.

Tex hustled after him and stopped him from falling all the way down to the bottom of the slope.

Nate tugged his kerchief off his neck and used it to blindfold Skleen. This time when they hoisted him to his feet, his knees wouldn't hold. Nate hooked one of his arms through Skleen's elbow.

Tex took the other side. They dragged him onward. Neither spoke a word. And Becky for certain wasn't talking. Skleen knew her voice.

They were a long time getting back to camp.

Becky saw the flickering firelight leaping high ahead of them and heard murmuring voices. She also heard a coffeepot clink against a tin cup, and soon she could smell the fire and the savory brew.

Long before they reached the campfire, Tex said, "Stay back." His warning was muttered well out of earshot of the camp, but it wasn't necessary. They'd discussed this at length. Becky and Nate would go straight for their horses and ride for the Idee alone while the Marshals took the men away. After some debate, she figured, based on where they'd made their capture, the Marshals would escort the outlaws to Fort Bridger to lock them up in the jail there.

The cavalry units that had guarded Mrs. Mussel and Mrs. Morris had come from there, so they were aware of the dangerous criminal gang roving the territory.

If the Marshals took their prisoners and rode south, they could reach the train station in a single day. If they found the train wasn't coming through soon, they'd have to push on to Fort Bridger.

They also said that if the train was heading east, they might just ride it to Laramie. A lot could change depending on what they found as they rode.

Keeping any of the outlaws from knowing of Becky and Nate's involvement was top priority.

Becky stood in the shadows with Nate at her side as they watched Sal jump up and help Tex carry Skleen to the tree they had surrounded with outlaws.

They tied Skleen up and let him slump to the ground. Out cold still, just as he had been for the past hour.

"He made a break for it. I knocked him halfway down the mountain." Tex's voice was low. Even with Skleen apparently knocked out, he didn't want to give the man much to go on.

Nate pulled her away. They headed for where the horses were tied. Brutus came up and silently greeted them.

Becky stroked the patient dog, and then she and Nate got their horses and led them slowly away from the men. They didn't want any of them, five outlaws in all, to realize someone was riding away. They'd never know anyone else was with the Marshals.

They walked a fair distance, fighting for the most possible silence. Nate took the lead. Finally, Nate stopped moving and whispered to her, "Nice work. *You* captured our suspect. And you did it in such a way that he won't know it was you. He didn't see me either. He was running from us because Tex stepped on a twig loud enough to warn him. Skleen took off, but before he could give us the slip, *you* stopped him by knocking him halfway down a mountainside."

It lifted Becky's heart to hear Nate speak so highly of her. Especially since she was starting to notice her whole body ached where she'd been wrenched while she clung to the tree and swung herself out to knock Skleen over.

"You did one thing wrong, though."

Becky narrowed her eyes and realized she could see him. It was still dark, but the coming dawn was starting to brighten the eastern sky.

"What did I do wrong in your opinion?"

"You made two highly trained U.S. Marshals look bad." Then he laughed. "I'm proud to work with you."

19

She matched his quiet laugh and wasn't ready at all when he kissed her.

A kiss in the dark from a man who'd kissed her before. She liked it even more this time.

She was a little surprised when she wrapped her arms around his neck and clung to him like a burr. His strength, the breadth of his shoulders, the muscles of his arm, the softness of his hair beneath his Stetson—they all called to her, a lure she wanted to chase after.

He smelled like the forest and the mountains, the wild, and some scent that was uniquely his. She drew the scent into her lungs even as she drew him into her arms.

His arms wrapped around her waist and lifted her to her toes. Her arms tightened, and her breath caught.

His head tilted sideways, and the kiss, which began much like the one he'd given her earlier, went deeper and gained power. It consumed all the space in her head until she could only think about and enjoy the kiss.

An owl swooped close overhead, enough to make Nate jerk his head up. Becky jumped out of his arms.

Then the silence returned, and Nate turned to Becky. It was no longer full dark beneath the canopy of trees on the narrow trail. His eyes gleamed in the morning light.

Brutus nosed Becky's fingers, and she remembered they weren't alone. The dog, the horses. A ranch waiting down the trail.

Nate took Becky's hand. "We both pretended that first kiss didn't happen. Or at least pretended it was a mistake. A cowhand hadn't oughta go around kissing a woman who can hire and fire him, after all. But I'm not going to be able to pretend this time, Becky."

She didn't know what to say except "I didn't do all that well pretending last time. Reckon there's no sense trying now."

His fingers, work-roughened and strong, held hers and gave her something she hadn't had in a long time. Maybe never. Someone to hold on to. Oh, she'd had Mariah and Nell, who were wonderful. But now, with them married, she realized just how lonely she'd been.

Which made her think of Pa.

"What's going to happen, Nate? You've worked with the Marshals. You understand them."

He tugged her closer. His other hand rested on her arm, slid up and down. A comforting stroke. "I'm not sure. I don't think they can just ride out to your pa's place, tell him we've arrested half his cowhands and now it's his turn."

"Finding those men heading out from the Circle J before the Marshals got into place made it harder, didn't it? There was no chance to study them, watch them confer with Pa. Maybe sneak up close and hear Pa discussing a plan with Skleen or any of them." Becky swallowed hard. "I wonder what happened to the Marshal who went in there to work? He wasn't among these men, or at least Owen didn't say he was. But all the hands must know what's going on, so how can a Marshal work there and not be found out?"

Nate's arms came around her again but without a kiss this time. He just held on. She felt as if she'd needed this for years, to be held and hugged.

"I chose a solitary life, mostly because of Pa."

Nate took a gentle but firm grasp of her upper arms and drew them around his neck, then went back to hugging her even more closely. "You needed to stand on your own. And you could afford to do that, thanks to the generosity of your grandparents."

That eased Becky's hurt a bit, pulling her thoughts away from Pa. "Ma took me to see them once when I was young. It was after my two little brothers died. I think Pa tried to stop her. I can't remember much about it except it was an unexpected trip. I think there was some shouting, but I might not be remembering that right.

"We rarely left the Circle J, even to go to town. But Ma took me, and we rode in a wagon to see my grandparents. It was a new world for me of hugs and smiles. Grandma and Grandpa lived in a big house with beautiful furniture and servants and delicious food of all kinds. They were, I now realize, rich. As a child I just felt their kindness and generous giving. And their faith.

My grandparents were churchgoing people, and when we were with them, my ma's faith showed itself in ways I'd never seen before. It was a wonderful trip. I didn't want to go back home."

Nate kissed the top of her head.

"Less than a year later, Ma was dead. A new baby went with her. And it was only Pa and me, alone. I went to work and became a ranch hand. I suppose it would've been more proper for me to tend the house, but Pa had no interest in propriety. I was too young to stay in the house alone, so I went to work with him."

Nate nodded. "And then your life with your pa became unbearable and you inherited a lot of money. Your grandparents were smart enough not to let your pa get his hands on it, and you were smart enough to set a life up for yourself." He kissed her again. "And reckless enough to go chasing after an outlaw gang . . . and wonderful enough to let me kiss you here as the sun's rising. A new day."

She rested her hand on his cheek.

"I think it's time you made some changes so you're not as alone as before, Miss Pruitt."

She smiled. "Oh, you do, do you?"

"Yes, I do." He stole a quick kiss. But then it wasn't stealing if she handed it over to him, now, was it?

"But let's talk about it back at the Idee. After we make sure the cows haven't stampeded down the trail chasing the rest of the herd."

Becky flinched at the thought. "They'd be all the way to Denver by now."

He grinned, his white teeth flashing. Then he let go

of her, stepped around his horse, and swung up into the saddle.

She was right behind him. Looking forward to getting home and talking more with Nate Paxton.

20

Nate was overwhelmed by what had happened between him and Becky.

His normally sensible mind had shied away from letting anything grow between him and his boss. It felt wrong, a poor man like Nate pursuing a wealthy woman like Becky? He was coming to her like some kind of beggar.

Yet he knew he was a good cowhand. He was helping her. She counted on him and trusted him. Even when she sometimes looked as though she wanted to punch him.

The things inside him that made him a strong man told him to ride away. Go make something of himself. Come back with some honor. But he couldn't ride away now, not when Becky's cowhands were all gone. The three Marshals who were using her ranch to set up the capture of the Deadeye Gang were also gone. And the danger would only increase if word got out the Marshals were connected to Becky, with the rest of the men at the Circle J setting out to punish her for her part in harming their criminal enterprise.

No, he couldn't leave, not now. But could he marry her?

Brand Nolte had married Nell, who was a woman of some influence around town, plus she'd made a decent living sewing together chaps for her cowboy customers. Becky had told Nate just how much money Nell made with her chaps, so there was good reason to believe she went into the marriage worth far more than her husband. Brand's sole possession was a homestead he was still four years from proving up on.

Nell had even homesteaded her own claim before the wedding; her homestead bordered Brand's. So, along with all her money, the business stretching out for years, and the power of being the town's justice of the peace, she'd doubled Brand's property holdings in one fell swoop.

Mariah, Becky's other good friend, had brought a blacksmith shop into her marriage. Clint was well established, though, nearly equal in wealth to his wife.

Nate had nothing. Not even a homestead.

He could offer to homestead and add a few acres, bring that into the marriage, but then he had to live on the land, and Becky already had a fine house. She wouldn't want to move to a homestead cabin, and Nate would never ask her to. Besides, would adding one hundred and sixty measly acres really mean much to a woman who already owned ten thousand?

He looked sideways at Becky. They needed to talk, figure such things out together.

Or maybe they needed to put off talking about anything serious. He just didn't know.

Becky, riding beside him, reached across the small distance between the two horses and rested her hand on his elbow. She smiled, slid her hand down his arm, and entwined her fingers with his.

"I can sense you over there thinking, mulling over big problems. You're worried about my pa, aren't you?"

Which told him *she* was worried about her pa. It made him disgusted with himself for the selfish direction his mind had gone.

"Do you think they can hold those men they arrested? Is it against the law to hide overhead of a trail? They didn't do anything. We can almost know for sure they were going to, but that's not going to survive a trial."

Nate thought it over. "Yeah, but those men are part of the Deadeye Gang."

"I agree, but—"

"Let me finish."

It was light enough now that when Becky arched one brow at him, he could tell she didn't like being cut off. He couldn't blame her.

"Sorry about that—I just wanted to tell you what was running through my head." Now that she'd distracted him from feeling quite so dishonorable for kissing his boss.

"Go on." He heard the humor in her voice. And just a faint note of irritation.

"My point is, you're right. We know a few facts, but that's not the same thing as having solid evidence. Up to now, this gang has gotten away with murder because no one survives their robberies. No witnesses. That's allowed them to stay in the same area and hit stagecoaches and freight wagons again and again. Well, those days are over."

"True. But if they leave the area to find new hunting grounds, we've just turned our problems loose on someone else."

Nate nodded. "Three of them are wanted men—that group's going to jail. They may even hang, depending on what they're wanted for. By the time the Marshals comb through the wanted posters, they might be able to hold more of them without having to prove what they were up to last night. As for your pa, I think what Owen intends is to separate those men and get them to point a finger at the others. Get the men without wanted posters to hand over information about the known outlaws—your pa and the other men at his ranch. Maybe more of them out there are known and wanted men.

"Thing is, we probably shouldn't've taken those men. We should've waited until we saw them drawing a bead on some passing freight wagon. Owen didn't handle this right." Nate shook his head. "But now that we have them, it doesn't suit me at all to arrest a bunch of killers and not punish them for the worst crimes they committed."

"They killed Mariah's pa and brother. They need to pay for that."

"They're hard men, and they aren't likely to fess up to their crimes or turn on their saddle partners. Not easily anyway. I'm sure, though, Owen has his methods to get them to cooperate. He may have information we don't know about. We just have to hope for the best."

They emerged from a heavily wooded trail to an open space just as the sun rose fully over the horizon. Their episode of spying and trailing and acting as lawmen was finally over.

It was back to ranching now, the life Nate loved. With a woman he respected above any he'd met before. A woman he could love forever.

Becky said, "Let's make tracks for home."

They picked up their pace, and with better, wider trails, they made the hours and days they'd spent following the outlaws shrink to a pleasant ride.

"You've created a monster." Leland stomped through the door to the courthouse.

Nell looked up. She was used to Samantha storming in, usually crying. This was new. "What happened now?"

"Samantha wants to become a suffragist. She wants to give speeches and travel from town to town like Mrs. Mussel is doing." His angry expression was suddenly overtaken by sadness. "She doesn't want to be married to me anymore."

For one terrible moment, Nell saw Leland's eyes glaze over with tears. First, Samantha wanted to leave him because she was homesick, or that was Nell's guess. Now she wanted to leave him to work for a great cause.

At the root of it, it seemed she just wanted to leave him. And they were both fine people. When they weren't bickering, they appeared to have a true affection for each other.

What was wrong with these two youngsters?

Nell sat at her judge's desk, which was really just an old dusty table she'd found in the upstairs of what was an abandoned building. She stared at Leland, prayed, thought for a moment, yet no great splash of genius occurred to her.

"What happened?" she asked Leland.

"You and Mariah told her to work for the paper. As if my wife needs to work. As if I can't support us both with my homestead. It's insulting."

"I work, Leland. Mariah worked until just recently with the baby coming. And she still does the more intricate work that Willie can't manage. Becky works. For heaven's sake, she may not have had a job on the homestead, but your ma was the most hardworking woman I've ever known. Why would you find it insulting to have your wife work? Especially"—Nell spoke quickly because she saw him getting ready to argue—"when she's not doing it for the money. She's doing it to use her mind, to sharpen skills she's still discovering she has. Frankly it's a very rude thing to say to me, a working woman, that your wife working insults you."

Leland opened his mouth to reply, then closed it and stared at Nell. Which gave her a chance to talk more.

"She can't have arranged to travel. How would she do such a thing?"

"No, she hasn't. It's all just talk at this point."

"And the trails aren't safe so long as the Deadeye Gang is around. It's doubtful we can get an entire cavalry unit to come and escort her every time she finds a place to give a speech. So she's not heading out anytime soon."

"You're saying I've got a wife who's not ready to leave me until the trails are safe? That's not comforting, Nell."

It truly wasn't.

Nell had no great ideas, so she just said what came to mind. "Go get Samantha and bring her here."

"She's with Mr. Kintzinger. He's teaching her how to

set the type on the printing press. She's been there every morning for the last four days. She comes home late. I've been cooking our meals. It's that or I don't eat. So now she's working and I'm not. Warren is doing more than his share around the two new homesteads just to keep things running."

Because Nell was a businesswoman, she asked, "How much money is Percy paying her?"

It'd better be more than a dime a day because Nell would pay her that. The orders for chaps kept coming, and her work as justice of the peace was taking up too many hours of the day. She was falling behind even with Cassandra and Michaela helping out. And Joy, Leland's sister and the new schoolmarm, was coming in, too. She'd asked if she could earn a dime a day, too, until school resumed.

"He's not paying her. She's so excited to learn about the paper that she's working for free. And she's writing stories about what she reads in *The Revolution*. She loves that, too. So she's doing it all just for the love of it." Leland's voice was laced with scorn.

Nell rather thought he had a point. "Well, you can't say she's not letting you support her. That part of your complaint isn't valid." Her thoughts grew dark. The newspaperman had found himself some free labor, and that didn't set right at all. "You said she's at the newspaper office right now?"

Percival Kintzinger had a printing press tucked into a corner of the land office.

"Yes."

"Leland, go home. I'll go have a talk with your wife and with Percy. I may be able to straighten this out." Nell had a few things on her mind concerning Percy's treatment of his employee.

Leland scowled.

Nell could see he was an adult man, one with his own homestead. He worked hard every day to provide for himself and Samantha. Still, she was tempted to give his ear a good twist.

"Let me see what I can do, Leland. You're right about one thing. This is at least in part my fault." It was not in any way, shape, or form her fault.

It was Mariah's fault.

Although both of them had to be declared innocent. If this were a court case, Nell would rap her gavel and hand out no punishment. Then she might rap her gavel a second time—over Percival Kintzinger's head.

21

Becky's chickens had indeed survived her absence. The cows and pigs, too. But then she'd fully expected them to get by without her.

She and Nate were alone at the Idee. While she scattered corn across the ground for the chickens and gathered their eggs, Nate cleaned out the coop, where he found a few of the hens nesting.

When at last they got the chickens cared for, Becky said, "Come on into the house. It's late for dinner, but I'm hungry. We'll have scrambled eggs. We've got a week's supply of them. And then we can talk."

He looked up and gave her the most serious smile she'd ever seen in her life. "I think we need that."

Becky got to work making enough eggs to feed two people who'd been living on meager camp food for three days. She filled glasses with milk they'd collected from her very disgruntled cows. She had five milk cows, but two had dried up and would stay that way until their calves were born.

Nate sliced bacon and brewed coffee.

After she'd set out butter, jelly, and a can of peaches, she divided the eggs between her and Nate while he split up ten pieces of bacon. A plateful of warm biscuits added to the homey, comforting meal. With a table and chairs, they had all the trappings of civilization.

They'd been so busy getting everything on the table that they hadn't said more than a few words to each other. Once they were seated at Becky's kitchen table and had a few bites of food in them to cut the worst of their hunger, Nate said, "I've got no right to think I'm fit for such a fine woman as you, Becky."

She dropped her fork, which went skidding off the table. Nate snatched it out of midair and handed it back to her.

"You're not fit for me?" She hadn't expected the conversation to go this way. Her heart began hammering away. She'd hoped for kind words from him, words of admiration. Instead, he'd insulted her. "Do I act to you and the men like I think I'm above you? Do you take me for an arrogant woman who looks down on the ones who work so hard for me?"

Nate, who'd taken another bite of eggs, started choking. After forcing the eggs down his gullet, looking frantic, he said, "No, I didn't mean that. I-I meant you're a wealthy woman with a prosperous ranch. I'm a ragtag cowhand without a spare penny to my name. I can't bring anything to a m-marriage."

He'd gone and said the word, and she hadn't realized she was expecting to hear it until that very moment. She'd figured he would speak of their sharing kisses, maybe talk of courting or doing *something* to further their personal acquaintance. But when Nate said *marriage*, she knew then she'd been hoping for that.

"Um—" she hesitated—"are you saying I'm unlikely to marry unless the man is a prosperous rancher or businessman? Because there aren't that many of either around these parts. Which would mean I'm destined to remain alone forever."

Nate quit eating and watched her, his eyes dark and thoughtful. "What do you think, then? Should we . . . uh, Becky, will you marry me? Can you respect me enough to tie yourself to a mere cowpoke?"

The two of them locked eyes. Becky thought of Pa and how much she respected Nate compared to him. Pa and his greed for her inheritance, his involvement with thieves and murderers. Pa was all about how much he could take. And here was Nate, worried about how much he wanted to give.

He didn't speak of love, but she was a realist and had spent too many years alone. She'd watched her two best friends marry and in many ways move on without her. Oh, they'd always be the best of friends. But their friendship with her was no longer central to their lives. And that was as it should be.

She sat at the head of the table while he was right around the corner from her. Slowly she extended her hand to his. He reached out and clasped their hands together. They sat there like that for a while, silently, but offering her hand was an answer, so there was no hurry for words.

Finally, she replied, "Yes, Nate, I'll marry you. What's more, I'd like to marry you right now. It's not even suppertime yet. Let's ride into town and find Nell before she closes up for the night and see if she'll supply the vows."

"And we can swing by Brand's cabin. If he's home, he can be part of our wedding. We can invite his girls and Mariah and Clint."

Becky nodded. "Let's finish eating and go. I don't want to spend another night alone."

Plenty still needed to be done around the ranch. There were cattle to check, though a quick look at the herds closest to the house showed them thriving. They could have cleaned stalls in the barn and pigsty. They could have worked hard for two days just to begin to catch up. Instead, Becky saddled up her palomino. Nate did the same with his black stallion.

Side by side they rode to Brand's and found him full of smiles at their news. His girls were already in town, working at Nell's dress shop.

Brand galloped ahead to invite Samantha and Leland to join the wedding guests. By the time they reached Nell's, Brand had spread the word. There was a little cluster of townsfolk waiting at the courthouse.

Nell had on her black robe and was grinning to beat all.

The sheriff and Doc Preston and his wife were also present. Mr. Kintzinger attended, apparently to report on their wedding, though the man had a subdued look Becky didn't quite understand.

No one knew about the capture of the Deadeye Gang. Becky and Nate had agreed to say nothing and never refer to their part in it. Sal, Nate's brother, had agreed to ride with the prisoners until they were locked up. Afterward he'd come running back, knowing how shorthanded the Marshals had left Becky and the Idee.

The other Marshals would join them as soon as they could, though they could be held up for a trial. They also needed to get back to round up the rest of the gang, so they'd be pushing hard to return.

As everyone took their seats in the courthouse, Nell tapped her gavel, smiled, and said, "This is my first wedding. I'm thrilled that it's for two people I think will be wonderful for each other."

Becky glanced at Nate. Her brow furrowed.

He turned to Nell and said, "Those aren't the normal vows. We want this to be legal."

Nell's eyes went wide. "This is the first wedding ceremony I've ever performed. Do you think if I say other than the strictly traditional vows, the wedding won't be legal?"

She eyed Brand. He shrugged. Then she looked at Mariah. "You and Clint haven't been married long—what was your wedding like?"

Leland spoke up. "My pa did a whole lot of weddings. He said generally the same thing, but he made the ceremony real personal. When Samantha and I got married, he spent some time welcoming her to the family." Leland looked down at Samantha, who gave him an affectionate smile.

The two of them must be getting along today.

Joy, Leland's little sister who'd wandered into the wedding service, said, "My ma told me once that a parson was a man legally recognized as having the right to perform weddings, granted to him by the state. She said if the parson wanted to, he could just sign a marriage certificate, have the bride and groom and two witnesses sign, and that would make it legal. The ceremony is more about standing before God and swearing to honor the vows taken before Him. Judge Nolte can't say a thing wrong in the ceremony, not as long as you all sign a marriage certificate. That can be a register in a church or maybe sign the docket here at the courthouse. The certificate isn't a formal document either, or it doesn't have to be. Ma used to create beautiful marriage certificates with a special pen and pretty handwriting. Maybe I can make one of those for you. In fact, I could take over that job for the town."

There'd been four weddings in town in the last year or so. Mariah and Clint, Nell and Brand, Samantha and Leland, and now Becky and Nate. Someone could take over that job and still have plenty of spare time.

"I'll make a note of this in my docket, Joy." Nell nodded. "I'm keeping you busy at the dress shop, but the wedding certificates would be considered part of my job as justice of the peace. You can work on them at the shop while earning your dime a day. And it would be nice if you'd make up four of them, one for each newly married couple."

"Thank you, Your Honor," Joy said. "I'd be glad to do it. I don't have Ma's fine hand with the curly letters, but I can make up a nice-looking document."

Nell listened some more to Joy's and Leland's opinions on vows, arranging to have legal papers drawn up instead of getting on with the wedding.

"I can't believe," Becky said, "that I've got such a rank

beginner performing my marriage that she's taking advice from a sixteen-year-old."

Nell turned to Becky and smiled. Then she shrugged and gave a firm nod of her chin. "I'm the justice of the peace of Pine Valley. What's more, I'm a woman of faith. I therefore declare that these vows make you legally married, and I challenge anyone who says otherwise to a . . . a sewing contest."

Mariah snickered.

Becky rolled her eyes. "Get on with it, Judge."

Nell went on to administer what sounded like tidy wedding vows, though Becky wasn't sure if they matched the regular vows she'd heard twice recently. While she'd missed Mariah's wedding, she'd been invited to both Nell's and Samantha's—both weddings handled by Parson Blodgett. These vows of Nell's sounded roughly the same. Love, honor, and obey. Sickness and health. Richer or poorer.

That gave her pause after Nate's concern about coming to the marriage with so little.

Next, Nell invited the gathering to stop the wedding if they thought this was a mistake. It popped into Becky's head to hold her breath until that part passed lest Pa storm in trying to do just that. Which also made Becky realize that all her earthly goods would be Nate's in the event of her death. Maybe they were his anyway. She wasn't sure how far the equality laws in Wyoming reached.

Even so, she wasn't at all worried about Nate taking her land and tossing her off the Idee. Instead, she wondered about the fact that she'd never made out a will. And until they finished their vows, if something happened to Becky, her pa would inherit everything.

She remembered again the need she'd seen in Pa's expression. He'd been willing to strike her. Would he also be willing to kill her? Just how bad was his need?

By marrying Nate, she was removing herself from the legal position of Pa being her only living relative and the natural heir to her ranch and money. She'd much rather Nate held that place, which amounted to more than the vow to love, honor, and obey. It amounted to *respect*. And that was something she could build a life on.

She respected Nate enough to appreciate his worries about coming into the marriage with far less wealth than Becky had. And she respected him enough to put herself in his care as a shelter against Pa, which was something of great value he did bring her.

She'd have to make sure he understood that.

"I now pronounce you man and wife. You may kiss the bride." Nell giggled, clapped her hands, waited for a second or two for the kiss to conclude, then flung her arms around the bride.

Becky hugged her back, and Mariah hit their little twosome like a very pregnant whirlwind.

"When's the baby due again?"

Mariah pulled back and rested a hand on her very round belly. "The doctor thinks it could be any time now."

"Shouldn't you be sitting down?"

Mariah giggled to match Nell. "Probably."

"You know," Becky said, "you two seem a bit overly happy about my wedding."

"Of course we are." Mariah embraced her again.

"We've been matchmaking for some time now." Nell gave Becky a kiss on the cheek.

Becky looked sideways at Nate, who was surrounded by the other guests. He caught her eye. "Did you know they were matchmaking?"

Nate's eyes closed and opened in the world's slowest blink. "When?"

"I didn't say we were any good at it." Nell stepped out of their circle and removed her judge's robe. She hung it on a nail behind her table, then returned to the group.

Clint gave Nate a firm clap on the shoulder. "It's too late to have any kind of party. It's already past suppertime and I don't have much I could prepare in this short of notice. But after church on Sunday, we'll have a reception at the diner. Everyone's welcome."

Nell said, "You're not doing this for the whole town on your own. I'll make a roast and a dessert for the reception."

"I don't want a big fuss," Becky said. She wondered how long it'd be before the townsfolk realized she and Nate were alone at the Idee, without the absent Marshals posing as cowhands. Because if all of Becky's cowhands had taken off, people were going to want to know why. And it would be tricky not to let on that things had been very strange out at the Idee.

So, until the Marshals got back, the quieter Becky and Nate were, the better. Best case would be that when they returned—at least the three Nell had met, Sal, Owen, and Tex—no one would have caught on they'd even been gone.

And they *would* be back because their work wasn't done. Their work concerning Becky's pa. Becky shook off the dark thoughts and focused instead on her wedding. She'd been distracted for too long.

"Potluck wedding party at the diner Sunday after church," Mariah announced with a raised voice. "For those wanting to come, bring a hot dish or a dessert, whatever you were planning for your own Sunday dinner."

"Mariah, no," Becky hissed. But her voice was drowned out by lots of excited thanks as the wedding guests filed out of the courthouse and hurried toward home.

Becky couldn't stop the ones already outside. A good chunk of these folks would be attending the reception, and the rest of them—the ones who'd hear her if she started shouting—would need a good reason why not.

Nate and I don't want to talk to any of you for fear a hint might slip out of what's going on around here . . . wasn't a good reason.

The courthouse was soon empty, with Nate and Becky walking out into the setting sun with their best friends. They stepped into a sight glorious enough to rob everyone of speech. The Wind River Mountains at twilight.

"Just look at that sky," Mariah said, sounding awe-struck.

Becky nodded silently. The sky was orange and red against a darkening blue, while the sun sent the last of its beams against the shoulder of one of the Cirque of the Towers. And the lake between the Towers and Pine Valley reflected the vivid sky.

"It's a good sign," Nate said as he took Becky's hand. "God has brought us into our new married life surrounded by beauty." He turned to his new wife and added, "I've married a woman of great beauty to match this glorious sky."

Becky had never heard such words before. She had long, straight brown hair. Her eyes were an odd color she'd heard called hazel. To Becky all it meant was they were a color that couldn't make up its mind. Green in some lights, brown in others. Her skin was tanned from her long hours working in the sun.

She hadn't donned a fine dress for the wedding but had worn her best black riding skirt. She never rode horseback in a regular skirt, considering it foolish. She wore her newest blue calico blouse, the one Nell had foisted on her last Christmas—a dark blue sprinkled with light blue flowers and green vines. She had on her best black Stetson and boots.

She thought she looked all right. But beauty to match this sky? She wanted to snort at the idea. To protest such nonsense. But it stroked a hidden place in her heart that hadn't heard kind words from a man ever before in her life.

She squeezed Nate's hand. "It's a fine omen from a loving God."

They smiled at each other, washed in the beautiful sunset, and walked down the steps to where their horses were hitched.

Mariah put a restraining hand on Becky before she could untie her horse. She nodded down the street at Samantha and Leland, who strode hand in hand toward home.

Becky shook her head. "What's going to become of those two?"

Nell came up beside them. "I had Percy Kintzinger arrested yesterday."

Mariah and Becky both turned to her sharply.

All Becky could think of was the Deadeye Gang. "Did you find out he was in league with the Wainwrights?"

Nell jumped, then gave Becky a strange look. "No. For heaven's sake, what made you think of that?"

Becky wasn't about to tell the truth, that the Deadeye Gang was close to all she could think about. "Sorry, they're just who needs arresting in these parts. What did Percy do?"

"He was making Samantha put out the whole paper, not just write stories. He'd taught her how to run the printing press. Then she delivered the papers herself. She was even selling ads, collecting payment for them and taking the money back to Percy. He was teaching her to keep the accounts for the paper, too."

"You had him arrested for giving Samantha a job?"

"No, for not paying her. She was working long hours every day, and he had tricked her into believing he was doing her a favor by training her. It's a wonder the weasel didn't try to charge her for doing the work."

Mariah looked at Brand. With some reluctance, she said, "I'm not sure it's a crime to find someone dumb enough to work for free."

Brand rubbed his hands over his face. But he didn't speak up in defense of his daughter, and he was a man prone to do such things.

"I had to let him go." Nell crossed her arms and scowled at the land office. Closed up for the night. Like the whole town, except for the saloon. Tinny music flowed from the saloon, the building next to the courthouse. They could hear "The Yellow Rose of Texas" clearly.

Kintzinger ran the newspaper out of the land office while also helping folks sign up for homesteads.

"He was held in a cell for four hours," Nell said. "I think that scared him but good. It was Mariah's idea that Samantha read *The Revolution* to learn about women's suffrage and write stories about it for the paper."

Mariah held up her hands as if to ward off anyone who thought this was her fault. "I wanted her to take a more mature approach to being married. I thought those articles might encourage her to stand on her own two feet. Deal with Leland in a way that would help their marriage."

Becky sighed. "I suppose it couldn't hurt."

"She was just too young for marriage," Brand said.

"Young or not, she's a married woman now and needs to settle down." Mariah tried to sound kind.

"Mr. Kintzinger let her write a few articles." Nell scowled as she talked. "He kept adding little jobs. By the time she'd been at it a week, she was running the paper, doing his job for him. For no pay."

Brand scrubbed his face again.

"When the sheriff unlocked the jail cell to let Percy free, I told the newspaperman to start treating his one-and-only employee better or I was going to financially support her while she bought her own printing press and went into competition against him. I can afford to buy another empty building in this town." Nell already owned two, her dress shop and the courthouse.

Brand gave Nell a nervous look. "I don't think her starting a newspaper would be that good for their marriage right now." He looked after his daughter and gave a worried frown. "On the other hand, I'm not sure things could get much worse."

Nell patted him on the shoulder.

Becky did her best not to laugh. She looked at Nate and said, "You're not going to be a troublesome husband, I hope. I'd hate to fall into Percy's devious clutches in an effort to save my marriage."

Nate sounded falsely gruff when he scowled at her. "Let's go home, woman. I can't wait to start managing you."

Becky grinned. "I can't wait to see you try it."

Telling their friends goodbye, they mounted up and rode for home. They'd have ridden with Brand and Nell, but they were a bit slower getting going.

After a few quiet minutes of riding, Becky asked, "When do you think they were matchmaking?"

Nate tilted his head as if searching for the answer. "That day they came out for coffee to spread the town news maybe? They didn't make a fuss about my coming in with you, but then I came in without their having to ask."

They rode on again in silence as they considered that. Finally, Becky said, "Nell was right. They weren't any good at it."

Nate laughed, and Becky joined him.

When the laughter ended, Nate said, "Let's get home."

"My first chance to obey my husband. So far I can handle it just fine."

They set their horses to a ground-eating gallop even as Becky had a shiver of nerves and wondered why they were in such an all-fired hurry.

But they sure enough were.

22

"We need more help." Nate nearly staggered as he reached the door to Becky's back entry. He held the door open, and Becky managed a thank-you smile. Her shoulders were slumped, though, her boots dragging.

He and Becky had been working since just after sunup. They'd've gotten started earlier except they'd welcomed the morning by spending some time . . . being married.

Finally they'd gotten on with the day, and both of them were now reeling from how hard it was to run a ranch of this size, just the two of them.

While Nate still regretted coming as a penniless cowpoke to a wealthy woman, it couldn't be denied that he'd been a big help to her.

"I've got an idea where to get the help."

Becky sank onto a chair at the table, dragging a canvas bag of jerky and water along with her. It was the same meal they'd had at noon. And they'd had it for a couple of snacks. It sure helped to be starving.

"This is all we've got to eat. I just don't have the strength to cook. We should've stopped hours ago, but as it is, we still left a dozen chores for tomorrow. And tomorrow has got its own chores. You're right—we need help. But I can't think of a single man around to hire. What's your idea?"

"What if we rode to town tomorrow to eat at the diner?"

"We don't dare. There's no time."

Nate took a strip of the jerked beef and dreamed of a meal at Clint's. "If we come home with some help, we can justify the time away."

"Who do you have in mind? And how will you explain our being here alone?"

Nate nodded while he chewed the tough beef, which tasted wonderful and helped mightily toward mollifying his terrible hunger. His belly had been so empty, his backbone was rubbing up against his navel. "The explanation is a version of the truth that leaves out the details. We had enough men when our main cowpokes headed out on the cattle drive. Then our skeleton crew took off and left us with no help."

Becky poured them both a glass of water and mulled over his idea, though not for long. "All true. Who'd you think of to hire, then? I wondered if Brand might come out for a bit. He'll frown on sleeping here. He has to ride to town to keep Nell and his daughters from being on the trail alone, so he couldn't stay too long."

"Brand's a good idea. Let's ask him. My idea is a little outside the normal way of thinking, I reckon. Let's see if we can get Leland and Samantha Blodgett out here. Maybe Warren, Leland's younger brother. Joy can come, too."

Until school started its fall term, Joy was busy making

chaps for Nell. She'd probably jump at the chance to stop punching holes in leather.

"Maybe Samantha and Joy can run the house," Nate suggested. "Leland and Warren are no cowpokes, but they can ride. We won't ask them to rope or brand. Not much need of that this time of year, and if a horse or cow comes up lame or needing help, we can do that ourselves. But they can help us move cattle to new pastures and check the herds. And they can do some of the chores around the ranch. Samantha and Joy, too. Homesteaders can always use a little cash money."

"They have things they're doing now. Leland and Warren are supposed to stay put on their claims." Becky was tossing out problems, yet Nate could see she was just thinking out loud, trying to see what might stop the youngsters from helping them. That way she'd be ready to solve any problems they presented her and Nate with.

"We won't keep them away long enough for it to ruin their chances to prove up." Nate picked up another strip of jerky but couldn't quite make himself eat it. He stuffed it back in the bag. "A week or two, maybe a month, and the Marshals will be back. Not much longer after that and your cowhands will return from the drive. We'll have to send the Blodgetts back home once we're a hideout for the U.S. Marshals."

"Warren or Leland can ride over to their homesteads and do their chores. Or maybe Brand would agree to go milk their cows and feed their critters."

He nodded and saw the exhaustion fade a bit from her eyes. He was finding himself mighty fond of his new wife. "We can pay them in cows if they want."

Becky smiled, seeming to like that idea. "Barter their time for beef on the hoof. I'm surely cow-rich. It might work."

Nate took her hand. "*We* are cow-rich, Mrs. Paxton. Not just you."

Becky turned her hand around to clasp his. "I find that notion appeals to me, Nate. It's nice being a *we* and not just an *I*."

They talked over what lay ahead as they filled their bellies. Nate saw that there was enough jerky left over for breakfast.

"If they agree to come and help us, maybe we can work them all so hard, Samantha and Leland will stop their squabbling." Becky drained her water glass, stood, and picked up the canvas bag she'd laid on the table.

"As one of the older children in my home, I often found working a pitchfork for ten hours a day settled a fretful mind down nicely."

"You mean you doled out hard work to control your little brothers and sisters?"

"No, I didn't mean that. Though now that you mention it, I did do that. What I meant was, Pa did that to me." He rose and took their glasses to the dry sink, rinsed and tipped them upside down to dry. "Cleaning up after a meal is sure easy when we eat this way."

Becky laughed quietly. "Let's get to bed, cowboy. I'm exhausted."

Of course she was. He was too. After all, they *were* newlyweds. "Too exhausted?"

Becky turned to look at him, then smiled in a way that was purely encouraging. "No, not too exhausted."

He took her hand, and they finished up their first full day of being husband and wife in a way that suited him very much.

He had the feeling it suited her, too. And that was enough to thrill a man.

They worked all the next morning, and when Nate came to drag her out of the barn where she'd been cleaning out horse stalls, she refused to quit.

"There's just no time. If we push hard, we can keep up with what all needs to be done."

Nate studied her. "You're doing a job an inexperienced cowhand could do."

Becky felt her spine go stiff. It was the honest truth that she didn't like anyone telling her what to do. And the fact that she'd just two days ago promised to obey him made her feel all the more stubborn because she was in the wrong.

But instead of snapping at him to get back to work, it occurred to her she ought to try being reasonable. "I changed my mind about bringing those kids out here, Nate."

"Because they'll notice the hands are all gone and talk about it in town?"

"No, our excuse ought to hold up."

"Because they might get crossways of the trouble around your pa and end up in danger?"

"I hadn't thought of that. But that is a good reason to keep them away from here."

"Then why?"

Becky glared at him, then remembered that she was going to be reasonable. "Because it's embarrassing that I've let my ranch get out of control. Letting others see the place like this, especially Brand, who won't be as gullible as those kids, stomps right on my pride."

Nate pulled his Stetson off his head. With one gloved hand he smoothed his brown hair back. Becky was watching pretty close, and she thought he was holding the hat so it covered his face, and smoothing his hair in such a way so his hand covered his face. But it wasn't that well covered. Nate was trying to hide a smile.

She jammed the pitchfork into a pile of dirty prairie grass she used for bedding and stalked right up to him. "Are you laughing at me?"

He clamped his mouth shut and shook his head. She was close enough now to jab him in the stomach, which shook loose a grin, then a chuckle.

"What's so funny."

Nate put his hat back on his head, smiling wide. "Why, Mrs. Paxton, I do believe you are guilty of the sin of pride."

She glared at him, but then a smile snuck onto her face. "Let's go back to that excuse you came up with about our putting those kids in danger."

"You do know that those *kids*, especially Leland, are only a few years younger than you."

Becky flinched. "Is he? Why does he seem so young?"

"He doesn't. Not to me. Samantha is sixteen, so you've got her beat by a little more than a few."

Becky tapped her toe on the barn's dirt floor, then whirled toward the stall where her palomino stood chomping grass.

"Let's go to town. It's close enough to noon, we can eat. I might start chewing on the barn walls if it's between that and more beef jerky."

Nate headed for his stallion. The two of them were saddled up and riding for town within minutes.

When they reached Pine Valley, neither of them talked about doing anything but eating. They entered the diner to find Samantha and Leland sitting at a table with Brand and Nell. Half their workforce was there.

The diner smelled like heaven. Savory and scented with onions and more unusual things. Spices Clint grew himself and added to his recipes. Becky had never heard of garlic or basil before Clint showed up. He used other words more exotic than those, and she'd seen him tearing up green leaves and odd little hard seeds, stirring them into the usual kinds of food like beef, pork, and chicken— producing something that lured folks straight into his diner.

Clint approached with coffee cups and pot in hand and placed the cups on Nell and Brand's table without asking. Nate grabbed two empty chairs from a nearby table and brought them over.

Samantha, sitting across from Leland, hopped up and slid her chair around so she could sit beside him and make room for Becky and Nate.

"Welcome, Mr. and Mrs. Paxton. Your meal is my wedding gift to you." Clint poured their coffee rather formally but with a big smile, then headed back to the kitchen without asking them what they wanted to eat.

Becky noticed the meal Nell's family was eating was some kind of chicken and vegetables. Her stomach growled at the sight. The food would be there soon, so she dove right in to what she wanted to say.

"We've got trouble, and we think the Nolte family can help us solve it."

Clint was back with plates of the chicken before anyone finished chewing.

"What can we do?" Nell was a woman to take small bites, so she spoke first.

Becky and Nate took turns explaining their problems. Leland looked hesitant about leaving his own place, but Brand encouraged him and Samantha to say yes. He offered to come out for daytime work and then he'd ride to town to pick up Nell, do Leland's chores, and Joy and Warren's too if they agreed to help Becky and Nate.

"I can't believe you have no cowhands, Becky. What happened?" Nell knew Becky well, and nothing like this had ever happened before. It was out of character for Becky to allow a situation like this to occur.

Becky shoved a bite of food in her mouth and chewed stubbornly, not wanting to explain any more than she already had. And especially not to Nell, her good friend.

"I feel responsible," Nate said. "One of the cowhands who rode off is my brother. We had three hands left after the bulk of Becky's cowhands rode out to drive the herd to Denver. Sal, my brother, said he needed to leave for a few days. I objected, but in the end he was going and promised to be back as soon as possible. That left us with two hands. Not enough, but we could get by.

"Once Sal was gone, the others left soon after. I think Sal would've stayed with us if he'd known the other hands would abandon us." Nate looked at Becky. "If you don't want to rehire him when he comes back, I'll support you in that. It's all such a mess, and it's mostly my fault. Becky, I'm sorry." Nate turned to the others at the table. "We'd sure appreciate the help."

Becky didn't look over at Nate because she was afraid her eyes might be shining. He was taking the blame. Sparing her any blow to her pride. Her sinful pride. Blast the man, he was a flat-out hero, and right now she was so happy to be married to him, she could barely keep from saying so out loud. She got her emotions under control and looked at Brand instead.

"I'll help," Brand said. "I'll come out every day until your hands come back."

"Thank you. Nell, I know you're getting help from Samantha and Joy."

"Leland and Warren work for me, too."

Good grief, she might be the town's biggest employer.

"Sewing dresses?" Nate asked.

Nell snorted. "No. They're all making chaps. But I'm getting closer every day to catching up on the orders. I can spare my helpers for a couple of weeks."

"Cassie might want to work, too," Brand added. "She's a hand with cattle. She can rope a bit, Samantha too. And both can ride, but they're nowhere near cowhands."

"Neither am I or Warren."

Becky nodded. "There are enough simple jobs you could do to help get us through until my men come back. What do you say, Leland? Will you come? Samantha, I hope you and Joy know your way around the kitchen so you can cook for us all. I've got a garden that's getting overgrown. I managed to gather eggs yesterday, but I was doing it around sunset. And checking the herds, that's a job a good rider can handle without too much trouble. Nate and I will do all the more skilled jobs."

"Will you teach me how to do some of those skilled jobs?" Leland asked. "I'd like to run my own ranch someday, if I can ever afford to buy the land. You could help me learn what all's involved, and what skills I'll need to do a good job of it."

Becky reached a hand across the table, and Leland shook it. He and Samantha looked into each other's eyes and smiled.

Samantha said, "It'll be good for Percival Kintzinger to write and print up his own newspaper for a while. It's so much better since I went to work there that he raised the price to three pennies from one, and he's printing more copies. But he's been a bad boss, and it'll give me pleasure to quit." She looked at Leland. "You were right about him treating me poorly. Thank you for standing up for me."

Leland nodded. "Working there is a fine thing if Percy treats you right. You're good at it." He turned to Becky. "And learning more about ranching will help us live a better life out here. Thank you."

Becky thought the two of them were a bit calmer than she'd seen them before. Maybe by the time they'd finished helping at the ranch, under the watchful eye of Brand during the day and with Becky and Nate on hand, they'd settle in to married life.

"*Why* aren't they back?" Joshua Pruitt snarled at Buck, his newest cowhand. A man of low morals but with decent cowboy skills. The perfect hired hand for the Circle J. Joshua, standing beside his barn, slammed a fist into the logs that formed its walls.

Buck shrugged and stared off toward the southeast—the direction the men had ridden. Joshua followed the direction of Buck's gaze and tried to imagine what was keeping them.

"The shipment must've been late," Buck said.

"It's been known to happen." Joshua knew this to be true, yet it didn't happen often. The man who'd supplied them with news of gold shipments and stages that carried payrolls was reliable. Only Skleen knew who he was.

"They sometimes change routes at the last minute."

"Could've happened that way." Joshua hit the barn with the side of his fist again. Slower this time. He tried to make himself believe it. "My men are waiting and watching. They're set up overlooking that trail. Hoping it's just delayed."

The fist kept hitting. He wore gloves, but still the pounding hurt his hand. "But for three days?" His voice rose. The power of his fist grew. "No, they wouldn't wait and watch for three days."

"For gold they might. If no shipment rolls through, they'll be back."

Joshua had a twisted feeling in his gut. Worse than usual. Something had gone wrong. His fist was raw now. He felt blood flow inside the leather. He finally quit pounding because he had to, not because he wasn't still going mad from the wait and the worry and the rage.

Something had held them back beyond delays. Had they seen a rich haul and divided it between themselves and headed for the hills? Or was it something less than treachery?

"It isn't the first time Skleen's brought back poor information." Grimly, Joshua crossed his arms over his chest. He did it to support his right hand. He had to wonder if he'd broken a bone. This would be the last time Joshua trusted Skleen. The man was arrogant, acted like he was the boss. Joshua intended to teach Skleen a lesson, and it would be the last thing Skleen learned on this earth.

Beyond the rage, the turmoil of waiting, and the pain in his hand, it was fear that drove Joshua the most. If his men came back with that gold, Joshua could finally pay off the man he owed and get his ranch back in his own hands. If they didn't show up, Joshua was trapped. Just like he'd been ever since Becky betrayed him.

He wanted out. He wanted to go back to making an honest living, like he was doing before his daughter stabbed him in the back. Joshua thought of Nate Paxton's cold eyes when he'd stopped Joshua from using his fists on Becky. He couldn't just ride over there and drag her home, not with Nate at her side.

Like a wild horse with the bit in her teeth, sometimes it took doling out a little pain.

Talk about treachery!

He looked over at Buck, sorry he'd shared his thoughts with the cowhand. He'd always been one to keep his own council. Yet another thing owing money to the wrong man had taken from him.

"Buck, get one other man and ride out to where that gold shipment was to pass through. You were there when we talked about the route. Find out what happened."

"You're sure, Boss? You'll be mighty shorthanded around here."

Joshua scowled. "Do as I say."

"On my way," Buck said, then turned and strode over to his horse.

Joshua stormed toward the house. Once he was inside, he'd bandage up his hand and do all his fretting in private.

When he reached the house, fuming about Becky, he considered how alone she was over there. Her crew had taken the cattle to market, and she always sent her foreman along with them. Knowing her, it was likely she'd not told anyone about the run-in she'd had with her pa in town.

Now Nate, who'd stood between a daughter and her pa, would be gone to Denver. A drive that long took more than a month.

Becky would have a few hands still, but few men would do as Nate had done.

Carefully, Joshua slid off his glove and assessed the damage he'd done. Ugly, the skin ripped up. He flexed his hand, and though it was injured, no bones had been broken.

He decided to give his men a few more days to get back with the gold. If they came, everything would be settled and he could return to normal life. If they didn't come, or if they hadn't gotten the gold, then Joshua was done waiting for Becky to come to her senses.

He'd pick his moment, head out in the dark of night.

He hesitated when he thought of those dogs, but then there were quiet ways to kill a dog.

Noisy ways too, yet that would give her a warning.

Poison? Bow and arrow? Traps?

He'd study on it, make some plans. If he had to, if his fellow gang members failed, he'd get his daughter and drag her home.

And if she refused to cooperate, a bitter-cold part of him took pleasure in knowing that he was her only heir.

23

Nate took Leland and Samantha to check one of the herds. Both were eager to work outside.

Becky took with her Brand, Warren, and Cassie. Brand was by far the best at ranching, but still not great. Warren was a decent hand, too. Cassie rode a horse well and willingly followed orders.

Not a one of them could rope a cow and throw her if she was limping or in any way needed attention, though Brand had animal-doctoring skills if Becky hog-tied any calves.

Joy went to the house to get supper cooking and do some cleaning. She also had orders to milk the cow, gather eggs, and feed the chickens and pigs, then check to see what was ripe in the garden. She didn't even flinch when they rode out and left her to it.

Becky was right now kicking herself for forking dirty straw out of those stalls in the barn. Warren wasn't much of a cowhand, but he could have handled that.

They all worked their hearts out through a long afternoon and into the evening. When they finally headed in for supper, Becky felt better. "I'm going to hold this ranch together, thanks to all of you. I appreciate that you came out here. I'm hoping Joy has a fine meal for all of us."

Brand tugged on his hat. "Glad to do it, Becky. But no supper for Cassie or me. I'm late getting myself to town, and Nell will be so weary making chaps for the day that she's bound to scold me. Cassie and I will be back early in the morning."

As Brand and Cassie headed for town at a gallop, Becky led her meager work crew to the barn, where they unsaddled. Before they were done, Nate came in with Leland and Samantha. They finished putting up the horses, then walked together toward the house.

"Can Joy cook?" Becky hadn't given that much thought.

"She's a hand in the kitchen," Leland said. "There'll be something hot to fill our bellies that won't leave behind an ache."

Becky thought that was less than glowing praise. But at the same time, it was all she felt like asking for.

With Michaela's help, Nell had finished an entire pair of chaps. It'd been a long day. When Brand finally showed up, the family rode home together. They ate a meager supper because it was too late to cook much. Cassie had moved into Brand's old room, while Michaela slept in the loft by herself.

Once they were settled in bed, Nell decided to cross-examine her husband. "So, what's going on?"

"Something strange for sure," Brand told her. "Becky having no cowhands at all? It's not normal."

"She's as smart as any rancher I've ever known." Nell didn't admit that she hadn't known that many. "She'd have never left herself with Nate and three unreliable cowhands. She usually keeps more hands at home from the drive, and the ones she keeps back are dependable. What's going on?"

Nell's asking the question the second time didn't help.

"Do you want me to guess?" Brand propped himself up on his elbow and gave Nell a quick kiss.

"I think it's for the best if you do. It's called brainstorming. Toss out ideas no matter how farfetched and then we'll see if we can't come up with something."

"This isn't how you act when you're a judge, is it? Don't you demand facts?"

"I'm guessing it has something to do with her pa."

"Why's that?"

"You're not doing it right." She kissed him back. "Build on my ideas. They say in brainstorming there are no wrong ideas."

"Guesses, not ideas." Brand sighed. "Okay, well, maybe her pa realized how few hands she had working for her, and new ones at that. And he came over in the dark of night and bribed them to come work for him so Becky would face trouble. Nate's brother probably wouldn't have taken a bribe, so maybe Joshua came over after he'd left. And he'd've known Nate wouldn't agree to abandon Becky. So he lured the two newcomers away, and that's how she ended up with no work crew."

Nell arched a brow. "That's a pretty good guess."

"Thanks, ma'am. Now it's your turn to guess."

"Maybe Joshua staked out Becky's ranch. Waited until

her two new cowpokes were separated from Nate and Becky . . . and then he killed them."

Brand gasped. "That's a mighty bloodthirsty guess."

She nodded. "Besides, he'd've probaby had to shoot them, and that would be noisy. Becky would've heard the gunfire. And what about the horses? If Joshua Pruitt has turned to murder and horse thieving, he could hang for it."

"A better guess than mine, not in the sense of it being right, but just for pure entertainment value."

Nell gave a little laugh. "Brand, I think Becky was embarrassed about hiring those kids today."

"Leland is about two years younger than her, and she started her ranch over two years ago. Calling him a 'kid' doesn't seem fair." Brand rolled onto his back and propped his hands behind his head. "I watched Nate and Becky work today. Those two are highly skilled. Roping and riding. Hazing cattle and handling green-broke horses. By their standards we were all kids." He stared at the ceiling.

Nell stayed on her side, tossing ideas around. "Could it have something to do with Mrs. Mussel and her speech?"

Brand's head snapped around. "What made you think of that? How could her speech have anything to do with this?"

Nell shrugged one shoulder. "It's just all I can think of that's happened recently that's different. And her pa causing trouble. That might've made him mad enough to do something nasty to Becky."

"That speech and the Deadeye Gang are all that's going on around here, seems to me. I don't know how the speech could have anything to do with stagecoach robbers." Brand rolled back to his side. "Do you have any ideas for sneaky questions I could ask tomorrow to try to trick some information out of them?"

Nell smiled. "Give me some time to think it over. I'll see if I can come up with something. One thing's for sure. Whatever happened to her cowhands, it wasn't normal. Becky wouldn't have let herself get into a situation like that to begin with."

Brand kissed her, long and slow. "While we were brainstorming, I had an idea that's got nothing to do with Becky and her problems."

Nell kissed him back. "They say there are no wrong ideas."

Their guessing game was over for the night.

"Clint, I think the baby is coming."

Clint's feet hit the floor with a hard thud. He turned up the lantern and spun around to stare down at his wife.

Mariah had to wonder if she was on fire or had turned purple or what exactly because Clint stared at her as if he'd been stunned beyond words. Then he shouted, "Doctor!"

He whirled around and took one step. His feet were tangled in the blanket he'd dragged off the bed when he jumped up. He fell face-first on the floor, so hard that the cabin shook. Mariah got up and rounded the bed. She always took the side nearest the window. She stared down at Clint, who seemed temporarily stunned. Then he began kicking himself free of the blanket, and Mariah figured she had only seconds to stop him.

"You're not going for the doctor. Don't even think about it. I shouldn't have even told you I'd had a labor pain."

"Not tell me!" Clint surged to his feet. "Did you really think you could get through the entire business of having a baby and I wouldn't notice?"

Mariah sighed. "You're mostly a very sensible man, but I can see this is too much for you. Fine. I'll be in charge. My understanding of having a baby is that it takes a long time. An entire day of laboring isn't unusual. I regret waking you up, but I was lonely."

Her heart pinched a little when she thought of how she'd wanted him to be with her through the labor. And now she was kicking herself.

"We are not going to wake Doc up and drag him out here so far in advance."

"You don't know anything about having babies." Clint came close, caught both her upper arms, and lifted her to her tiptoes. "We should get the doctor and let him tell us what to do. He can come over and visit with us for a while, then come back later if he decides it's too early."

Mariah looked out the window. She saw a familiar constellation to the south. "Come and sit outside with me for a time. Just sit. It's a cool night, after a hot day."

"That's another thing. It's not the end of September. The baby is coming too early." Clint's voice was rising. She had to distract him before he went into a panic.

"It's not that much too early. Let's go." She took his hand, found she had to rip it off her shoulder, then dragged him out of the bedroom toward the front of the house. They had two rocking chairs out there.

221

"Mariah, we're not going outside. You need to get back to bed."

He sounded stern, but whether he just couldn't bring himself to haul her back to the bedroom or was so addled he didn't notice what his feet were doing, Clint came along quietly.

She stepped outside, where starlight peeked through a light cloud cover. A cool breeze ruffled her oversized night-gown made of white flannel. A gift from Nell. The moon was so bright that the stars close to it looked overpowered. At the edges of the sky, the stars shone more faintly. She tugged Clint to his chair and pushed him into it, then sat down beside him.

They faced the town. A clump of trees blocked their sight of the town, but it was close by. They walked into the diner most mornings.

Mariah gazed up at the Cirque of the Towers. No snow-capped peaks, but the mountains gleamed white in the moonlight. Their chairs faced the Towers, and Mariah thought she'd let Clint have a minute to get ahold of himself. She hoped she could tell him about what she was going through. After a few moments of silence, she thought he might be ready.

"I've had about ten labor pains."

Clint shot out of the chair. "Ten? And you just woke me up now?"

Waking him up was a major mistake, and one she wouldn't make when their next child came along.

"Sit back down, honey, please? Try and relax. It only makes me fretful to watch you jumping around. Surely I'm the one who should get to do any worrying. Bringing

222

this baby into the world falls much more heavily on me. So calm down."

Clint slowly, reluctantly sat.

"Doc's wife told me what to expect. She said the pains would be a fair stretch of time apart at first, and mild-like. In fact, I think I've been having these pains since just after the noon meal. When I say I've had about ten, in truth I didn't recognize them as such until just recently. I've had two since we went to bed. Once I realized I was in labor, I thought back, and I now believe the mild cramps and back aches that had come and gone all day are all part of my laboring. I didn't deliberately keep anything from you—I just didn't recognize it."

Her stomach tightened again. "There goes another one." She reached across between the chairs and took Clint's hand and pressed it against her belly. "Feel how tight it is?"

Clint's hand, at first reluctant, relaxed and rested on their child. "You're sure it's not just the baby moving? Sometimes I think I can feel her little head, and it's hard like this."

"Her?"

Clint met her eyes. "Daughter or son, it doesn't matter. I'm not sure why I said *her*."

"We'll know more before another day is out."

"No breakfast or dinner for the fine people of Pine Valley."

She patted his hand. Together they felt her stomach relax. "You might well have time, but I'd like you here with me."

"You think it'll be that long?"

Mariah shrugged. She wasn't that thrilled about it taking that long herself. "Mrs. Preston said some come fast, some slow. The first one is usually the slowest of all. She said twelve to twenty-four hours is normal."

"Twenty-four hours?" Clint collapsed back into his chair. In the moonlight she saw the horrified expression.

"Or twelve. And if these pains started at noon, then I'm almost at twelve hours already."

"You can count the ones you didn't know were happening?"

Mariah shrugged. "I'm counting them. If it's twenty-four hours, we'll have a baby at lunchtime."

"Seems appropriate."

"When morning comes, I'll want you to go fetch the doctor. I'd like it if Nell could come, too. It would be nice to have Becky here, but she's a long way out and it sounds like she's shorthanded. Best not to pester her." She leaned forward and rested a hand on Clint's precious face. "And you. I want you here. We're going to be all right."

Clint drew in a deep breath and exhaled slowly. "Let's say a prayer. Then we'll sit here and see if your labor pains—that's a terrible name for them, by the way—come closer together or get stronger. We'll sit here and get through it together." He leaned forward and kissed her. Holding both her hands, he said a heartfelt prayer that almost brought tears to her eyes.

And with those tears held inside, she said her own quiet prayer. Before she could finish it, her voice broke and she quit talking, hoping Clint hadn't noticed.

He was watching her too close. He took her hand and

asked quietly and so calmly it was a wonder, considering how he'd been acting, "What's the matter?"

"It's st-stupid."

"Well, I reckon I've been acting stupid since you woke me up. Thanks for taking a turn. Tell me what's making you cry."

Mariah's throat felt thick until she couldn't talk. Tears escaped her eyes. She was so determined to handle this child-birthing business calmly. And now . . . "I w-want my mama."

A sob cut off whatever other foolish thing she'd been going to say, and she wasn't able to fight the tears at all. Sobbing, she was barely aware of Clint's arms tightening around her. Soon she was sitting on his lap.

He pressed a handkerchief into her hands. Surprising he had one when they were both sitting outside in their night clothing.

Clint held her close, gently but firmly, pressing her right against his body. They rocked for a long stretch of minutes while Mariah cried out her foolish tears. Might as well wish for a magical flying horse to swoop down and carry her to the doctor's office . . . or wherever magical horses took a person. She imagined, in this one case, the horse would take her to heaven to see her mama.

Finally, her tears ebbed. They rocked in silence for a while longer, through another labor pain.

Clint whispered in her ear, "I want my ma, too."

She started crying all over again.

They passed the night that way—rocking and praying, whispering and, sometimes, Mariah crying.

Once all her tears were shed, they sat in the cool mountain night, looking out at the magnificent mountains. Clint rested his big, strong hands on the curve of her belly and prayed each time a pain came. When at last the sun brightened the land and washed the peaks of the Towers in a dazzling red, her pains coming closer and stronger, Mariah said quietly, "It's time to fetch Doc Preston. Help me inside first. And please ask Nell to come out, too. If it's too early for her to be at her shop, leave a note."

Clint lifted her into his arms, carried her inside, and sat her in the rocking chair before the fireplace. He kissed her and said, "I'll be gone no longer than ten minutes."

She nodded.

He spun around and ran for the door.

24

Brand came galloping alone into Becky's yard, much earlier than she'd expected him. She knew he had to ride Nell to town, then come back out.

He had a frantic look in his eyes that made Becky's breath catch. "It's Mariah. The baby's coming. She'd like you to be there."

Becky's eyes shot to Nate, who said, "Brand, ride back to town with her. I'll handle the ranch for today. Don't worry about us."

Becky was sprinting toward the barn.

"Give your horse a drink. Cassie didn't come with you?" Nate looked down the trail and saw only dust.

Brand got down and led the horse to the water trough. It really wasn't that far of a ride, and after a breather, his horse could handle the ride back. Brand looked startled. "I took off and left both my youngsters in Nell's care when she's got a baby to help bring into the world."

He punched himself in the head. "I'll bring both out with me when I come back. We got to town and found Mrs. Preston on the steps of Nell's shop with the news the doctor had just been called to Mariah's laboring. Mariah wanted Nell and Becky to be there."

Nate nodded. "Don't worry about coming back out if you want to stay close." He gave the barn an anxious look. He sort of wanted to stay close, too.

"No sense in my hanging around town fretting all day."

"All day?" Nate dragged his Stetson off his head and almost dropped it in the water trough.

"I've got three. It takes a good part of the day to get them born." Brand pulled his horse away from the water before it could founder itself. He swung up into the saddle just as Becky, riding her palomino, came out of the barn. "I'll be back, Nate. And I'll bring my girls with me."

The two horses thundered out of the yard. Nate stood staring at the dust being kicked up behind them. Then his cowhands walked over and wanted to know what all the ruckus was about.

They got right to work because it was driving Nate crazy to stand around thinking.

"I'm not staying around here any longer—you don't need me." Sal Paxton crossed his arms and faced Owen.

"I do need you."

"For what?"

"I want every man here to tell his part at the trial of how this arrest was made."

Sal shook his head. "We left Miss Becky with no help

on her ranch. With one cowhand, my brother. I told him I'd ride along to make sure the prisoners didn't escape. You needed me for that. But that's done now. And the prisoner I caught has a wanted poster. You don't even need a trial for him."

Of the six men they'd brought in, they'd found a wanted poster for five of them. And the sixth had been urged to talk about his saddle partners, enough that he implicated himself in past Deadeye Gang robberies.

They'd questioned all the men separately. A couple of them had slipped and told small details that definitely cast suspicion on Joshua Pruitt. Enough to arrest him. As if six men, including five with wanted posters, wasn't enough to cast suspicion.

"If you ride off right now, I'm going to complain to the Marshals Service and get you fired."

"Give me a good reason I should stay, Owen."

Sal watched him and was struck by the notion that Owen just didn't like anyone disobeying his orders. Or if he had a better reason for not letting Sal leave, he wouldn't admit it. Which meant it was probably one of those twisty-turny reasons that amounted to Sal not needing to know.

Owen didn't answer.

"Pruitt is already on edge. The men he sent off to stop a gold shipment didn't come back. You know he's feeling the heat. And 'on edge' to a man like Pruitt will come out as rage to anyone who crosses him. Add in the one man we didn't catch. That lone youngster we didn't have enough men to bring in. He'll have gone back, and who knows what story he told."

Owen scowled, though for the first time Sal thought

the man might be thinking of something besides locking their prisoners up for good.

"We believe no one saw Miss Becky or Nate. And none of our prisoners have been given a chance to get word to their boss. But what if we're wrong? What if they did get word out somehow? What if they didn't see Miss Becky or Nate, but they did see me, or you or Tex? That would be enough to connect the Idee Ranch to the gang vanishing. Becky and Nate might be in danger and so shorthanded that they could be cut down without a fighting chance."

Sal grabbed the top of his Stetson and lifted it off his head in a mockery of doffing it. He dropped the hat back in place. "I'm leaving. If you get me fired, so be it. I'm getting tired of riding after outlaws anyway. You know you need to sneak back onto the Idee. You know you should be treating Miss Becky with nothing but respect and gratitude. You're asking a lot of her to set her own pa up for prison, possibly for a hanging. And you're going to ask more because you *will* go back and use her ranch as a setup to arrest Pruitt?"

Owen glared and didn't answer. Which was an answer in itself.

"When I get back, I won't tell Becky and Nate how you tried to hold me here. I won't do any one of a dozen things that might convince them you're not fit to use her ranch for your plotting. Goodbye, Owen."

Sal strode away from the ruthless boss and was surprised by how much lighter he felt with each step he took. The lawman work had been weighing him down for a long time, he realized as he headed for the stable where he'd boarded his horse. He didn't have to go to the hotel where he'd slept last night because he had little but the bedroll he brought with him, intending to head back fast. They hadn't left the Idee to stake out the Circle J with any intention of being on the trail for over a week.

He quick saddled his horse and rode out of the stable. His last glance at Owen as he hit the trail to Pine Valley showed the man standing in the middle of the street, glaring.

Becky charged up the steps to Mariah's house and burst through the door to find . . . calm.

She'd been running in a flat-out panic ever since Brand had come for her, and her friend couldn't at least have the courtesy to look a little frazzled?

Instead, Mariah, sat in a rocking chair, fully and neatly dressed. Clint sat at the kitchen table with Doc Preston, both drinking coffee. Nell stood at the stove cracking eggs into a sizzling skillet, Cassie and Michaela at her side. Everyone looked as placid as a windless lake.

Becky jammed her hands onto her hips. "I thought you were having a baby."

Brand pushed past Becky to go pour himself a cup of coffee. He went to the stove for it and spoke quietly to Nell.

Mariah smiled bright enough to shame the sun. She stood from her rocking chair.

No one rushed to stop her. Or to catch her if she fell. No one yelled or even moved, though Clint looked hard at her, and Becky noticed his knuckles were white as he clutched his coffee mug.

Mariah came to Becky and threw her arms around her. "I told them not to bother you. I know how busy you are with the ranch. But I'm glad you came."

Becky hugged her very round friend tightly. Before the hug could end, Mariah said, "Here comes another one."

Becky stepped back. The doctor hurried over and rested a hand on her belly. "You should sit down. They're coming faster. You'll need to go to bed soon."

Mariah had one hand still on Becky's arm, and suddenly Becky felt a crushing grip. Mariah's face was slowly losing its calm cheerfulness. Nell, scraping eggs onto a platter, looked nervously at Mariah.

Clint came to Mariah's side while Brand patted his wife on the shoulder and said, "I'll head back to the ranch now. You don't need so many people underfoot. Becky, I'll see to your horse over at the smithy first."

"Thanks, Brand." Becky appreciated that her friend Nell had married a good man. Then Becky thought of how Nate had sent her off to her friend and said he'd handle everything at the Idee. She'd done well for herself, too.

"Thanks for bringing her, Brand." Mariah spared him a single glance.

"Glad to help. I'll be praying for you and the baby. For God to care for you." He nodded. "I'll take Cassie and Michaela with me. We'll do what we can to help." He left the room just a little too fast, his girls in tow.

Mariah, leaning hard on Doc Preston, with her right hand still sunk into Becky's left arm, moved to the chair. Becky came along because it seemed like the wrong time to be wrestling with her friend.

Mariah sank into the chair. Becky crouched down because

she really had no choice. Clint dropped to his knees in front of his wife and took her hand in his. Becky saw his lips moving in what she knew had to be a prayer.

The doctor was on Mariah's left, and Nell came behind Mariah and rubbed her shoulders. Far too many minutes passed if the amount of pain Mariah appeared to be in counted. When she relaxed, she said, "Only a couple of minutes between the pains now. And it lasted almost as long as there was space between them. I think I'll go to bed. I want to be lying down for the next contraction."

Nell patted her shoulders. "Good idea."

Becky got her arm free from Mariah's claws.

Clint wrapped an arm around Mariah's lower back and helped her stand with such love and gentleness that Becky felt tears clog her throat. And she wasn't a crier. Not even close. All three of them had done very well for themselves.

"Who do you want back there, Mariah?" Becky spoke to her from the side Clint wasn't on. "I'll stay right with you through it all if you want. But I'm content to be out here, waiting and praying."

Mariah's eyes met Becky's, and Becky saw the truth in them and smiled. Without making her ask, after she'd come riding in at such a tear, she said, "I'll wait out here. Clint, you should wait with me."

"What? No."

Doc Preston said, "A baby being delivered is no place for a father. It would be best if you waited out here."

"I will not—"

"Clint!" Mariah cut him off. "Please let the doctor handle this. Stay out here. But stay close. Please."

Clint had the look of a man torn in half. A man who

wanted to be with his wife with a towering passion. And a man who wanted to let his wife have anything she might possibly ask for.

"A birthing is distressing," Doc added. "And many a man gets mighty upset to see his wife in the last stage of it. Having you in there will make it harder for Mariah because she'll be so intent on not distressing you. And she shouldn't have a single thing to worry about except delivering the baby."

Clint stepped away from Mariah as the doctor took his place. Nell followed Doc and Mariah into the bedroom.

"Why does she get to go?" Clint looked at Becky. She saw such hurt in his eyes.

She knew now that taking care of Clint was as much of a help to Mariah as helping with the birth. Becky was grateful she was here.

"Let's get some coffee and eggs and sit outside," Becky said. A cry came from the bedroom. Another labor pain was building. "Doc Preston is right. She doesn't want to upset you. You know that's right."

The devastation was replaced with a flash of anger. Clint hissed the words more than spoke them. "Well, she *is* upsetting me."

He didn't speak loud enough for Mariah to hear. Which was its own generosity, considering how badly he wanted to be with his wife. He moved to the kitchen and dished up a couple of plates. Becky poured two cups of coffee.

They headed outside and closed the door to the sound of Mariah's cries. Becky settled into a rocking chair while Clint sat on the top step of the porch, looking as taut as the skin of a drum.

Mariah's laboring was still loud. "We can hear her, but she can't hear us. That's a way to help, Clint."

He muttered something, and Becky decided she didn't want to know what it was.

They sat there for what seemed like ages. Once, when the shouting inside had stopped, Becky went in, got the coffeepot, and brought it back out. Together, they drank coffee and watched shadows move as the sun rose and shone down on the eastern slopes of the Cirque of the Towers.

Becky spent time in prayer. She wished the town had a parson. Were he still here, Parson Blodgett with his long experience ministering to his flock and his kind, cheerful nature, would have helped them through this.

Clint sat waiting, his shoulders tense, his foot tapping and his knee jiggling.

At last, when the sun was high overhead, the door opened, and Nell stepped out with a tiny bundle in her arms. Clint shot to his feet and rushed to look at his newborn child.

"You have a son, Clint," Nell said, beaming.

"How's Mariah?"

"She's perfect." Tears welled in Nell's eyes. "Your son is perfect. Everything is just perfect. Doc said to give him a few minutes before you come back. Do you want to hold him?"

The dreadful tension ebbed out of Clint. "I got a lot of experience with younger brothers and a sister. I'm a hand with babies. I've even changed a diaper or two—or two hundred—in my life."

Nell smiled through her tears as she handed the baby

over to the proud father. "Mariah said you agreed to name him Garret after your pa, and Theodore after her brother. *Garret Theodore Roberts*, meet your pa."

The baby reached a tiny hand up toward Clint, who took him from Nell with impressive skill. He lifted the little boy up until Garret's searching hand rested on Clint's nose.

A single tear rolled down Clint's cheek. His eyes shone brighter than the noonday sun.

Doc stepped out of the bedroom. "She's ready to see you now, Clint."

Clint, even carrying the baby, almost mowed the doctor over. But it was clear Doc had done this plenty of times before because he was nimble as he stepped out of the way.

Mariah saw the two greatest loves of her life come into the room. Exhausted, aching, not feeling altogether wonderful, she found a smile that went all the way to her heart.

Clint came to her bedside and sat carefully on the edge. "You're all right?"

"Tired, but yes. I'm fine."

"I'd say you're wonderful." He blinked, and she saw the tears in his eyes. And thought of how her pa would have acted if he ever saw a man cry.

She decided she liked Clint's way of handling things better.

Clint touched the little one's hand, and those impossibly tiny fingers clutched his one single finger. He lifted the baby's hand to his lips and kissed it. "Garret Theodore

Roberts, meet your ma and pa, together with you for the first time."

He bent close to Mariah and offered her those tiny grasping fingers. She kissed her son just as Clint had, then looked up and met Clint's gaze. The three of them, a family together for the first time.

"I love you, Mariah. I love our little Garret. I love the life we can give our son, the two of us together, raising him in faith and teaching him everything we know." A smile snuck onto Clint's face. "Do you suppose he'll be a cook or a blacksmith?"

Mariah smiled back at him. She felt tears burn her eyes. "They both involve fire, so let's not push him into either too soon."

Clint chuckled as he slid an arm behind Mariah's head, and the three of them shared a hug.

25

Becky managed to spend a good chunk of the day in town. She had to wait a while to see Mariah, of course. And Clint didn't come out for a long time.

That seemed to be a good sign. Surely if there was the least little thing to worry about, he'd come running for the doctor.

The doctor had left a while ago but said he wouldn't go far.

Becky gladly waited.

A pa needed to spend some quiet minutes with his new baby. She wasn't sure how long it'd be before she could see Mariah, but she didn't go in and demand a turn.

Instead, she and Nell talked quietly, buzzing with happiness about the new baby. They cooked their usual meal. More eggs, only this time they added toast and bacon. By the time they had their leisurely meal ready, Clint came out.

Becky said, "Can I have a turn with the little one?"

Clint was empty-handed and wore an expression of

dazed joy, like a man who'd just witnessed a miracle. "Go on in."

"Sit a while, Clint, and eat a meal you didn't have to make yourself." Nell carried a plate for him to the table. Clint stared at the plate as if he'd never seen food before.

Nell looked up and met Becky's smiling eyes. Becky poured him coffee while Nell filled three more plates, and the two of them took the food and went in to see Mariah.

It was a beautiful day, and Becky didn't want it to end.

Finally, Brand and Nate came for her and Nell. They both got to meet baby Garret and shake Clint's hand. Cassie and Michaela clamored to visit as well, and Mariah welcomed them into the bedroom to see the baby.

Nell offered to stay the night with Mariah, but she was sent home with many thanks.

As the six of them went out and mounted up, Brand said quietly to Nell, "She'll probably say yes if you offer to stay tomorrow. Babies can be exhausting."

Nell nodded. "I'll be sure to offer again tomorrow."

Becky fell in beside Nate, bringing up the rear, with the girls ahead of them and Nell and Brand leading.

"How did the day go?" Becky asked.

Nate had a lot to say. Things weren't running as smoothly as she'd wished, but all things considered, things weren't too bad. By the time he'd made a report on the day, they waved goodbye to the Nolte family.

Then they had a few more minutes to ride in blessed quiet.

Nate looked at her and said, "It was a good day, then?"

"Wonderful day. Why do you ask?"

"You have a ridiculous smile on your face, like nothing

I've ever seen before. Not even when that new colt was born colored like your palomino."

Becky laughed. "It was such a wonder, Nate. I suppose I saw my little brothers when they were born, but that was a long time ago, and I was so young myself, I have no memory of it. That makes little Garret the only baby I've ever seen. What a tiny miracle he is. And he comes into the world in that tiny package but has everything he needs to grow into a man. God made a wonderful world for us. I've spent so much time worried about outlaws and the Marshals and working the cattle while being shorthanded, I forget how blessed I am."

"Well, I've been feeling mighty blessed since you agreed to marry me, Becky."

That got a wide smile out of her. As they approached the last curve before arriving home, she said, "Marrying you was a fine idea. Fine indeed."

"I'm hoping Sal comes back in just a few days. Maybe he'll bring some of the Marshals with him. More skilled hands would sure help around here."

Becky reached over and rested a gloved hand on Nate's wrist. "We'll manage. Right now I'm only going to think of blessings. Time enough to go back to fretting tomorrow."

They rounded the corner to see Samantha and Leland go into the house hand in hand.

"I think keeping those two working hard and exhausted by the end of the day is the answer to their marriage woes." Nate twisted his wrist just enough that he and Becky were holding hands as they rode toward the barn.

"If that solves marriage problems, we ought to get along just fine for the rest of our lives."

Nate stretched from his horse to hers and kissed her. "I'm counting on it."

Once they got the horses settled for the night, it was suppertime, so the two of them headed toward the house.

The Kid came running into Joshua's house, gasping, his eyes so wide, Joshua could see the white all the way around them. The Kid looked like a frightened horse.

"Buck and Harvey found me and dragged me back here, but I should've stayed until I found the men. They just vanished, Boss. All of 'em!" The Kid was shouting now.

Joshua lurched to his feet, his desk chair slamming against the wall behind him. "The gang vanished? Were they captured, killed, or did they run off?" His thoughts were reeling. "Wait. Was this *after* you got the gold shipment?"

"No. We all rode out the night before just like we'd planned. We got into our positions. I stood there overlooking the trail and watched the freight wagon pass through. I was on the far south end of the canyon wall, and I was supposed to be the last to get into the fight. But there was no fight. No guns were fired. The wagon, loaded down heavy with a fortune in gold, just rolled on by while I stood there wondering what had happened."

"Why are you just coming home now?" It'd been nearly a week. Sure, it was a long ride to the overlook for the robbery and a long ride back, but The Kid should've returned before now. It made Joshua furious to think they'd let things drag on this long.

"I searched everywhere before I gave up and came back.

241

I tried to follow their tracks and thought I'd picked them up a couple of times, but I was never sure. I'd follow a faint trail for a bit, then lose 'em. I was days searching, ridin' in all directions. But it's like they vanished into thin air."

A chill ran up Joshua's spine. The Kid made it sound as though they were talking about ghosts, like dark magic was at work. Had the devil himself come for his own?

What was Joshua supposed to do now? Skleen was the one who knew which stagecoaches carried payrolls, or in this case, a wagon loaded with gold. Without Skleen, Joshua wasn't sure how to learn when another stagecoach would come through.

He felt trapped . . . and with a big note coming due soon.

He'd sent his most experienced men on this robbery. The ones he had left, including The Kid here, all needed help. And his best help had vanished.

Panic like Joshua had never known avalanched through him.

Then, out of pure fear, an idea came to him. Give it up. Ride away from this life of crime he'd never intended to lead. Lose the ranch and start up new somewhere else. An honest life.

He hated the fear he felt. It erupted into rage.

Rage needed a target, and he found one in a snap.

Becky.

Mostly alone at her stupid ranch, and he was her only living relative. The only one with a claim to inherit everything she owned.

He'd give her one more chance to be reasonable.

He looked hard at The Kid. Made no effort to conceal

his rage. The Kid backed up a step, expecting Joshua might kill the messenger.

"Tell the men to saddle up."

"Where we goin', Boss?"

"Go. Now!" Killing the messenger was an idea with merit. The Kid might not have been in on whatever his gang had done, but he hadn't found the varmints either. And he'd taken too long getting back here.

The Kid scrambled out of Joshua's office at a near run. Joshua tamped down his rage. The amusement of making a man run for his life was like a balm for his temper.

He thought things through calmly and decided he wouldn't change a bit of his plan. He strode from the room to ready his horse. Joshua never went along with his gang, but this time he would. This time he'd settle up with his selfish daughter.

He figured she'd have maybe two or three hands at her place, no more. Good, they would have them outmanned.

Just like always, they'd leave no witnesses alive.

26

Becky took Cassie and Michaela with her. Nate got Samantha and Leland. Brand stayed at the house to do chores.

Becky really had to stomp down hard on the boss aspect of her relationship with Brand. He was worried about his daughters, thinking they might be so incompetent that they'd try Becky's patience. And that was possible.

But Becky had no dangerous tasks set for the morning. She had a herd at one of her farthest pastures and just wanted to ride out and make sure the grass was holding up. The creek, which sometimes got low by the end of the summer, was running fine because they'd had lots of rain in the past weeks. Still, a rancher kept a close eye on her grass and water.

"If the cattle need to be moved," Becky said to the girls as they rode along, "we'll come back for them. It's a pasture with rocks and trees and a steep bank along the creek. We won't try to haze those stubborn cows out of that tough ground alone. Even if I find a cow that's come up

lame, I don't intend to doctor her, not with just the three
of us. But if they're comfortable, we'll just ride amongst
'em, stir them up enough to move a bit so I can see how
they look. For now, we'll ride out and back home—that's
what I'm hoping for."

It was a nice ride. She enjoyed spending time with the
girls. They were good riders and mostly quiet. Michaela
especially was careful, easy in the saddle, but she took no
risks and wasn't really relaxed.

Cassie stuck on her horse like a little burr. She was no
young child, but with a little training, she'd be a solid
cowhand. Nell liked having the girls around, Becky knew
that, but it was tempting to ask if she could have Cassie
out to work regularly and train her for ranching.

Occasionally the girls would leave off their quiet ways
to talk about the baby. They were delighted with little
Garret. Becky had to admit she was, too.

They reached the edge of her property. This was the
land that shared a boundary line with Pa's. She shuddered
at the memory of Pa getting ready to hit her before Nate
stopped him.

She thought of how he'd tried to stir up trouble the day
of Mrs. Mussel's speech, and how he'd been taken down
by the cavalry. Bound and gagged and left lying at the back
of the crowd, along with the rest of his cowhands, until
the speech was over.

When the speech concluded and Mrs. Mussel and Mrs.
Morris had left town at a sharp speed and were well away,
with the crowd having dispersed, the sheriff finally untied
the men and let them return to their homes.

Becky had slipped into Nell's shop to get away from

whatever ugly thing her pa might say to her. She watched him through the shop's window; he was red-faced with humiliation and furious as all get-out.

All those unpleasant memories rode along with her now, and she almost turned back. Pa's range was vast, Becky's almost as big. There was next to no chance Pa would be anywhere near this one pasture. Even so, she unhooked the thong on her pistol holster. Best to ride ready for trouble, whether from Pa or his men or a feisty Angus bull.

They rode around the pasture and found nothing to worry about.

"The grass is getting worn out here, but that's normal for September. The cattle will be all right for another week or two, and by that time all my hands will be back."

The girls acted interested in learning, especially Cassie.

"Let's head home." Becky reined her horse toward the Idee, probably an hour or more away by horseback. They'd started early and would be home in time for the noon meal.

If they hurried.

"Let's make tracks," Becky said to the girls. "We're past the roughest part of the trail. I want to get home. I'm hungry."

The girls both gave her a shocked but delighted look, then kicked their horses into a canter.

Becky gave them a few paces head start before spurring her palomino into a ground-eating gallop.

Out of nowhere, a loop sailed straight at her, roped her tight, and jerked her off the horse. The palomino, its blood up for the race, didn't seem to notice she was gone and vanished around a curve in the trail.

She hit the ground so hard, it knocked the wind out of her. "Let's get out of here."

She didn't recognize the voice. Stunned and gasping for breath, she wrestled with the rope, clawed for her gun . . . only to find it wasn't there. The unhooked thong had allowed her pistol to come out of its holster.

Then a man was on her so fast, she couldn't get the lasso free.

"We gotta get those kids. No witnesses, remember?"

"They didn't see nuthin', and I'm not gonna hurt a couple of little girls. Let's just get this one out of here, and fast. They won't notice she's missing until after we're long gone."

"Boss ain't gonna like it."

"Then keep your mouth shut."

Becky kept her mouth shut too, praying the girls would ride for miles before they noticed her horse was riderless.

They'd get home, Nate would see she was missing, and he'd light out for her. Surely one of the best trackers in the territory would find her.

"No witnesses . . ."

Her stomach wrenched at those words. The only folks she knew of who had a reputation for such a thing was the Deadeye Gang. But they'd been arrested and hauled off to jail. The usual gang was four or five, maybe six outlaws. Had they made a mistake in capturing those men? Chased after some other robbers who weren't part of the dreaded gang?

Did Pa have some bad men working for him who weren't in the Deadeye Gang, but who might take part in a holdup? If so, why come after her?

Becky realized she didn't really know who belonged to the gang.

No witnesses meant they were taking her somewhere to kill her.

She needed to think. To plan. To be ready to make a break for it if the chance ever came. And yet all she could think about was that she was possibly in the clutches of the most murderous gang in Wyoming.

Her heart pounded. Tears burned her eyes.

A bag was thrust over her head. Now she couldn't witness anything. Being blind was a horror, but not letting her see anything might be a good thing. It might mean they intended to let her live and didn't want her to identify them. It cleared the panic enough for her to ask them, "What do you want?"

She struggled to free her hands, which were bound with rope so tightly that it cut into her wrists. She noticed how the man who'd tied her up had the skill of a cowhand.

"Shut up. You'll find out soon enough what we want." The man doing the talking laughed.

The other one, who'd refused to go after the girls, said, "I'll hang back and cover our tracks."

She was lifted to her feet. Her knees buckled, and she'd've fallen if they hadn't caught her. She got draped across the saddle on a restless horse that snorted at the odd, wiggling package on its back.

"What are you doing?" She shuddered to think of being carried away. Yes, Nate would come. Yes, he'd find her. But how long would she be in the hands of these two men?

The horse shifted again, the saddle creaking. She felt

the man swing up behind her and lash the horse. They took off at a gallop.

Where were they going? She tried to guess the direction. With the sun nearly straight overhead, she couldn't get a sense of north, south, east or west.

But she knew her land. She felt them round a curve, then ride straight, then climb for a while. They entered a wooded area and slowed down. The trail was narrow here. Woods, because the temperature dropped here, which said shade to her. And narrow because she got slapped in the head or feet occasionally by limbs hanging over the trail. She felt the slope going up the side of a mountain and struggled to recognize the area. It might have been desperation, but it felt familiar.

What good would it do her to know anyway?

Maybe if she fought her way free, she would know which way to run home. But even without figuring out her location, she tried because it was occupying her mind, pushing back against the fear.

There was no shortage of narrow wooded trails around here, so she had no idea what direction they'd ridden.

Nate heard thundering hooves riding too fast for any good purpose. He'd come this far from the ranch, checking cattle, when he'd come across a baby calf in need of attention.

His head spun around to face the danger just when Cassie burst out from a clump of trees, Michaela right behind her. Next came Becky's palomino.

The horse was riderless.

Nate leapt to his feet and charged for his horse. He mounted up and rode over to meet the girls.

"We don't know what happened to Becky," Cassie said. "We were galloping for home and got ahead of her. We'd been running a long time when her horse caught up. Since we were closer to here than where we'd started running, we came for you."

"I know where you worked today. I'm going to find her. Get to your pa. Stay by the ranch house."

"You'll need help. Pa's a hand with doctoring cattle. What if she fell off her horse? She might need him."

"Just stay to the ranch house. I don't want any of you in danger." Nate slapped the reins against his black stallion's rump and headed for the distant pasture.

Brand dashed out of the chicken coop when he heard galloping.

His girls appeared on horses so tired they were lathered. Becky's horse veered toward the barn and trotted inside.

"What happened?" Brand asked.

The girls shouted at him, explaining and pointing. He sprinted for the barn. The girls' horses were spent, the palomino as well. The girls followed and kept talking as he saddled the horse he'd ridden in on.

Then a new set of hooves sounded, coming from town.

He led the horse outside, swung up, and saw a cowhand riding in. Brand had seen him a couple of times. Nate's brother, Sal. The men from the cattle drive weren't due back for weeks. Sal was one of the men who'd abandoned the ranch.

"What's going on?" The sharp voice and, what's more, the sharper eyes made Brand wonder what kind of man this was.

"Becky's missing," Brand answered. "Nate's gone after her. Are you a tracker?"

"Better than Nate. Let's go."

27

As they rode on, Becky tried to get a sense of where they might be headed. Her first thoughts were of Pa and how ugly he could act. But were they on the trail to the Circle J? She wasn't sure.

Draped over a saddle, her belly hurt, her blood rushing to her head. A tree branch hit her hard, which left her feeling dizzy and fighting to stay conscious.

Into that dizziness and confusion, that sense of being lost, that knowledge that she might soon face a horror, a still, small voice whispered the words *"Whom shall I fear?"*

A Bible verse whispered into her terrorized mind by a loving God.

"Whom shall I fear?"

A psalm. She couldn't remember which one, but she was sure it was from the book of Psalms.

"The LORD is my light and my salvation; whom shall I fear? The LORD is the strength of my life; of whom shall I be afraid?"

She dug deep into the words of the verse. Yes, she might

be facing death, but she didn't fear death. Her growing desperation, her rabbiting thoughts as she tried to place herself, the idea she'd have to overcome two armed men to escape—they were all based in a fight for life.

But that verse was a great truth, for her faith was in the Lord. Her desire to stay alive was about this life when the most fundamental wish of a believer was to be with Jesus. To stand in the presence of God. To pass from this life to the next and be in heaven.

Becky knew in that moment that her faith was true.

She loved her life. She loved Mariah and Nell and that precious new baby, Garret. She loved her ranch, her independence, her own strength.

And here, as she dangled in utter defeat, it blew through her like a fresh mountain wind that she loved Nate.

Yes, God had allowed her to build a wonderful life here in Wyoming. A place of beauty that was beyond imagination.

But what waited for her in the next life was glory.

The fear left her. Because these men couldn't hurt her.

"To live is Christ. To die is gain."

Never had God and her Savior been more present for her. She was surrounded by the Spirit of God, His power, strength, and wisdom. And the peace she felt . . .

It was glorious.

All the struggle left her. No more thrashing. No more shouted questions.

Oh, she'd still fight if she got a chance. She'd bring these men to justice if possible. But whatever she did, she'd do it fearlessly.

"The Lord *is my light and my salvation; whom shall I*

253

fear? The Lord *is the strength of my life; of whom shall I be afraid?"*

Certainly not these men.

She could almost smile because the peace had swept away all her fear.

And she hung there and waited and prayed.

Bent low over his horse's neck, Nate read the girls' tracks. He read their fear, their rush for help.

He read the palomino's tracks, a horse with no one holding the reins. No Becky.

He saw where they'd ridden out to the distant pasture at a steady pace, but the tracks back were frantic and racing.

Keep cool. Keep your eyes wide open.

Thinking that didn't slow his pounding heart. Or his twisting, turning thoughts.

He knew where they'd planned to spend the day, so he only read the tracks to confirm he was going the right direction. It was a stretch of land close to the Circle J.

Joshua. The image of him drawing back a fist to hit his daughter was right at the front of Nate's mind. If someone had Becky, Joshua's place was where Nate would look first.

Or had she fallen off her horse? He hoped and prayed that he'd find her knocked to the ground. Maybe a low branch had swept her out of the saddle.

But Becky wasn't there. More than that, he could see the palomino had been galloping along riderless all this way.

His horse pounded along her back trail. Finally, with

the fear churning inside, he reached the rugged pasture where he found . . . more tracks. The tracks of strange horses.

Nate slowed but didn't dismount. The ground was churned up where someone had fallen. Becky almost certainly. It looked as though she'd been caught and taken away by two riders.

Nate stared at the ground. He could read sign like the written word, and these tracks told a story.

A deliberate grab for Becky. Two horses wheeled around and ridden hard to the northwest, the opposite direction from the ranch house. One horse left behind deeper tracks because it carried a second rider.

It carried Becky. They had her.

His throat swelled until he fought to breathe. But even that didn't slow him down.

The girls started out in the lead.

Brand didn't know the Idee. He had no idea where Becky had been working today.

Sal held back but not for long. "I see the tracks. Let me get in front."

Brand had to get better at tracking. He prayed for more skill. In a situation like this, more skill could be the difference between life and death.

Then he prayed for more than that.

What had happened to Becky? He'd've liked to question the girls further, but he didn't know where to begin.

Then Sal started peppering the girls with his own questions, which caused them both to keep up with him.

Though Brand brought up the rear, he kept close enough to hear them.

"I know that pasture well." Sal twisted in the saddle and gave Brand a grim look. "Borders her pa's land. Her pa's up to mischief. I wonder if Becky saw something she shouldn't have. Or if they're afraid she did."

Saw what? Brand couldn't imagine. What did Sal know that he could imagine something awful?

"She should've had more sense than to go so close to his property."

"Why? What could she have seen?"

Sal twisted again in the saddle. "Nothing. Just thinking out loud." Then he faced forward and urged his horse on.

Seconds later, they were all picking up speed until soon they were galloping. Brand watched Sal use his knees and his hand, slapping his horse on the rump, every move speaking of tremendous skill. Nate was a skilled cowhand, so why wouldn't his brother Sal be the same?

But it was more than that. Something beyond mere cowboy knowledge. Sal was talking like a man who'd faced more than his share of trouble. And he was too young to have served in the war.

Now he was leaving all of them behind, and Brand would be hornswoggled if he'd call for Sal to slow down. Instead, Brand slapped his horse with an open hand like Sal was doing. He crept up on his girls, hesitated because he didn't want to leave them to bring up the rear, then decided the trouble they faced was ahead of them. Better that he put himself between the girls and whatever might be waiting down the trail.

He drew even with the girls, and for a few moments

the trail was wide enough for them to ride three abreast. He urged his horse to ride between them and glanced to his left and right. His Cassie, the tomboy, cool in times of trouble. His delicate little lady Michaela. Right now, their faces were pale as milk. But pale or not, he saw pure grit in their eyes. They knew trouble was coming but were doing their best not to shy away from it. Instead, they were pushing hard toward it with no fear except the fear of what might be happening to Becky.

Brand rode past the girls and gained on Sal as the trail narrowed. A few minutes later, it turned rocky and they had to slow down to protect the horses. He shuddered to think of the breakneck pace his girls had set to go for help. Glancing back to check them, he saw Michaela with Cassie close behind her.

Finally, they reached the distant pasture. Brand only guessed this was it, as he'd never been here before. But it was distant for a fact, and Sal had slowed to a walk, his eyes on the ground.

Game trails headed off into the trees every so often. Brand only saw them because Sal paused by each and studied the tracks. All of them were more rock than dirt. Occasionally, Sal came to a full stop. They were moving at a crawl now.

The girls came up to his side. He saw grim determination in Cassie's expression. Michaela had tears streaming down her face. When she saw him looking at her, she shook her head fiercely, swiped an arm across her eyes, and moved on past him to make offering comfort impossible.

"Sal, look there." Cassie pointed at a nearby tree.

Up high on the trunk, Brand saw the letter N carved into the bark. The carving looked to be recent.

Sal's eyes darted to where Cassie had pointed. He smirked and said, "Nate's mark. I should've remembered." He turned to Cassie and nodded. "Good work."

Brand noticed his daughter sat a little straighter in the saddle as they followed a trail that took them up a steep incline and into thick woods.

"We're not headed for the Circle J," Sal muttered.

It hadn't occurred to Brand that Becky's pa could have anything to do with her disappearance. In Sal's view, there was something about Joshua Pruitt that amounted to trouble.

They moved up the trail at a fast walk. It was all they dared for fear of a horse stepping wrong and hurting its leg. Sal paid more attention now to the trees and not just the trail.

Brand thought of the few hands at Becky's place. After Nell had gone out to see the men off on the cattle drive, she'd told him that Becky had a skeleton crew. Which was typical. What wasn't typical was that they were strangers. Sal was Nate's brother, but there were a couple of others. He hadn't seen them at her place when they'd rode out to support their wives on their matchmaking whim, but Nell had.

She'd left Becky with the men alone because she trusted her friend's judgment. And she figured Nate and Sal to be dependable. But when they'd up and vanished, quitting with no warning, they left Becky with no hands to help her besides Nate. And Nell had very seriously wondered what was going on out there.

Then came Becky wanting to hire children and an in-experienced hand like Brand. Brand appreciated the work and was always willing to chip in for a day or a week here and there. Cash money was tight on a homestead, though marrying Nell had eased all of that. The woman was prosperous. Still, Brand did his share, and working out at the ranch was part of it.

Next, Sal came riding in, taking charge and acting like Becky not coming home was more than just her falling from her horse. In fact, he'd acted like that the second he'd heard there was trouble. According to the girls, so had Nate.

And now they were *not* heading for the Circle J . . . and Sal had sounded surprised. Which meant Pruitt was a threat. Sal certainly thought so, and likely so did Nate because brothers would understand each other's way of thinking.

It made no sense, but then Brand was on edge—even more so than a few minutes ago. He fingered his six-gun but left it in its holster. And he braced himself for trouble.

28

The horse Becky was being carried on came to a halt.

She felt the saddle horn gouge her stomach, nearly knocking the breath right out of her.

Whatever was going to happen would happen now. She clung to the peace she'd found while she was being kidnapped. But it wasn't easy. Her heart sped up. Her throat went dry.

"To live is Christ. To die is gain."

As she silently repeated the verse, she realized she fully expected to die.

A jerk on the back of her shirt sent her tumbling feetfirst to the ground. Though her ankles were tied together, she hit the ground standing up before falling, which lessened the impact.

She lay there on the ground, helpless. Bound like a maverick calf. The men dismounted. The horses were led away. She curled up on her side as she heard another rider approach. Her heart pounded harder. Her breaths came fast and shallow.

This was why they'd taken her here. It was to meet this man. *"No witnesses."* She'd heard one of them say that again.

She understood that when it came to her soul, no one could hurt her. But there was the physical pain to fear, and she was dreading what she would have to face.

A boot rolled her onto her back. No, a boot *kicked* her onto her back.

"Anyone follow you?"

Pa.

Pa had done this to her. Her fear was less and her anger more. Whatever he had planned—no doubt it'd be cruel— she'd survive it. She'd get a chance to tell Nate she loved him. With the sack over her head, tied up and helpless, she felt herself smile.

The bag was yanked off her head. She squinted in the sunlight and looked up.

Joshua Pruitt.

Pa standing over her. He was a big man. And it was him who'd kicked her.

"No one followed. And you know I'm good at hiding tracks."

She recognized the voice, but in her addled state, she couldn't place the name. One of Pa's new cowhands. And most of the ones they'd arrested were his old established hands. He'd sent the best to rob the gold shipment.

"Set her on that rock over there," Joshua said, pointing. He watched this man rip the gag away. It'd been knotted so it snagged her hair. They were rough with her, inflicting pain. Pa didn't care.

The one who'd spoken, skinny and tall, and the other man, shorter and stouter, lifted her by her elbows and set her down hard on the waist-high boulder. Her feet dangled like a child sitting in an adult chair.

"Pa, for heaven's sake, what are you—?"

He slapped her so hard across the face, she'd've fallen from her perch if the kidnappers, Pa's men, hadn't caught her.

They sat her up straight again. The bald skinny one, older and tough as gristle, laughed.

"Put the gag back on," Pa said. "I don't wanna hear another word."

The skinny man put it back on, tying it so tight it forced her mouth open. She bit down on the kerchief.

He'd brought her here today to hurt her, that much was clear. Maybe even kill her. It hit her hard that Pa was a killer.

There was no proof he ever went along on the stage-coach robberies, but even to know of them beforehand and do nothing, that made Pa a killer the same as if he'd pulled the trigger.

The truth of that twisted something deep in her heart. She'd listened to Owen and the Marshals and was forced to admit that those who'd robbed the gold shipment came from Pa's ranch.

Until now, she hadn't borne the full weight of Pa being the boss, the brains behind the Deadeye Gang and their thieving and murdering.

Pa was a killer. And now she was in his hands.

How good was Skinny Man at hiding tracks? Nate was good too, but could he find her in time? Becky searched hard for that soul-deep peace she'd discovered and hung on to it.

Then she settled in to find a way to survive long enough to tell Nate how much she loved him.

Nate slid back into his saddle. Stopping to mark the trail was probably a waste of time. The girls wouldn't see it. If they came with Brand, he might.

Didn't matter. Nate didn't want a kindhearted but far-from-tough homesteader and his two young daughters at his side in a gunfight anyway.

If Sal were here, they'd have a chance to follow his trail, yet he was a day's ride away.

The prints he was following were hard to make out. One of the riders was hanging back, brushing out marks. They'd done a decent job of finding the rocky paths and sticking to them.

Still, they weren't perfectly hidden. More than that, Nate could see the effort made to hide the tracks. The tracks themselves might be gone, but a trail swept clear was its own clue.

He came upon a stretch of solid rock where the trail split off, then split again. He stopped and dismounted, afraid he might take the wrong path. As he crept along slowly, his heart began pounding at the thought of doing so. He took a moment to pray. It was a strange feeling, though, a terrible feeling to be so dependent on God. He wasn't a man used to needing a miracle. He was a strong

263

man. He took care of himself. God was for faith. For his innermost soul.

Not for finding a trail. That was something he did for himself.

It struck him hard that he didn't bring God into his daily life. And that was wrong. A strong man needed to fall on his knees—as he was right now. To accept that he needed God every day, every hour, every minute. As he bent to his task, there on his knees, he prayed.

And that was when he saw a twig snapped off close to the trunk of a tree. It was freshly broken.

Twigs could snap for reasons other than a kidnapped woman being carried past. But his eyes landed on just that spot in the midst of his prayers. With a leap of faith, he chose a trail.

With wavering confidence, he marked his trail as he had before. Praying with every breath, he rode fast, hoping to reach a spot with dirt blown across it. A spot he could be sure was right.

Then he saw it. The stretch of blown soil. The scratch marks of tracks wiped away. He was elated to know he was on the right track, but riddled with fear to think of Becky being dragged away for who knew what purpose.

Inside, he was twisted up by churning emotions to the point he wanted to roar like a hungry cougar. He pushed onward instead, bathing his torment with more prayer. Nurturing his hope.

He approached a sharp peak in the trail and slowed, not sure what he'd see on the other side. Each time he reached a bend in the wicked trail, he hoped he'd round it and see

Becky, alive and well. But it made the going slow because this rattlesnake of a trail was full of bends.

As he moved toward the summit, he heard something strange that didn't fit.

The next second, he dove to the ground.

29

There's another one, Pa." Cassie was turning out to have eyes like a hawk.

They were making good time. Sal was leading, who was also on the lookout for marks. Yet Cassie was right behind him and spotting them first.

"How did he choose this trail? There are no marks. Not even his. It's solid rock."

"I think he's taking a good long time figuring it out," Cassie said.

Brand had no idea how Cassie could tell anything like that.

"His marks save us a lot of time."

Sal looked at Cassie and nodded, then pushed his mount up the narrow, rocky trail.

"Another one." Cassie pointed down this time. "See that broken twig? I'll bet that's what he saw that made him choose this trail."

Brand had some questions he wanted to ask Sal. About

abandoning Becky. About the other men running off. About Sal mentioning Pruitt. What was going on?

Not the right time, though.

And Sal Paxton had a hard look about him, something in his eyes that didn't match the cowpoke who'd wandered in to see his brother and then stayed.

Brand kept it all to himself and focused on the trail. When this was over, he was going to ask Nate to give him some schooling on wilderness skills. It was all very impressive, the way Sal followed a trail, the understanding between the brothers, and Nate's ability to read a direction from clues Brand couldn't begin to discern.

Brand knew about farming the land, about caring for animals, but there was so much more to know out here in the wilderness. And some of it could be the difference between life and death.

"Here, Sal." Cassie pointed high this time. "This direction."

Sal turned toward a steep trail of solid rock, narrow enough to scare off a mountain goat. Their horses, mountain-bred mustangs, were sure-footed and so didn't hesitate to follow the dangerous trail. Sal's horse, which looked like a thoroughbred, did hesitate at first. But it was a well-trained critter and kept climbing.

They spread out in single file. Then Sal stopped so suddenly, Cassie's horse almost walked into him.

Brand looked down the line of riders and saw a body sprawled flat on the ground.

Dead.

"This is your last chance, girl," Pa said. "You either go into partnership with me today or you'll reap the consequences of refusing me."

Becky's eyes widened. That's what this was about?

She started to shake her head, but then she saw that poisonous look again in Pa's eyes. She remembered the need she'd seen in him before. An almost desperate need. But how could a rich, powerful rancher like Pa *need* her money, her land? He'd never needed anything in his life. Want, yes, but need?

And she knew from that look of poison that he expected her to say no. Almost wanted her to. And then what? Would he beat her until she said yes?

Becky watched him. If she said yes, it wasn't even legal. Her understanding of the law, even in a forward-thinking place as Wyoming, was that upon her marriage, her land became Nate's property. Her signing something served no purpose because she couldn't sign away something she didn't own in the first place.

That had to mean Pa didn't know she'd gotten married. What with planning the gold heist and staying away from town after the humiliation he'd suffered during Mrs. Mussel's speech, he might not have heard about it.

No great voice from heaven gave her instructions about what to do. No finger of fire carved commands to her into stone. Not even a still, small voice whispered on the wind.

But because she'd thought of the ownership question and decided her agreement wouldn't be legal, she nodded.

Satisfaction flashed in Pa's eyes . . . and maybe a hint

of disappointment. She suspected he'd looked forward to beating cooperation out of her.

Pa took a folded-up paper out of his front pocket. It was creased and soiled but new. He hadn't been carrying it for long. He'd gotten the papers in order and then kidnapped her. Not waiting one minute longer than was necessary.

One of his hired thugs hurried to Pa's horse and pulled an ink bottle and a pen from the saddlebag.

Pa had come prepared.

"Untie her hands but stay close by."

It struck her then that Pa was afraid of her. How could he be? She wanted to ask him. She also wanted to tell him he was wasting his time.

She wanted to announce her marriage.

The gag was probably a good thing because it helped keep everything she considered saying inside. Which was for the best.

A hard tug on her arms and they were free. Both of Pa's cowpokes stood so close that it would've been near impossible for her to tear the gag free and tell Pa his legal document didn't carry any legal weight.

She didn't attempt to do a thing other than obey him.

She reached for the pen. Opened the ink bottle and dipped it in. Pa unfolded the document and smoothed it with his hand. Most likely a partnership agreement.

Then the words at the top of the paper caught her attention as they were no doubt meant to. In large print that couldn't be missed, she read, *Last Will and Testament of Becky Pruitt*. Her eyes rose from the paper and met Pa's eyes.

She knew then she was going to die.

"Nate!" Sal rushed for his brother's body.

Brand came after him fast just as Nate twisted on the ground and hissed, "Get down."

Sal dropped to his knees, then flat on his belly. Brand thought it was more than obeying Nate. Like Brand, Sal had feared his brother was dead. His knees were already wobbly with grief.

Brand crouched low. His girls caught up to him and were kneeling on the ground without another order being given.

Nate saw Sal and gave a grim smile of satisfaction. Sal came to Nate's side and reached out a hand. They shook hands in a way that Brand would've guessed they were brothers even if he hadn't already known it.

Nate jabbed his thumb toward the drop-off just ahead. He whispered, "Becky."

Sal, still lying on his belly, drew his six-gun. He crawled forward and peered over the ledge. Brand saw that Nate had his gun drawn, too. Brand crawled forward just as Sal had.

Sal was on Nate's right while Brand came up beside him on his left. His girls did the same, moving to Brand's left.

Brand drew his gun just as Nate and Sal had.

God have mercy, he'd brought his children to a gun-fight.

God had mercy.

He'd sent Sal just when Nate needed help the most.

Nate's heart lurched with hope, then sprang to a height he hadn't thought possible.

Sal was here. After one firm handshake, Sal came up beside Nate, and the two of them looked down over the ledge they were sprawled on in time to see Becky's hands cut free, the piece of rope falling to the ground.

Nate didn't waste a second planning with his brother. They were both top marksmen, fast and tough.

But to go over this ledge . . . they'd be in plain sight. Joshua Pruitt and his two hired men would open fire immediately. And Becky would be right in the cross fire.

And to shoot from up here, to try to pick them off, Becky was still in the cross fire. But at least no one down there would be running, diving to the ground, and using Becky as a human shield.

Two shots when there were three men.

Nate watched Becky as she took the pen Joshua thrust at her. She read over the paper presented to her and then . . . stopped and looked up at her pa.

Her face turned pale. Her lip was bleeding, and there was an angry-looking red mark on her cheek. The fury Nate felt to know she'd been struck . . .

He gathered himself to go hurtling over the ledge.

Becky couldn't say a word, but she knew in that moment, Pa intended to kill her. She'd sign this paper, then a second later she'd die.

It wouldn't be legal, though, and for the same reason her signing partnership papers wouldn't be legal. The ranch belonged to Nate. Yet she couldn't tell her father that fact because of the gag. Instead, she looked hard into his eyes—into the dark pit of his soul.

How had he come to this? He'd always been a ruthless, cruel man. But now he'd turned plain evil. Robbing stages, murdering witnesses?

And it seemed he intended to kill his child. His only child. How did a man sink to such depths of sin?

It didn't matter if she signed or not, for the end was the same. She held the pen in her hand and was sorely tempted to drive the tip of it into his heart.

But the men who'd brought her here were too close, too watchful. She'd never so much as scratch Pa. So she shook her head and threw the pen to the ground.

Pa drew back his hand, as if he wanted badly to make her bleed before killing her.

Sal met Nate's eyes. He clamped a hand on Nate's gun hand.

A movement behind Sal brought Nate's head around to see Brand, and . . . good grief, Brand had brought his children to a gunfight.

Brand came up beside Nate, looking horrified. Like a father ought to in this situation. Soon his daughters were beside their pa and peering over the ledge.

Like the others, Cassie studied what was going on below, watching Becky. She whispered, "I'm going to stand up on this ledge and take just a few steps. Make sure they see me. I'll act like I've been following Miss Becky. They'll come for me, and that'll draw them away from her enough that you can get a shot off."

Nate quailed at the thought. But Cassie had been out there, so it wasn't outside of impossible that she might've trailed them.

He looked around and saw a good-sized boulder along the trail just a bit. "No," Brand said. "Absolutely not."

The little girl had outsized courage. Nate had seen it. Calm in times of trouble.

"We can't risk it, Cassie," Sal said. "They might just start shooting."

"No, they'll hesitate. If one of you men shows himself, bullets will start flying. But me? They'll want to know if Michaela followed, too. I'll show myself by that boulder there. If one of them pulls his gun from the holster, I'll be out of sight before they can fire a single bullet. Either way, if they start shooting and I hide or they come to grab me, it'll draw them away from Miss Becky. It'll give you three men a chance to pick them off. Pa, Pruitt is farthest away from her, you'd better take him—unless the other men move away from him. You're a good shot, but I'm guessing not as good as Nate or his brother."

"Cassie, no. I'm not going to let you—"

Brand stopped talking when she jumped to her feet, ran around the men, and stepped out beside the boulder. She stood there in full view of those below, who were at least a hundred feet down the mountain slope from her.

No one noticed her. The three men were focused on Becky. Nate took aim.

Sal and Brand, too.

Nate was relieved that Brand didn't chase after his daughter and show himself. Watching below, Nate saw Becky shake her head and toss the pen to the ground.

The two cowpokes grabbed Becky's arms. They were too close to her. Taking the men down without hurting Becky was going to be risky. But they might well have to take the risk.

"Miss Becky, what's going on? What are you men doing to my boss?"

Cassie's voice cut through the crystal mountain air.

All three men whirled around.

"Don't hurt her!" Cassie shouted and took a step forward.

Nate heard Joshua say something, but couldn't make out the words. One of the men grabbed Becky's hands and quick tied them in front of her.

Nate saw Becky look up at Cassie. His wife was a savvy woman. He sincerely hoped she didn't think Cassie was out here alone.

Cassie shouted again, "Michaela, stay back!"

More guttural words from the cowpokes. The men shoved Becky to the ground.

All three of the outlaws were watching Cassie when Nate saw Becky reach into her boot. She pulled out a knife and cut the rope from her wrists with one swift jerk of the blade. But she stayed there on the ground.

Two of the men rushed up the trail toward Cassie, who stood there in plain sight, wringing her hands. Such a scared little girl. Nate almost laughed.

The kid had the heart of a Sioux warrior.

In one sudden move, Becky lunged at her pa with the knife. She seemed to aim for his heart but missed. He dodged her, knocking her aside.

Becky lay sprawled on her back on the ground.

"Get back here! Kill her!"

Joshua Pruitt's shouts had the men wheeling around.

Nate shot Joshua dead.

Sal took the first outlaw, the one closest to Cassie. Then he shot the second one.

Brand had his gun out but never fired a shot.

Nate stood and sprinted toward Becky.

Brand was a pace behind him, rushing for Cassie.

Sal ran over and checked both cowpokes while Nate kept an eye on Joshua, which was the hardest thing he'd ever done because everything in him was drawn to Becky.

Finally, Nate went to her side and dropped to his knees. He eased the gag from her mouth and used her knife to cut the bonds on her legs.

She hopped up, flung her arms around his neck, and said, "I love you."

"Becky, I—"

A moan from behind had them both spinning around.

Pa's eyes were open, staring overhead. He bled from a bullet wound in his gut and a knife wound on his shoulder.

His eyes slid to look at Becky.

Nate swallowed, licked his lips as if they were too dry to move.

A hoarse growl came from deep in her pa's throat. "Betrayed by my own daughter. No loyalty. Should have partnered with your pa. Betrayer."

Becky, kneeling on the ground, crawled the few feet to his side. She frowned as she gazed into her pa's eyes. She tried to see into his heart.

Stupid to feel betrayed herself. The man who was supposed to love her first, love her fully, hated her and had planned to kill her for money.

"Why did you do it, Pa? What happened that you needed money bad enough to support the Deadeye Gang, cover up all those murders?"

"Created the gang because I borrowed money. Hired cowhands who rode the outlaw trail. I demanded no witnesses be left alive, so no one could ever describe a face or the Circle J brand."

Becky exchanged a quick look with Nate. Pa had just confessed to forming the gang, and they'd both heard it.

"I knew your ma's folks were rich. I kept track and knew your grandpa was long dead and your grandma dying. After she died, her money didn't come. I didn't know why but knew it would sometime. I expanded, borrowed against that inheritance. Borrowed from a man who collects at the point of his gun. Then the money went straight to you."

"So you turned to murder? You were always a hard man, Pa, but you were honest. Weren't you?"

"Honest is a good way to stay poor."

He said nothing more as his eyelids dropped shut.

"Who did you borrow from, Pa? Is he dangerous to me?"

Pa swallowed, shook his head. Did that mean she wasn't in danger? Seconds stretched to a full minute, with Pa's breathing becoming shallow. He didn't speak again, but he was still alive.

Becky had all the answers she was going to get. She had

to wonder if this man Pa owed would come and claim the ranch. But that was a worry for another day.

"Pa, you're dying. You lie here hating me, full of greed. Hungry for money you have no chance to spend. You're full of sin, deep in your soul. Stop now. Stop the evil you're steeped in and face eternity. Are you ready for eternity, Pa? You're going to face God now. Turn your heart to things that matter. Face judgment with some wisdom and humility."

Deep in his throat, a huff that might've been a mockery of laughter was his only response.

Becky didn't want to pray for him. She didn't want him to even have a chance at salvation. And that struck her as her own ugly sin. So she rested her hand on Pa's heart and prayed. Asked God to reach the hard, unrepentant heart of her earthly father.

They were frozen like that. Becky on her knees in prayer. Pa silent, his breath rattling. Nate at her side, his arm around her shoulders.

They stayed as they were until the last breath escaped Pa's body and he died.

Becky sat back on her haunches and let her hand fall away. With her head bowed, her eyes filled with tears. They weren't tears of grief for her cruel pa, but tears for all that had never been. And now never would be.

The tears didn't fall, though, because it wasn't Becky's way to cry overmuch. And certainly not over the death of a man who'd planned to kill her.

Finally, she lifted her head and looked at Nate.

He pulled her close and wrapped his arms around her.

She saw Brand and his girls and said, "You brought two young girls to a gunfight?"

Cassie grinned. Michaela wiggled her fingers in a wave. Neither of them looked anywhere near tears, and they'd just watched a shootout.

"Cassie saved you, Becky," Nate said. "Smart kid."

"Michaela's a tough one, too." Brand, standing between his girls, rested his hands on both their shoulders.

"Samantha is gonna be so jealous." Cassie leaned against her pa. "She missed everything."

"Yep, she missed being in a gunfight." Brand shook his head ruefully. "Lots of good about the West, but some things are mighty hard, too."

Becky noticed Sal loading the two no-good cowpokes on horses he'd found somewhere. Circle J brands. Each of the men with a bullet to the heart.

Becky got to her feet.

Nate helped her, then touched the corner of her mouth and drew away a finger tinged with blood. "How many times did he hit you?"

Becky launched herself into his arms. "All I wanted was to stay alive long enough to tell you I loved you. He hit me twice, and I stabbed him. And you shot him." She lifted her chin. "It was you, wasn't it?"

Grimly, Nate nodded. "It was me."

"So we evened the score."

Sal came up with another horse. Becky recognized Pa's favorite stallion. "He owed someone money. He could've sold the ranch, paid off his debts, ridden away and started new somewhere else. Instead, he turned to murder. He admitted it to me and Nate."

"I heard it," Sal said.

"We all heard it," Brand added.

Sal laid Pa over his saddle and tied him on. "We need to go to the Circle J and arrest every man there." Sal looked around. "Easier to go there than ride all the way back to town. And we've got a man at the Circle J. I'd like to get there fast. Maybe he's still alive."

They all rode together, including two little girls. Once there, they left Pa and his hired men behind in the woods and rode up cool as you please to Pa's ranch house.

There were two men standing by the corral. Their expressions when they saw Becky told her they knew exactly what Pa was up to today.

They didn't have time to do anything before Sal and Nate had guns trained on them. They were bound and gagged and tossed into the barn. Over the course of the long afternoon and evening, the rest of Pa's men rode into the Circle J two by two, and each pair was captured, tied up, and hidden. When the last pair arrived, one of them pulled his gun and aimed it at his saddle partner.

"Good to see you, Sal. We've been riding all afternoon, searching for Miss Pruitt."

"It's Mrs. Paxton now."

"Nate, that you?"

"It's me, Buck. We were afraid for you."

Sal said, "We've sent a man every night to the meeting spot, and when you didn't show up, we were afraid they'd found you out and killed you."

"Pruitt sent me out with another one of his men to check for the gold shipment. I couldn't slip away. They've been on edge, so I didn't dare risk it."

Buck told them everything.

"We got Pruitt and two others." Sal led the way to the barn. "All three dead. And six men here in the barn. Are there more?"

"Nope, that's the lot. The crew he sent out to hold up the gold shipment over by South Pass City vanished—all but one kid. I hoped that meant you'd gotten them. When I went searching for them, I found one man left. I brought him back."

Buck looked over the prisoners and pointed to the one glaring up at them. "That's him. Told us the others vanished. Ran off. He didn't know what happened to them. Sent Pruitt into a rage. That's when he cooked up his plan to kill Mrs. Paxton here so he could inherit her land. Sent us to scout her property, grab her, and bring her to the spot Pruitt picked to kill her."

Buck shook his head. "I was mighty scared for you, Mrs. Paxton. I was determined to find you and protect you, even knowing it'd blow my cover at the Circle J. Reckon you saved yourself, though."

While they talked, they loaded all the prisoners on horseback, stopped to pick up Pruitt and his cowhands, and started out on the long ride to Pine Valley.

"I'm going to ride ahead," Brand said. "Nell will be frantic. I'm hours late coming in from Becky's."

Sal nodded. He'd taken charge by loading up their captives between two horses tied together, each with a man draped over the saddle. "I reckon we've captured every outlaw in the territory. Tell the sheriff to make room in the jail cells."

"We've made Wyoming safe." Brand smiled, and then he and his girls galloped toward town.

Becky thought Sal and Brand were overly optimistic. But they'd sure as certain thinned the herd.

Sal leading one string, and Buck leading the other had slowed the two Marshals down enough that Becky and Nate rode ahead of them.

"When you told me you loved me, I didn't answer you back." Nate glanced over his shoulder to make sure they were out of earshot of Sal.

"I noticed." Becky, her hair out of its usual braid, tangled from her long, hard afternoon, tossed her head, then glared at him.

"I wanted a minute alone with you, and now I've got it . . . I love you, Becky. I've known I'd taken a fine woman to be my wife. I knew I respected you and liked spending time with you. I knew I admired and had affection for you. But today, when you went missing, I knew I loved you. I knew the world would be a dark place for me without you. I love you, Becky. I'm so glad you're safe so I can spend the rest of my life showing you how much."

They were a long time riding into town, and before they reached Pine Valley, they met the sheriff, Deputy Willie, and two other men riding out to help.

Nate said, "Sal and Buck are U.S. Marshals. They know more about this than I do. I want to take Becky home, Sheriff. She's had a tough day."

Sheriff Mast, who'd heard it all from Brand already, looked at the bruise rising on Becky's face and nodded. "I'll need to talk to both of you, but tomorrow would be soon enough."

Becky and Nate turned off at the next available trail for the Idee and rode for home.

Maybe finally the Deadeye Gang were all dead or captured, and peace could come to the equality state at last.

At least for tonight.

Epilogue

They'd all gathered in the diner to wait out the vote count.

Nell's reelection bid had them strung tight. All except Nell, who was quietly snoozing in a rocking chair. Brand was holding their two-month-old son, Brandon Nolte Junior.

The voting had closed at eight o'clock. The sun had set on the chilly November day. The town council was busy counting ballots, all 227 of them, or so Nell had been told.

Women had lined up to vote with smiles galore and boasted one after the other that they'd voted for Nell. Quite a few of the men said they had, too.

Confident she'd win, and not that worried if she didn't, Nell dozed. Not fully asleep. She was aware of the friendly group gathered around, sharing a pot of chili soup, which Clint had begun to feature regularly in his diner. A perfect spicy feast for a cool night.

Nell had encouraged everyone to go home, especially Becky and Nate. But they stayed anyway, as did Parson Blodgett and his family.

The Blodgetts had returned to Pine Valley six months ago, just as the weather was letting go of winter. With them were Mrs. Blodgett's mother and sister. He'd since gone back to his job as parson. He was urged to regain his job as justice of the peace, but he wanted Nell to keep the job. He had agreed to fill in for her until the baby started sleeping through the night.

Having the Blodgetts back in town had helped Leland and Samantha settle in to married life. They were now a happy couple with a six-month-old daughter.

Joy Blodgett had married Mr. Betancourt and helped him now at the general store. Cassie had become the new schoolmarm, but Nell noticed the way Warren looked at Cassie and suspected they'd need a new teacher soon.

Warren became skilled at making cowboy hats, as good-looking as any Stetson.

Leland had learned boot making, and neither of the brothers could keep up with the orders. It provided the money they needed to fund their homesteads until they were established and producing well.

The door to the diner opened and closed.

Nell managed to lift her heavy eyelids and saw that Samantha and Leland had left with their sleeping baby.

Mariah's little Garret, now twenty months old, was asleep in the cradle they kept in the kitchen. Mariah was growing round with their second child.

Becky was expecting her first and had grudgingly agreed not to rope cattle or bust broncos until the little one was born. It made her feel a little unneeded, yet she knew such things weren't safe for the baby.

Nell smiled to think of how much Nate made Becky feel needed all the time.

The door opened again. Doc Preston led the way in, with Mayor Clint and Sheriff Mast right behind him. Their wide smiles told Nell all she needed to know.

"You won!" Doc raised his hands in victory.

"Congratulations, Your Honor!" Clint said, then went to check on his chili soup simmering on the stovetop.

The sheriff came in looking excited and proud. He'd been the main force behind appointing Nell and gloated over what a great idea it was.

Crime really had gone way down in their part of Wyoming Territory. Nell received at least a bit of credit for that, though she certainly hadn't captured the Deadeye Gang. But she had prosecuted them.

It turned out she didn't have to order their hanging. Pruitt had drawn in outlaws from far and wide, and they were all wanted. Over some objections from those who thought the Deadeye Gang should be hanged for the crimes they'd committed right here, Nell shipped them to where they were being hunted, took all the reward money and distributed it very fairly, and didn't have to sentence a single man.

She knew the day might come when she'd have to make that decision, and she prayed that God would balance justice and wisdom and mercy within her.

Nell smiled at the excitement that erupted around her. Then the ruckus woke up Brandon Junior, and she said, "All right. Time to get home." So long as Junior was awake anyway, she let herself be hugged by everyone.

Last but not least, by Becky and Mariah. An awkward

hug around Becky's very round belly, a baby in Nell's arms, and a toddler bouncing in Mariah's arms. Somehow they managed it, and with a lot of joy.

They were getting good at it.

Brand slid an arm around Nell. Clint came up and relieved Mariah of their daughter. Nate took Becky's hand in his.

"It's a fine thing to go riding in the evening and not be afraid." Brand gave Nell a long look. She nodded.

"Let's go home." Becky knew tomorrow would be another busy day. And she knew she'd face each Wyoming sunrise with love for her husband, trust in God, and a lasso in her hand.

Turn the page for a sneak
peek at another exciting
read from Mary Connealy

Chasing the Horizon

Book One in the new series

A WESTERN LIGHT

Available in the spring of 2024!

JULY 1869
CHICAGO

Elizabeth Rutledge crept out of the alley when she heard the creaking of the wagon wheels. The man driving the garbage cart, the same route every night, slowed to a near stop as he turned onto the last lane to take the trash and dump it on an ugly pile that would soon be added to by the garbage created by the Horecroft Asylum.

"Sir, can you help me?" Beth was dressed in what looked like mere rags, clothing even the servants in her father's home would look at with disdain.

Her voice was laced with fear, and she put a tone of begging into it. The fear was easy to come by. The thought of what she was doing made her heart pound until she felt it in her ears.

If this failed, she'd almost certainly end up locked away with Mama.

"I've dropped a nickel in a crevice between the cobblestones, and I can't get it out. I need it, sir, to feed my children."

The garbage man pulled his reeking cart to a stop and jumped down. He rounded the dapple-gray nag and crouched down beside Beth. She saw evil in his eyes, even in the nearly pitch-dark of the street, which was lined with crumbling brick buildings.

She'd studied this man and knew far more about him than he'd ever suspect.

He'd help her all right, yet she'd never regain possession of her coin. She felt the weight of the gun in her pocket and hoped the man was just a thief and not something much worse.

While the two of them struggled with a little stick to lift out the coin that Beth had lodged thoroughly in the tight crack, Beth heard a faint rustling coming from behind her.

It was nighttime near a garbage dump. Any rustling sounds were usually made by rats, and this man didn't strike her as the smartest.

He ignored Mama as she climbed out of the back of the wagon and slipped into the night. Beth thought Mama had made a bit more noise than would be expected, but she didn't dare turn to look. That was all it would take for Mama to be discovered, then taken and locked away.

Again.

Swallowing hard to make her dry throat work, she saw the garbage man finally dislodge the coin. He held it up with a smirk.

"Oh, thank you—"

His laugh cut her off as he closed his hand around the nickel. "It's mine now."

"No! Please . . ." She had to make a fuss or the man might become suspicious. "If you take it, my children won't have anything to eat. Please!"

But he ignored her, clambered onto the wagon seat, and

slapped the reins on the swaybacked horse. He laughed as he rolled away.

When his laughter had faded in the distance, Beth whispered, "Mama?"

A shadow shifted in the narrow alley across the street. Beth hurried over.

"Elizabeth." Eugenia Rutledge flung her arms around Beth. Mama smelled just like the man's garbage wagon.

Beth only hugged her tighter. The feel of Mama hugging her thickened Beth's throat with tears. She fought them until Mama burst into tears herself.

Beth clung tightly as she wept. Several minutes passed before Beth was able to regain her composure.

"Elizabeth, my darling girl—"

"Shh. And it's *Beth* now, Mama. And from this moment on, you're *Ginny*. My older sister, Ginny Collins."

Even after three years in an insane asylum, Mama was youthful-looking, her hair still fully brunette with no sign of graying. She was far too thin, though, and Beth had to wonder what the food was like in that house of horrors, Horecroft.

The plan was for them to pass as sisters. Beth prayed for a lack of curiosity among those who encountered them.

"You've given us Oscar's surname? Beth and Ginny Collins . . . Yes, of course we need new names." Something fell off Mama's head. Beth thought it might be a cabbage leaf.

Another shadow emerged, and Beth grabbed for her six-gun.

"I-I brought someone with me," Mama explained. "She's a friend. I couldn't leave her in the asylum."

A woman so frail that she looked absolutely breakable shuffled to Mama's side.

Beth was speechless. She'd made plans, detailed plans. For two.

"Let's go. I've held us up too long as it is. There's no time to waste." Mama didn't know the plans, but she did know everything was urgent.

"I'll go by Kat," the delicate blond woman said. She was so small, she looked more child than adult. "I'll do whatever I need to do to stay out of that horrible place."

Beth didn't have much choice in the matter. Time was severely limited. She'd plan their next steps on the walk to the wharf.

"Let me get my satchel," said Beth. "It has everything I believed I'd need for two women—sisters down on their luck, working their way downriver to Independence, Missouri." She'd have to find additional clothing for Kat that might fit the woman, who was slender to the point of starvation, and not raise suspicion.

Beth would think of something before Kat needed a change of clothing. She had until they reached Independence, where the wagon train should be heading out of town right about now.

Their transportation to the West.

They'd go and find a place beyond Thaddeus Rutledge's reach, and they'd hide for the rest of their lives.

She'd told Oscar not to wait for them. She and Mama, and now Kat, would have to catch up sometime later.

And to get there, they'd be working their way westward.

Mary Connealy writes romantic comedies about cowboys. She's the author of the BROTHERS IN ARMS, BRIDES OF HOPE MOUNTAIN, HIGH SIERRA SWEETHEARTS, KINCAID BRIDES, TROUBLE IN TEXAS, WILD AT HEART, and CIMARRON LEGACY series, as well as several other acclaimed series. Mary has been nominated for a Christy Award, was a finalist for a RITA Award, and is a two-time winner of the Carol Award. She lives on a ranch in eastern Nebraska with her very own romantic cowboy hero. They have four grown daughters—Joslyn, married to Matt; Wendy; Shelly, married to Aaron; and Katy, married to Max—and seven precious grandchildren. Learn more about Mary and her books at

maryconnealy.com
facebook.com/maryconnealy
seekerville.blogspot.com
petticoatsandpistols.com

Sign Up for Mary's Newsletter

Keep up to date with Mary's latest news on book releases and events by signing up for her email list at the link below.

FOLLOW MARY ON SOCIAL MEDIA

Mary Connealy   @maryconnealy   @MaryConnealy

MaryConnealy.com

More from Mary Connealy

After surviving a brutal stagecoach robbery, Mariah Stover attempts to rebuild her life as she takes over her father's blacksmith business, but the townspeople meet her work with disdain. She is drawn to the new diner owner as he faces similar trials in the town. When danger descends upon them, will they survive to build a life forged in love?

Forged in Love
WYOMING SUNRISE #1

Widowed seamstress Nell Armstrong finds solace in helping widower Brand Nolte's daughters learn to sew. But she's more than a seamstress, and her investigative skills from her late lawman husband come critical when a robbery survivor arrives in town. As danger encroaches from all sides, Nell and Brand must discover why there appears to be a bull's-eye on their backs.

The Laws of Attraction
WYOMING SUNRISE #2

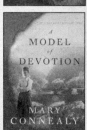

When the Stiles sisters discover their stepfather's plans to marry each of them off to his lecherous friends, they escape to find better matches and claim their portion of their father's lumber dynasty. While trying to stay one step ahead of their father, the sharp-minded sisters must use their wits to deal with troublemakers, find love, and obtain their rightful inheritance.

THE LUMBER BARON'S DAUGHTERS: *The Element of Love, Inventions of the Heart, A Model of Devotion*

◊ BETHANYHOUSE

Bethany House Fiction   @bethanyhousefiction   @bethany_house   @bethanyhousefiction

 Free exclusive resources for your book group at bethanyhouseopenbook.com

 Sign up for our fiction newsletter today at bethanyhouse.com